Honey Yor

Unbelievab

She steppe ver—

sweet geezus— water on her

arms.

He reached up and loosened his tie.

Fuck.

Yeah. Right. They'd done that, and seeing her again only proved what he'd done a pretty damn good job of denying for the last four months: Once had not been enough.

Not even close.

And it pissed him off.

He didn't need this.

"Ms. York's safety and comfort are going to be your top priority for the next two days," the flack was saying. "Nothing, and I mean *nothing*, is going to come between you, and absolutely *nothing* is going to happen between you, so get those thoughts out of your head, and if you bring her back here with so much as a single hair out of place, you will find yourself back at the *bottom* of the food chain. Do I make myself clear, Mr. Rydell?"

"Crystal."

ON THE
LOOSE

TARA JANZEN

A DELL BOOK

ON THE LOOSE
A Dell Book / November 2007

Published by
Bantam Dell
A Division of Random House, Inc.
New York, New York

ISBN 978-0-440-24384-7

Printed in the United States of America
Published simultaneously in Canada

www.bantamdell.com

OPM 10 9 8 7 6 5 4 3 2 1

"Piense como el cazador, pero piense como el conejo, tambien . . ."

Bob MacKenna

Always good advice, from the Central American highlands to the Mideast desert sands. For all the change, things seem to stay pretty much the same, don't they?

K.K.

ON THE
LOOSE

PROLOGUE

C. Smith Rydell refocused his spotting scope on the three men exiting a canvas-walled hut nearly hidden in the trees below. He recognized two of the men coming out of the hut, had worked with them a few months ago on another U.S./Peruvian joint reconnaissance mission, and no way should either one of the agents be at this remote airstrip hanging off an Andean mountainside so steep it defined the word "dizzying."

Halfway to heaven and headed straight to hell, he thought.

"Mendez," he said, keeping his voice low. "Coming out of the hut. Wearing a black shirt."

A dozen other men, all heavily armed, were working in the encampment, stacking cargo and doing maintenance on the eight-hundred-meter stretch of dirt that had been hacked out of the forest.

"Old Julio Mendez?" his partner asked, swinging the lens of his digital camera away from the men on the runway toward the canvas-walled hut. A Peruvian counterdrug agent, Rufio Cienfuegos, was stretched out flat on his stomach next to Smith in the OP—observation position—they'd been manning since daybreak. A thick blanket of clouds hung in the air below their hiding place, obscuring the deep green valleys of the Rio Vilcanota and giving the landscape a surreal otherworldliness. Sky above them, glaciers off to the south, rugged mountains jutting out of a sea of white—Smith felt suspended in air, just him and Rufio and a full crew of *narcotraficantes*.

"Old Julio," he confirmed. "And Carlos Moreno, tan shirt, black pants."

"Moreno, too?" Rufio said with disgust, adjusting the focus on the camera. "Yeah, that's Carlos, all right."

Too many things had been going wrong with the DEA's counterdrug operations in Peru over the last year—missions gone bad, information leaked, two agents killed—with the problems all pointing to a traitor somewhere inside Joint Ops Central in Lima.

"Didn't Mendez put in for vacation this week?" Smith asked.

"Yeah," Rufio said. "He was going to visit his sister in Miami, but this ain't no fucking Miami."

It sure as hell wasn't.

After the last agent had been killed, Smith's former masters at the DEA had "requested him to volunteer" through his new unit for a joint saturation airfield reconnaissance mission. Their intelligence had obtained credible information that numerous undetected flights were being made between Cali, Colombia, and a series of remote Peruvian airstrips hidden in the mountains around Cuzco. The cocaine cartel based in Cali had the lock on drug traffic in the Cuzco region. The two dead agents had both been assigned to the Field Command Post in Cuzco.

There were no coincidences. It was all connected. Someone in Lima had been giving away everything the Cuzco post had been coming up with to fight the increase in drug-related crime flooding the city, and people were getting killed because of it.

Find the damn traitor, find the damn airstrips, and find the damn pilot who was making the border-hugging, below-radar flights without slamming nose first into an Andean mountain—those were Smith's orders, straight from General "Buck"

Grant, his boss at SDF, Special Defense Force, a group of black-ops warriors based in Denver and deployed out of a hell and gone annex of the Department of Defense in Washington, D.C.

"*Pendejos,*" Rufio swore softly, tracking the men through his camera, taking picture after picture. "They're going down."

Yeah, they were assholes, all right, and they were definitely going down.

Smith's bonus task on this operation, as requested by the Agency analysts, was to find the damn plane and take pictures. The analysts were concerned that the type of aircraft performing the theorized flight profiles could not be identified in terms of aviation industry standard production. Aircraft with the necessary service ceiling and range did not have the agility required to negotiate the rough terrain at such low altitude. Furthermore, the analysts' computer simulations indicated that even if an airplane with all the required attributes existed, the success probability of such flights was on the order of sixty percent. The rest of the time, according to the simulations, an aircraft attempting such profiles would either be forced up to a radar-detectable altitude, or it would crash. No one could fly that low and stay off the rocks, not consistently, not in the Andes. The odds of two or more pilots with such an unusually high skill level being in the same place at the same time were even slimmer.

No, the Agency analysts had concluded. It was one person, one pilot—but who?

It was Smith's job to find out, and as soon as he nailed the bastard's ass to the wall and had him behind bars, he'd be happy to tell him how impressed the Agency analysts were with his flying. Until then, he was looking for one helluva plane, one helluva pilot, God knew how many airstrips, and at least one son of a bitch—or he had been. Today had gotten off to a good start, with him and Rufio up by one airstrip and two sonuvabitches.

The distant drone of a multi-engine airplane coming into earshot brought a grin to his face and drew his gaze upward, away from the scope.

Perfect.

Make that one airstrip, two sonuvabitches, the freakazoid plane no one could tag, and whoever in the hell was flying it, he thought.

A very good day, indeed.

"Bango," Rufio said.

Smith's grin widened. "Bingo," he corrected, scanning the bank of clouds stretching from peak to peak across the valley. Wisps of the white ether rolled along the edge of the airstrip and drifted into the trees, adding a complication factor of about a hundred to any move the pilot might make. This was going to be either one hell of a landing, or it was going to be one hell of an explosion if the bastard finally missed. Either eventuality worked for Smith.

Unless the damn plane came down on top of him and Rufio.

His grin faded. Yeah. That could happen. It could happen in a heartbeat. When the wind kicked up, *he* could hardly see the airstrip, and he was practically on top of the damn thing.

Fuck.

He scanned the clouds again and hoped the mystery pilot was on top of his game this morning— way on top.

And where in the hell was he? The plane's engine note reverberated in the narrow valley, growing louder, but Smith couldn't pinpoint a direction of approach. Under the current conditions, if he'd been the pilot, he'd be following the valley upward, beneath the clouds, and would try for a straight-in landing.

But he was no hotshot Cali cartel pilot getting paid in gold, land, and more money than he could count.

The sound of the engines suddenly broke free in the morning air, and Smith caught a blur of motion off his left shoulder. *Geezus.* He ducked, for all the good that would do him if the pilot miscalculated anything—anything at all. But okay. Fine. The guy had made his point. This cartel flyboy was doing things the hard way this morning, popping straight up over the jagged peaks at Smith's back and dropping down out of the sky, right on top of the hidden airstrip—and on top of Smith and Rufio's OP—and doing an amazing job of it.

The sleek twin-engine Piper Seneca came in steep, then leveled off and streaked along the opposite edge of the strip, hugging the base of the slope through the clouds. The plane's camouflage paint caught Smith's attention for a second, but then blended into the mist as the pilot banked hard right, standing the plane on its wingtip and losing altitude. Smith could only watch its ghostly outline, impressed as hell. He knew pilots, he knew planes, and this guy was worth every dollar, ounce, and acre he was getting paid—and then some. With perfect timing, the pilot snapped the plane level in precise alignment with the strip and simultaneously throttled back just over the treetops three hundred meters from the landing threshold.

Something about the way the guy was flying sent an odd sensation sliding across the back of

Smith's brain—odd and disconcerting, not quite a memory, but close enough to give him a nanosecond's worth of pause.

He glanced at Rufio, making sure his partner was recording everything with his camera. Whether the pilot made his landing or not, Central was going to want it all in pixels and JPEGS.

But the landing was a done deal. Smith could tell. This pilot didn't make mistakes, not on the job. There was no hesitation in the aircraft's approach sequence, no second passes, no second guessing. This guy knew exactly what he was doing.

Exactly.

The odd sensation returned, stronger, twisting into a cold knot in the pit of his stomach—and he watched. Watched the plane clear the tree line with 25-degree flaps. Watched it flare three feet off the deck and touch down without even the barest hint of a bounce. The instant the wheels were solidly planted, the three-bladed props reversed pitch at full throttle, and the craft slowed to a halt with runway to spare.

Eight hundred meters wasn't much, but it was more than enough for this pilot, and Smith had seen it all before. The way the airplane spun a perfect one-eighty and taxied to the fuel drums at the edge of the strip without the slightest waver. The way the pilot pivoted the aircraft smartly counterclockwise, facing the left passenger hatch toward the fuel drums and holding the plane with the brakes, keeping power to both engines.

Smith had seen the skills, seen the confidence—seen the sheer, unadulterated arrogance more times than he cared to remember.

The cold knot turned to lead in his gut and started to tighten.

He'd seen the fucking plane, seen the custom camouflage paint job, the top of the craft a dull, mottled brown and tan, the underside a bluish gray, both sides making the aircraft difficult to track whether the observer was looking down against the ground or up against the sky. The dull texture of the paint indicated a radar-absorptive substance, which wouldn't make the craft completely stealth, but would further diminish a weak radar return.

Yeah, he'd seen the plane. He'd seen it explode on contact with a piece of Afghan real estate during Operation Enduring Freedom.

Or so he'd thought.

The Piper Seneca was replaceable, the paint job easily duplicated, but the landing sequence was a signature piece, literally, as if the pilot had written her name across the sky.

Her.

Irena Polchenko.

Every emotion he had froze inside him, froze like ice, because he wasn't going wherever this boatload of crap wanted to take him.

This was impossible. She was dead—and if she'd had her way, he'd have been dead, too. She'd personally arranged it, his death, put quite a bit of personal effort into it, *very* personal, the black-hearted bitch.

Yeah, she'd fucked him, and then she'd *really* fucked him. And then she'd died. He'd seen it, six years ago, watched the whole thing happen in a remote valley high up in the Hindu Kush Mountains, and even hating her, it had torn his guts out to watch her crash, to watch her plane fall out of the sky and be so helpless to stop it.

But win and move on was what he did, against the odds, to the very best of his ability, every time. It's what he got paid to do, and once he'd walked away from the site, he'd never looked back.

Never.

He was looking now, though, and wondering what he'd missed, wondering if they'd all missed something. Wondering if, so help him God, his betrayer really was in the Piper's cockpit.

A large, swarthy man carrying an assault rifle opened the hatch and surveyed the edge of the strip. Mendez, Moreno, and two of the other narco-guerrillas materialized out of the tree line and exchanged recognition signals with him. Satisfied, the man turned and gave an "okay" hand signal to the pilot, who then shut down the left engine and throttled the right engine back to an idle with the prop at neutral pitch.

"Looks like we've got a party," Rufio whispered, his camera trained on the plane.

The left prop came to a stop, and the reception committee placed a short ramp beneath the passenger hatch. The big guy with the rifle emerged, followed by a trim, dapper man carrying a briefcase.

"*Guardia de seguridad,*" Rufio said. *Bodyguard.*

"*Sí, y principal.*" *Yes, and the principal,* the guy who needed protection. Smith forced himself to take a good look at the men, and it took effort, too much, to tear his gaze and every atom of his attention away from the cockpit.

"You getting all this?" he asked Rufio.

"Everything," Rufio confirmed.

The Peruvian agent was young, but smart, and as tough as he needed to be.

"We need the pilot," Smith reminded him—unnecessarily, he knew, but *goddamn*. He trained his 40-power spotting scope squarely on the cockpit, waiting for the worst—and the worst was exactly what he got.

After the makeshift ground crew of armed guerrillas secured the main landing gear with chock blocks, the pilot opened the cockpit's hatch and stepped onto the left wing's antiskid pad.

Smith didn't need to wait for her to remove her helmet before he recognized her. She was unmistakable: tall and slender, five feet nine inches of pure, man-eating female inside a black flight suit—and he'd loved her.

The helmet came off and a cascade of silken, raven black hair fell almost to her waist.

Fuck. Of all the stupid crap he could have picked to remember upon seeing her rise from the dead, that he'd once been stupid enough to love her would have been his last damn choice. And it had been the whole goddamn problem. He'd been in love, so impressed with himself for winning her over all the other guys who'd trailed her like a pack of hounds, and she'd been working him right from the start.

She'd worked them all, and with that face, with that body, with that whole kick-ass, take names, do-me-if-you-can—and you probably can't—attitude, she was still working men. He didn't doubt it for a second.

Rufio let out a soft, low breath, proving him right, buying the whole Irena package, hook, line, and sinker in less than three seconds flat.

She was lethal, literally, and the boy was out of his league—way out.

So was Smith.

He felt gut-punched just looking at her.

A lot of people would want to know she was alive, a lot of agencies, a lot of governments, especially his. The Peruvians wanted the Cali cartel pilot who was going in and out of the Cuzco region, and sure, the U.S. government wanted that pilot, too, but even more, far more, they'd want the contract aviator who'd worked for the DEA in Afghanistan and sold out Agent C. Smith Rydell to a mountain warlord to seal a half-million-dollar heroin-for-SAMs—surface-to-air missiles—deal. They'd want to string her up and jerk the ropes tight—especially the rope around her pretty little neck.

Goddammit. Irena Polchenko.

She stepped down off the skid pad and visually checked the wheel chocks, before heading for the group of men convening around a table set up near the trees. Smith watched her cross the runway, every long-legged stride. He didn't hate her anymore. He didn't care enough to hate her.

She'd been dead to him for six years, and he wanted her dead again. That was all. It wasn't personal, not anymore. Not really.

Not very.

Right.

The only question in his mind was how he could best accomplish the deed to the DEA's benefit. They were the ones writing the check for this mission. And they'd want a nice long chat with Irena, all of it in a detention cell somewhere, with plenty of spooks and analysts to ask plenty of questions and guaranteed to get plenty of answers. So she wouldn't die today, not even with him only a measly two hundred and fifty meters above her with a clear shot and an M4 locked and loaded at his side. A joint Peruvian/U.S. QRT, quick reaction team, was waiting ten air minutes away, with enough agents to secure the airstrip and everyone on it, and that's what the DEA would want—her capture, not her death, not yet. All Rufio had to do was make the call.

He signaled the Peruvian to get on the horn, and out of the corner of his eye saw Rufio open the case on their compact HF radio unit . . . *but that's Irena down there,* he thought, the girl who didn't make mistakes, and if her new Piper Seneca was exactly like the old one, she'd have a—

Dammit. He turned toward Rufio to stop him,

but was too late. The Peruvian agent had already pressed the "send" key.

A high-pitched screech immediately rent the air.

She'd have a goddamn radio direction finder, he finished his thought, watching her snatch the screeching receiver off her belt and hold it up to viewing angle. *Fuck.* He knew exactly what she'd see: an HF radio signal transmitting on the Peruvian Federal Police band, fifteen degrees off the nose of her aircraft, originating at ground level with a strength and clarity that put it right on top of her position.

And that pretty much screwed the whole fucking surveillance op, *goddammit,* and Rufio knew it as well as he did.

The Peruvian agent instantly switched off the HF transmitter, but again, it was all too late. The girl was sprinting for her plane, escaping, *dammit,* and shouting over her shoulder. *"Peligro! Aborden el avión!" Danger! Get on the plane!*

The bodyguard reacted instantly, scooping up the briefcase with one hand, and hauling his principal out of his chair with the other. Irena was already at the cockpit's hatch, still shouting, this time at the confused reception committee.

"Hay intrusos encima de la loma alla! Encuentrenlos y mátenlos!" There are intruders on top of the hill there! she yelled, pointing directly at

Smith and Rufio's OP, which was suddenly way too damn close at a measly two hundred and fifty meters away. *Find them and kill them!*

Mátenlos—kill them.

Ah, yes. Those words had such a lovely, familiar ring, especially coming out of her sweet mouth, and for the record, he wanted to officially correct his memory of her to *bloodthirsty,* black-hearted bitch.

Shit. He switched on his emergency extraction beacon and started to quickly and efficiently stow his gear. Rufio was doing the same. They weren't particularly worried, despite the spatter of gunfire and all the excited chatter coming from the airfield. Their escape scenario had been well planned. They could elude their pursuers during the time required to get an armed aircraft on station, after which the bad guys would be too busy to interfere with their extraction helicopter.

He gave the airstrip a quick glance, and swore to himself. Irena and her passengers had already boarded the plane and closed the hatches. Talk about a well-planned emergency scenario. In seconds, she'd throttled up the right engine and spun the plane away from the OP's direction, while simultaneously cranking the left engine.

Yeah, the girl knew what she was about. She'd always known.

In less than a hundred meters, she was at full power, with three hundred meters of runway left, more than enough for liftoff. There'd been no time to refuel, so the plane was light, and with Irena at the stick, the Piper easily cleared the trees at the end of the strip—and in the next moment, it disappeared, vanishing into the mist of the valley below.

Goddamn. Smith slung his rucksack over his shoulder and checked the chamber on his M4. Rufio was doing the same, and half a minute later, they were on their escape route at a dead run.

CHAPTER ONE

One day later, the Blake Hotel, Panama City, Panama

Unbelievable.

Smith stood stock-still at the edge of the hotel's pool deck, staring at the bikini-clad blonde
testing the water with the perfectly polished toes
of her right foot.

Tilting his head slightly to one side, he sized
her up from a different angle, not that it made
any difference. She was perfect from every angle,
absolutely perfect. *Geezus.* His life couldn't possibly be this complicated, this crazy. He should
be with the guys at Joint Ops Central, hot on the
trail of two traitors, a notorious drug runner with
global connections, and a plane the DEA analysts were still drooling over. He shouldn't have
been rousted out of his hotel room in the middle
of the night and shoved on a flight leaving Lima

before dawn, and he sure as hell shouldn't have been reassigned to a lousy Personal Security Detail, a PSD, not for any reason—but especially not for this reason.

Panama City, hell.

Standing next to him, a State Department flack rattled on about being held personally responsible for any mishaps or screwups, of which there had better be absolutely none, zero, or Smith was going to get his ass handed to him on a platter. The stakes were high, the flack said; Rydell was being tagged for a job that he no way in hell deserved, and he damn well better remember it.

Yeah, yeah. Smith had heard it all before, and like everyone else who'd ever tried to sell that line, the State guy had it ass-backward. Guys like him never got tagged for jobs they didn't deserve. They got tagged for the jobs nobody else could do or the jobs nobody else wanted. Neither reason of which actually applied to the current situation, he silently admitted. Every guy in the world wanted this job. Guys dreamed about a PSD like this one, fantasized about them, and there were hundreds of badass knuckle-draggers out there who could do it at least as well as he could, and probably a few who could do it better, because at fifty feet he was already going down in flames.

Honey York.

Unbelievable.

She stepped down into the pool, bent over—*sweet geezus*—and splashed some water on her arms.

He reached up and loosened his tie.

Fuck.

Yeah. Right. They'd done that, and seeing her again only proved what he'd done a pretty damn good job of denying for the last four months: Once had not been enough.

Not even close.

And it pissed him off.

He didn't need this.

"Ms. York's safety and comfort are going to be your top priority for the next two days," the flack was saying. "Nothing, and I mean *nothing,* is going to come between you, and absolutely *nothing* is going to happen between you, so get those thoughts out of your head, and if you bring her back here with so much as a single hair out of place, you will find yourself back at the *bottom* of the food chain. Do I make myself clear, Mr. Rydell?"

"Crystal." The single word was cold, succinct, and in no way indicative of his current internal condition, which was hot under the collar and veering toward some sort of epiphany he was sure he didn't want to have.

But, *dammit,* strings had been pulled somewhere to get him taken off the Peruvian mission, and those same damn strings had to have been bought, sold, and horse-traded in dark alleys in order to get his butt landed on the pool deck of the most exclusive hotel in Panama City for a baby-sitting job—strings a whole helluva lot bigger than the ones holding Honey's bikini together.

String bikini.

Black bikini.

An if-there-were-a-hundred-and-four-square-inches-of-material-in-the-whole-damn-thing-he'd-eat-his-hat bikini.

And he couldn't take his eyes off it or the curves it did absolutely nothing to contain—which wasn't doing a damn thing to improve his mood.

"The itinerary for Ms. York's tour is in your portfolio, including all departures and arrivals and the names of every major coffee grower in the highlands. She's especially keen on meeting the plantation owners."

Smith slanted a glance down through his Ray-Bans at the shrimp-sized flack in his bespoke suit and handmade leather shoes. Brett Jenkins III had Yale written all over him, and asshole written all over that.

"Coffee? Tour?" Nobody had said anything about coffee to him. Nobody had used the word "tour."

High-priority personal security detail was what he'd been told, orders straight from the top, code red, a full-court press requiring the utmost discretion and a covert operator from SDF.

He let his gaze stray back to the woman leaning over the side of the pool and taking a sip from a piña colada with enough fruit in it to qualify as a side dish.

Discretion, his ass.

There was nothing discreet about Honoria York-Lytton in a black string bikini, nothing discreet about the huge pair of rhinestone-studded black sunglasses perched on her nose, nothing discreet about the hundred and one shades of blond hair she'd twisted up into a perfectly disheveled pile of wild curls on top of her head.

A hair out of place? Give him a break. She didn't have a hair *in* place. What she did have was a tiny black cocktail umbrella tucked in her wild blond curls. When she took the pink umbrella out of her piña colada and stuck it in her hair, too, the picture was complete: bimbo, party girl, five feet two inches of pure plaything.

He wasn't fooled for a second.

If she'd taught him one thing in San Luis, El Salvador, it was to never underestimate a woman in platform heels and a polka-dot dress—especially if that woman's family had come over on the *Mayflower* and her father and two uncles had been United States ambassadors, especially if that woman held an advanced degree from Harvard and her dating pool started on Madison Avenue in Manhattan and ended at the State Department in Washington, D.C.

She was connected, all right, and he hadn't called her, not once since the wild night they'd hooked up in the old Hotel Palacio in San Luis. He'd had Skeeter, one of his SDF teammates, track her all the way home to Washington, D.C., and confirm her safe arrival, and then he'd done his best to put her out of his mind. He hadn't written her, except once, but never sent the letter. He hadn't sent flowers, though he'd been damn tempted to more times than he wanted to admit, and he hadn't returned her panties.

Nope. The panties were still his, still in his possession, still in his rucksack, the sheerest, prettiest, most expensive piece of lingerie he'd ever seen, ever touched, ever whatevered.

Perfect. He had her silk underwear, and she'd sicced the State Department on him. Oh, hell no, this was no accident.

"...limo will be here in about forty-five minutes to take you to the air base to catch a flight scheduled to leave in two hours and arrive at Ilopango International Airport this afternoon. From there, you'll be taking a private vehicle up into the mountains of—"

"Ilopango?" Smith interrupted, his attention and his gaze snapping back to Jenkins. "Ilopango is in El Salvador." And no way in hell had anybody said any damn thing about the mission being in El Salvador.

"And so are the coffee plantations Ms. York is scheduled to visit in Morazán Province along the Honduran border, near the Torola River. Ambassador Hasbert himself has arranged the introductions."

Smith's eyebrows arched above the curve of his Ray-Bans. The Torola? Jenkins had to be kidding. Didn't the man know what in the hell was going on up in the hills of Morazán? Hadn't he done any goddamn research on this PSD at all?

Obviously not.

Smith's gaze shot back to Honey, and he swore silently to himself. She knew, so help him God. She had to know, or she wouldn't have needed

him, because, *dammit*, there was only one reason for there to be any connection whatsoever
between the pampered, pedicured, and pedi-
greed Washington, D.C., socialite and a Third
World backwater in the Salvadoran highlands.
Only one, goddammit, and it was nothing but the
kind of trouble somebody should have stopped
before it got to the point of him staring at her
bikinied bottom in Panama City.

Geezus. Just how the hell much trouble had
her sister gotten herself into this time? And who
in the hell had Hasbert arranged to introduce
her to? The Salvadoran government-sanctioned
coffee growers, or the rebel leader trying to blow
them off the map, Diego Garcia, because,
frankly, Ms. York didn't need an introduction to
Diego Garcia. She and the guerrilla captain had
met in San Luis the same night Smith had met
her, four months ago, in a church, over a table
piled high with the quarter of a million dollars
Honey had smuggled into El Salvador and had
been handing over to a dissident priest who
hadn't wasted a second in handing it over to
Garcia—U.S. cash, all in fifties bundled together
by rubber bands into two-inch stacks.

Mission of mercy, she'd called it, a mission of
mercy for her sister, a trust-fund-baby bride of
Christ who was sacrificing her life as an impov-

erished nun in El Salvador. But all hell had broken out on the border in the last four months, and more times than he cared to remember, Smith had wondered if he should have stopped the illegal cash transaction in the sacristy when he'd had the chance.

Not that he'd had much of a chance. The money had been on the table by the time he'd gotten to the church, and he'd been a little low on firepower and authority. One .45 cartridge, that's all he'd had for the ancient pistol he'd been packing. One lousy cartridge for one old gun, because Honey had stolen his Sig Sauer, his extra magazines, and about half his brains by then.

And there she was, sipping a piña colada and cooling her cute ass in the pool, waiting for him to take her back into El Salvador.

Smith cleared his throat before he spoke.

"Has Ms. York been advised of the guerrilla activity on the Salvadoran side of the border, specifically along the Torola River?"

"Thoroughly advised," Jenkins said, his narrow jaw firming up. "That's why *you're* here."

Perfect.

Smith checked his watch and wondered if the Peruvian transport he'd come in on was still at the airport, and whether or not he could get his butt back on it. His work with the DEA was damned important, and he'd like to get back to it, just as soon as he nipped this circus in the bud and got Honey York headed in the right direction. Which was north. Way north. Much farther north than El Salvador. Closer to Canada was what he had in mind.

"All you have to worry about is doing your job, Mr. Rydell," Jenkins continued. "You can rest assured that I am doing mine."

No, he wasn't. Not if Honoria York-Lytton was traveling into the mountains of El Salvador.

"I think we need to speak with Ambassador Hasbert," Smith said. And anybody else who'd been in on this deal. A personal security detail in Panama wasn't exactly a vacation, but in Morazán, it was combat duty, and Honey had no business going into combat. Somebody had to know better than to let this thing fly, and he needed to find that someone. If it wasn't Hasbert, then he was going straight to General Grant. Honey had jerked somebody's chain to get him assigned as her personal bodyguard, and Grant was the guy who could jerk back.

Because this was crazy.

"Ambassador Hasbert will not return to Panama and be in residence again until the end of the month," Jenkins said. "Until then, I am in charge and have personally verified Ms. York's itinerary."

Okay, it was worse than crazy. It was dangerously crazy—Honey heading into Salvadoran guerrilla territory, and the idiot in charge of the embassy in Panama facilitating the trip.

"You know this is wrong," Smith said. Anybody could see how wrong it was, allowing her anywhere near the Torola, coffee plantations or no coffee plantations, and he wasn't buying for a minute that the damn fiasco had anything to do with coffee, not with Diego Garcia in the area.

No. This disaster had Sister Julia's fingerprints all over it.

Jenkins's jaw firmed up even more. "What I know, Mr. Rydell, and what you apparently still need to learn, is that it is in everyone's best interests to follow the orders they are given. Mine are to turn Ms. York over to you, and yours are to guarantee her safety while she is in your care, at the sacrifice of your own life, if necessary."

The tight little smile Jenkins gave with his summation of the situation made it clear that, for his money, the quicker Smith could arrange to sacrifice his life, the better. Unfortunately, given the situation, Smith could see the odds on that were heading exactly where Jenkins wanted them to head.

Or not.

He glanced at Honey again, and this time, she was looking back. A frisson of something or another skittered through him, hitting places he was trained to ignore, and ignore them was what he did. Steeling himself, he stepped past Jenkins and headed for the swimming pool. He was the professional here, the guy they'd called for help. Taking charge was what he did for a living, and he was damn good at it.

He crossed the pool deck with long, sure strides. If the State Department pencil pusher didn't have the brains to stop this thing before it blew up in his face, or the guts to stand up to a five-foot-and-next-to-nothing blonde, Smith was going to do it for him.

Kee-rist. Irena Polchenko was alive and on the loose, running drugs for the Cali cartel. That was about all the bad news Smith could handle this week. Honey York needed to get her butt back home—and he was just the guy to tell her.

CHAPTER TWO

Smith didn't look happy.

Honey took another long sip of her piña colada, then slowly stirred the drink with her straw, watching Mr. Determination and Coolness Under Pressure bear down on her from behind the safety of her sunglasses. Oh, no, he didn't look happy at all.

She didn't blame him. She wasn't very damn happy with the situation, either.

Lifting the glass to her lips, she licked a bit of sugar off the rim and let it melt on her tongue.

He did look good in a suit, though.

Damn good.

Dove gray, tailored to perfection, crisp white shirt, robin's egg blue tie striped in pink and gold, the Windsor knot a little loose around his neck. He looked very *GQ,* very tropical . . . and cold, even in this heat. Cold, calculating, and in control, she noted; hard, unforgiving, and dangerous.

Good. She needed him to be all those things and more, and despite how determined he looked, she didn't give a damn what he needed, or wanted, or what he had to say. This was a done deal. He was hers for as long as it took, and it had better not take a minute longer than the forty-eight hours she'd been given to contact the *Cuerpo Nacional de Libertad* troop making their base near the Torola River.

Seven, eight, zero, four, four, two.

Forty-eight hours.

Six numbers.

Five suitcases.

And one bodyguard built like the Rock of Gibraltar—that's what she was taking into the mountains of El Salvador with her, and she'd be damned if she came back out empty-handed. He was her ace in the hole, even if he hadn't called her, not once in four months, not even to see if she'd made it home okay, the jerk.

A one-night stand—that's all she'd been to him, but that was about to change, big-time. *Dammit.*

She reached up and clasped the pendant

strung on a silver chain around her neck. The small ivory-colored piece of reticulated quartz was the one thing she'd been given to guarantee his complete, total, and instant cooperation.

Fortunately, it was the only thing she needed— a small comfort as he got closer and closer and the urge to run got stronger and stronger. It took effort, dammit, to hold her ground, which was ridiculous for reasons she wasn't about to explore. Honoria York-Lytton did not run away, ever. She was the one with all the cards here. Not him.

At the edge of the pool, he stopped and looked down at her through his sunglasses, his expression unreadable, and yet somehow, his message clear: disapproval with a strong dose of "You've got no business being here."

She wished he was right, but he wasn't, far from it, no matter how much he glared, and that's exactly what he was doing behind his glasses. She could feel it.

Slowly, without taking her eyes off him, she brought the tiny cocktail straw in her piña colada to her lips . . . and sipped. The seconds ticked by in utter silence, one after the other, with the sun shining, the palm trees swaying, the water lapping at her butt, and him not moving a muscle, just standing there, broad-shouldered and broad through the chest, looming over her in a beautiful suit and a pair of perfectly polished loafers.

She knew his name now, his full name. She'd read it in the report she'd been given, a cursory résumé that had dead-ended two years ago at a place referred to only as SDF. God only knew what he'd been up to since then, besides being in San Luis one night—God and the man who had given her the piece of quartz.

That man knew what he'd been up to. That man knew everything, even about her...*everything*, which had not made her happy. Oh, no, not at all.

Among a few other tantalizing tidbits, like him growing up in Little Rock, Arkansas, and going to the University of Wyoming in Laramie, the report on Mr. C. Smith Rydell had contained his physical stats, but she'd already known how tall he was—tall enough that in two-inch platforms, she barely came to his collarbone. She'd already known how much he weighed—enough to cord his body with layer upon layer of hard muscle, enough to rope his shoulders with a dozen of those layers, enough to six-pack his abs and burn the memory of him into every single cell she had. His hair was darker than it had been in San Luis, still blond in a few streaks here and there, but mostly a tawny shade of brown, just as long, but better cut. She remembered his eyes were a dark hazel with thick, dark lashes, and his mouth—

Oh, yes, she remembered his mouth.

She remembered too much about a man who had put her on a plane and never given her another thought.

Letting out a resigned sigh, he knelt down and brought himself almost eye level with her.

"This better be good, Honey."

She took another sip, long and slow, then licked the end of the tiny straw.

Oh, it was good, all right, good enough for the United States government to make a case against her and against him, good enough to send her into exile and him into jail, good enough to get them both killed, if they failed.

She wasn't going to tell him that, though, not until he knew he didn't have a choice. Not until he knew that come hell, high water, or a Salvadoran death squad, he was going to be right by her side—because she didn't have a choice, either, and not just because of the damn CIA and their damn threats.

Finished with the straw, she stuck it back in the drink and set the glass down next to his feet.

"A man in Washington told me to give this to you, that you would know what it meant— *exactly* what it meant," she said, reaching up and slipping the necklace off over the top of her head. She held it out, and the pendant dangled between them, with the bright, tropical sunlight shining through the quartz and glinting off the silver chain looped around her fingers.

He didn't make a move to take it, just grew very, very still and stared at the damn thing.

She understood. She'd been more than a little unnerved by the stone summons when it had been given to her—and it was nothing less. A summons: for her, a command she ignored at her peril; for him, she'd been promised, a call to duty he would obey, no questions asked.

And yet he didn't reach out to take it.

"I want a name," he said, when he finally spoke. "I want to know who, what, when, where, and how in the hell that came into your possession." His words were slow and measured, his voice the stone-cold definition of don't-fuck-with-me authority.

And she loved it—*oh, yes*. It was exactly what she needed, all his growl and grumble, all the sleek menace he could muster, and even with all that on her side, she was scared spitless by what the man in Washington expected her to do.

But Mr. C. Smith Rydell didn't need to know she was scared, ever.

Pushing her sunglasses down on her nose, she

looked up at him from over the top of the frames, giving him a cool once-over, and sure as hell not bothering to tell him who had given her the necklace. The name was hanging in the air between them, and he knew it.

So she held his gaze, quiet and steady, until he got *her* message.

"No way," he said, shaking his head, a slight, disbelieving grin curving the corner of his mouth. "You're not that connected. Nobody is *that* connected. You didn't get to that guy."

"You are so incredibly right, as usual, Mr. Rydell," she said, pushing her sunglasses back up. "I didn't get to him. He got to me."

Another silence ensued, another discomfiting, tension-filled silence, and Honey could tell it was going to be one helluva long forty-eight hours— one helluva long, dangerous, and no doubt unbearably hot and sweaty forty-eight hours.

God, she hoped she had the strength for it.

Sonuvabitch.

Smith stared at the necklace, stared at the sun-shot piece of quartz, and in his head, he kept swearing, one cold-edged curse after another.

Honey, he could have handled—his gaze dropped down the front of her—maybe. But the stone was nonnegotiable, an ivory-colored pendant carved into a chess piece, a white rook, and with her standing in front of him, and Peru hell and gone behind him, and damned Jenkins handing out orders like candy at a parade, the piece could only have come from the one man with the authority to make even General Grant jump: White Rook, *the* White Rook, a shadowy figure in the stratosphere of U.S. government who had created SDF eleven years ago with a stroke of his pen.

And White Rook had sent him Honey York.

Goddammit.

The situation was starting to give him a real bad, edgy feeling, and he hated it when he got a real bad, edgy feeling, especially before lunch.

He picked up her piña colada and looked to either side of the pool before taking a long swallow. There were a hundred people milling around the area, and he didn't know a one of them besides the idiot at his back and the piece of work at his feet—and that could be good, or bad, or mean absolutely nothing.

"This hasn't got a damn thing to do with coffee, does it?" he said, setting the drink down on the deck and letting his gaze fall back on her. Blond, rich, too damn beautiful for anybody's good, and nothing but trouble—if anyone needed a body-guard at the Blake, it was definitely Honey York.

"A little, maybe," she said, "but not really."

He swore again, a bit more crudely, then took the necklace and slipped it into his pocket—because he didn't have a choice.

"Come on, Ms. York," he said, extending his hand to help her out of the pool. "Let's go some-place where you can explain to me why I shouldn't put your butt back on a plane headed home, no matter how much jewelry you've packed into Panama."

He had to accept the assignment, whatever it actually turned out to be, but that was the only thing he had to do. The planning and execution of an SDF mission was strictly up to the operators—in this case, him—and in his book, there wasn't one reason in a thousand for her to be any part of whatever happened next, especially if it was going to happen in El Salvador.

He let his gaze slide down her body as she came up out of the water—okay, he could think of one, but that was not going to happen, not on a mission.

The minute she was solidly on the deck, he let go of her hand and took a step back, keeping a safe distance, if that was even possible with her, which he seriously doubted. She'd been nothing but trouble since the day they'd met, even if they hadn't even spent a whole day together. He never had understood what in the hell had compelled him to leave a perfectly good beer, in a perfectly good cantina, and cross a lousy street filling up with bad guys in order to save her from potential harm.

Potential, hell.

There'd been nothing "potential" about it. Those bad guys had been gunning for her, and everything inside him had said "intervene" in big block letters. Sure, she'd gotten herself into trouble that day in San Luis by wandering off the beaten tourist path, but he had not been able to let the mistake stand and take care of itself, not when he'd seen her and instantly known what was getting ready to happen.

So here he was again. *Dammit*.

He let her precede him to a nearby chaise longue and waited while she slipped on a pair of black-sequined sparkle sandals and tied a sheer black sarong low around her hips, and he tried not to be too interested in the process, especially the whole wrapping-something-around-her-hips process.

Right.

Now all he had to do was debrief her, get all the pertinent information out of her little steel trap of a brain, and then send her on her way, because there was nothing that could need doing in El Salvador that he couldn't do better, faster, and more safely without her.

No, he wouldn't be taking Honoria York-Lytton with him into Morazán. No way in hell.

CHAPTER THREE

No fucking way in hell.

Smith picked up one of the photographs Honey had set out on the table in her garden bungalow, listening to her brief him on the operation and her part in it, and all he could think was *no fucking way in hell.*

"The mayday call came in two days ago, and my *butt* was on a plane out of Dulles last night," she said. "The failed mission was diplomatic, top priority."

Weren't they all? he thought, but kept his opinion to himself. He'd been on a few "top priority" diplomatic missions, a couple where the rate of fire had exceeded the rate of diplomacy by a hundred to one.

He took off his sunglasses and gave the photo a closer look.

"The CIA knows the guerrillas found their downed plane, the pilot, and the courier's pouch he was carrying," she said. "What they don't know is if Diego and his men found—"

"Diego?" he interrupted, shifting his attention from the eight-by-ten glossy of a plane's broken tail section and pinning her with his gaze. *Diego?*

"Diego Garcia, the guerrilla leader."

Yeah, yeah, he knew, but *geezus.*

"You're on a first-name basis with the commander of the Cuerpo Nacional de Libertad? The CNL?"

"We met that night in San Luis, in the sacristy at St. Mary's. We had dinner together."

"I remember." Clearly, but he sure as hell hadn't considered it a friggin' social engagement.

"And we've . . . uh, corresponded a few times since."

He stared at her, dead silent.

Correfuckingsponded?

"So, uh . . . well," she continued, glancing at the photographs and absently straightening one edge of the pile, "what the . . . uh, CIA doesn't know is if the CNL found the flash drive the pilot was also transporting. It wasn't mentioned in their list of demands. But the Agency wants it back, and after we retrieve the courier's pouch, we're supposed to get the rebels to take us to the plane, unless this Campos guy can, so we can search for—"

"Stop," he said, lifting his hand, his jaw suddenly so tight he could barely speak. "Stop right there."

If the CIA wanted their damn courier's pouch and their damn flash drive back, great. Fine. He'd call Kid or Creed, and they'd go get them. But nothing about the op made sense, if Honey was involved. He couldn't think of a better way to get himself killed, because there was no better way. Oh, hell, no. Taking a hothouse blonde into Morazán to hook up with a bunch of jungle runners to go search the friggin' cockpit and fuselage of a crashed Cessna was a guaranteed goatfuck.

And there she'd be, right smack-dab in the middle of it, with her little sparkle sandals and her cocktail umbrellas, and all the power and money she had at her beck and call not doing her one goddamn bit of good.

Hell, no, nothing about it made sense—except for one little thing.

"Corresponding," he said, dropping the photo back on the table. It was a question, and he damn well expected an answer.

"Notes," she said. "Well, note cards. Embossed. A couple of them."

Embossed.

Of course.

"And, uh . . . he writes back on that really thin paper that you can almost see through."

Smith bet the CIA had loved that.

"And what do you two write each other about?" he asked.

"The weather."

Bullshit.

"And the hardships of camp life."

More bullshit.

"And Julia."

Bingo, bango, bongo. Game over.

"Get packed," he said, slipping his sunglasses inside his jacket pocket. "Whatever trouble your sister has gotten herself into, you're not the one who can get her out. You're going home." And if this was the kind of plan the spooks at Langley were running down the back side of State, it might be time for a desk job somewhere. Either that, or he needed to be carrying more ammo.

"I can't."

"Then I'll do it for you," he said, turning on his heel and heading for the closet.

"I mean I can't go home. The ticket they gave me, it was only one-way."

"Then we'll buy another one." He'd have Skeeter expense it out to the U.S. Embassy in Panama. Brett Jenkins could thank him later, because, man, he was doing the boy a favor. Far better to get stuck with the tab on an international airline ticket, than to have to explain how you lost the daughter of a former ambassador in the wilds of El Salvador. Jenkins would be stumbling over that one for the rest of a very short-lived career.

"It's not that easy."

"Yes, it is." With an American Express card and a passport, nothing could be easier.

He reached the closet, with her hot on his heels, swung the door open—and stopped cold.

What the fuck?

The closet was a walk-in, and there were eight frickin' Louis Vuitton suitcases in it. Five of them the big ones.

"What—" he started, then stopped. "What" was not the question.

"Why" was the question, as in why would any one person need so much stuff? Anywhere? Anytime? To do anything? And he was about ready to ask it, when she dropped another bomb.

"No, it's not easy. Not at all. They're not going to let me back in."

Feeling that bad edginess growing stronger

and starting to crawl up the back of his neck, he turned to face her. "*Who* isn't going to let you back in *where*?"

"The CIA is not going to let me back into the United States, not without slapping a charge of treason on me, not unless I bring them the courier's pouch, the missing flash drive, and Diego Garcia's assurance that the Campos coffee plantation in Morazán will not be part of the CNL's next push down the Torola River."

She'd done it again, struck him dumb—but okay, all right, he was starting to get the picture, and it was way bigger than Sister Julia and two embossed notes. Treason, *geezus*, and the rest of it—well, hell, he knew the Campos plantation, had deployed out of it once. Alejandro Campos had a knack for working all sides toward the middle without getting in the line of fire or on anyone's demolish-and-destroy list. The guy was deep in the game, brokering power between his base of operations in Morazán and dozens of points north and south across Central America and beyond; a player, a drug dealer, an arms dealer, whatever people needed him to be, ally or enemy, and Smith couldn't imagine why the CIA wanted Honoria York-Lytton to run interference for him with the CNL. Hell, knowing Campos, he'd probably financed the rebel group's last sortie—and knowing Campos, he'd probably sold them out three times while doing it, which would explain the CIA's vested interest in keeping him in one piece. That kind of talent was hard to find.

But treason, *Christ*, that was all too easy to find. The sacristy of St. Mary's had been full of treason that night in San Luis—at least it could be construed that way by someone with a motive, like an agency who needed to retrieve a goddamn courier's pouch and a fucking flash drive from a guerrilla group in the mountains and, for a thousand reasons, didn't want anyone to know it was them doing it, or that the whole goddamn problem was theirs, a description that fit every single thing the CIA did.

His gaze dropped down Honey again, from the top of her devilishly wild blond curls to the ten little hot pink toes peeking out of her sparkle sandals, all five feet two inches of one hundred percent pure girly-girl, the high maintenance, high-octane version.

Right.

That's who he'd send into the jungle to get his stuff back.

Not.

Not for any reason on God's green earth, which begged the question.

"Why you?"

"Diego requested me. There have been a few...well, events that have taken place recently. They've left people on edge, upset the balance so to speak, and apparently I'm the only one he trusts right now."

No surprise, not really. A couple of "recent events" in the Salvadoran highlands had made the back page of the world news section in *The New York Times*, and there had been casualties, with both instances being part of the "all hell breaking loose on the border" situation he'd been monitoring for the last four friggin' months.

So, okay, he could almost buy it. Honey had hand-delivered a quarter of a million dollars to the bad boy. Throw in a saintly sister saving highland village orphans, and there was definitely enough to grease a few wheels and set up a relationship, and odds were that Garcia and the CIA had hit a few rough spots in their dealings with each other over those "recent events." So, sure, he could see a murdering rebel bastard asking for a sweet-assed *gringa* to deliver his payola next time.

Fuck.

Somebody at the CIA needed to be shot.

"How much money are you carrying?"

Her brow furrowed. "About four thousand dollars. For incidentals and things."

Yeah. Sometimes, when he was out of town for a couple of days, he needed a few incidentals, too, but four grand's worth of incidentals would have to include his mortgage.

"I mean for Garcia."

"I don't know."

Great.

If there was anything else he was going to hate about this mission, he'd like to know it now, while he still had a chance to bail out.

"I have a lading document for the equipment that's supposed to be waiting for me at the airbase, and half the combination to a black briefcase they gave me marked with the letter Z," she continued. "Nobody told me what was in it."

Lading document?

Okay, he hated that—and the whole briefcase thing? He hated that, too.

"Who has the other half of the combination?"

"Alejandro Campos."

And he definitely hated that.

"Why Campos?"

She just looked at him, long and hard, her gaze narrowing on him like a very angry...very angry kitten. It sucked, it really sucked, but that was about all the "big bad dangerous me" she could generate. And it wasn't enough. Not for what she was expected to do.

He needed Red Dog. She was a sweet-assed *gringa*, too, but that girl could deliver a heart-stopping boatload of "big, bad, and dangerous" on demand, in one second or less—literally.

But he didn't have Red Dog. He had Honey-pie.

"I am sure, Mr. Rydell," she said, planting her hands on her hips, "that when you're given a job to do, you're also given all the wherefores and whys, all the how-comes and this-is-the-reason-becauses—but I was not. All they gave me was a rather frightening lecture on the legal parameters of treason, an hour to pack, a one-way plane ticket, half the combination to a briefcase, and a scurrilous threat tacked on to a warning not to fail."

A scurrilous threat. She was right. He'd never been given one of those. All the threats he'd been given could be measured in calibers.

And *geezus*, she'd packed all that crap in the closet in an hour? That had to be some sort of record.

"Jet lag?" he asked.

"Whiplash," she said.

Yeah. He could imagine. Whiplash with a bull-whip—and she still looked good enough to eat.

Fuck.

"Let me see the lading document."

She handed him a standard U.S. Air Force load manifest from off the table, and the farther down he read, the tighter his jaw got.

There was enough gear on the damn list to outfit a recon platoon for a week. Cases of it, as in gun cases. Boxes of it, as in ammo. Rucksacks of it, as in no way could one of them possibly be meant for Honey York to carry. And ordnance. *Christ*. His gaze strayed to the closet and all those damn Louis Vuitton suitcases, then came back to the list of military weapons and supplies. Yeah, he knew what this was—a Paris Hilton black op.

Sure. A Paris Hilton black op looking for a place to happen, a Paris Hilton black op that was not going to happen in El Salvador, not with Honey York attached to the luggage.

He swore under his breath, one succinct word. Whether she knew it or not, she had an international arms deal on her hands, which would make another, and far more serious, treason charge for somebody, like maybe the CIA, to hang over her head.

"Show me the briefcase," he said, folding the manifest and slipping it inside his suit jacket. *Geezus*.

She stepped by him and unzipped one of the

smaller suitcases. By his estimation, she rustled through half a ton of clothes, the kind of girl stuff with lots of tiny straps and tricky closures, before she uncovered the briefcase.

"It's heavy," she said, dragging it upright.

He reached down and took it from her, then set it on the table and checked the locks—cipher locks, two of them, one on each side of the handle, a custom piece. The damn thing looked beat to hell and was surprisingly heavy, which he knew might have more to do with what it was made of—leather-covered sheet steel—than with what was in it.

Anything could be in it.

And he didn't like not knowing what.

The being beat to hell could mean a couple of things: a rough passage, or a whole lot of rough passages. Given who had the rest of the combination, his money was on the briefcase having been taken back and forth over a whole helluva lot of borders a whole helluva lot of times.

He didn't know what to make of the capital letter Z hand-tooled into the top in an ornate, flowing script. It wasn't production work, but another purely custom feature, which meant he had a mystery on his hands, and he hated mysteries.

"Do you know what the Z stands for?" he asked.

She crossed her arms over her chest and gave him another considering look. "I'm hoping Zorro, but given the way my luck has been running since yesterday afternoon, I've got serious doubts about a masked man showing up at Campos's plantation."

Yesterday afternoon, *geezus*. Her head had to still be reeling. White Rook had snatched her out of her life and thrown her into this mess in record time—and he wouldn't have done it without a damn good reason.

Tasking civilians with vital missions involving weapons, locked briefcases, and the CIA was the surest road to disaster Smith knew, especially if the civilians were cute-assed blondes with no training and no practical skills.

He shifted his attention back to the briefcase. The design of the letter definitely had that Zorro look to it, but like her, he doubted there were any legendary heroes running around Morazán Province, ready to save the girl and the day. No, that job, if and when it needed doing, was going to be all his, and he could only think of one way to pull it off.

"Plan A, the way you've outlined it, is unacceptable to me," he said. He didn't give a damn who had put it together. "So we're moving straight to Plan B."

"Which is?"

"You tell me your half of the combination," he said, visually checking the briefcase before running his hands carefully over the top, "and I fly into Morazán alone to meet with Campos and Garcia. I'll get the courier's pouch and the flash drive, while you stay here at the Blake, sunning yourself by the pool and drinking piña coladas. Maybe Brett Jenkins can take you out for a nice dinner."

Not surprisingly, Plan B was met with silence.

Tough. He liked it, and she was just going to have to live with it. He'd given her a way out, and by all rights, she should be grateful.

He finished checking the briefcase by sliding his hands along the edges. He didn't feel anything unusual, but if it was rigged to explode, the thermite and the trigger mechanism would all be inside. When he was finished, he looked over his shoulder at her. She was still standing in the walk-in closet, arms crossed, mouth tight, her rhinestone sunglasses perched on top of her head with the cocktail umbrellas sticking up behind and her hair all wildly topsy-turvy. She should have looked ridiculous.

She didn't.

She looked put-together, not falling apart, her skin like satin, her bikini, what little there was of it, hand-tailored right down to the strings. She looked in over her head, but still holding her own. She looked in control of herself, even if the situation was out of her hands.

She looked like it would take a crowbar and two sumo wrestlers to get the damn combination out of her.

And *goddammit,* she looked like something he'd lost. Something he should have been more careful with—but that was an epiphany he wasn't going to accept delivery on, not here, not now.

"Why me, Honey?" That's the question he needed answered. Contrary to what she'd said, he didn't have a wherefore or a because anywhere in sight, and nothing she'd shown him had a damn thing to do with him, except her.

Without a word, she strode back to the table, the tiny heels of her shoes clicking on the hardwood floor. Once there, it took her all of ten seconds to blow him up again.

She spread the photographs out with the palm of her hand, then pulled three out of the lower end of the stack.

"This is you standing outside the window of the sacristy that night in San Luis," she said, handing over the first photo. "Please note the pistol in your hand—both hands, actually—and the intent expression on your face as you watch what's going on inside."

He glanced down at the picture, and that's all it took to prove her correct and for all the implications of the photograph to become absolutely crystal clear.

"And then here's the same shot again, but zoomed in on the window. Please note the illegal cash transfer taking place on the other side of the window, inside the sacristy, with me and Diego Garcia clearly identifiable. For the record, I hadn't known a camera could take such good photos at night."

He had, but he hadn't known anyone in San Luis had been taking pictures of him—and he should have, goddammit.

"And the last one"—she handed it over—"is of you and me getting in the cab the next morning, and yes, they know exactly how I got out of the country. In fact, they know more about the pilot and the plane you put me on that morning than I do."

Yeah, the fucking CIA knew everything, and they'd obviously tagged him when he'd entered El Salvador, which meant that even after the big favor Steele Street had done them four months ago, retiring one of their rogue agents, the CIA was still tracking SDF operators, and it meant—

"You blew my cover," she said.

Yeah. That's what it meant, and her cover had been perfect: ditzy blond tourist with a tote bag. Perfect, because it had almost been the truth.

Almost, but not quite. She wasn't ditzy, and she hadn't been a tourist. Like him, she'd been in El Salvador on a mission, except hers had been a mission of mercy, taking money to her sister, so Julia could repair an orphanage.

"In essence, then," she continued, "this is all your fault, and you have nobody to blame but yourself."

Typical.

"And I'm blaming you, too."

A foregone conclusion in his life whenever a woman was involved—but she was just getting warmed up.

"Because nobody cares if Honoria York-Lytton hops from Puerto Vallarta, Mexico, to San Luis, El Salvador, for a few days on the beach, but apparently the CIA cares very much where *you* are, and they cared very much about what *you* were doing that night," she said, her voice rising a bit, which he knew from a lot of rising female voices in his past was not a good sign. "And because *you* followed me, and they followed *you*"—and the whole "you" thing, that was not good—"*my* butt is in Panama with a bunch of guns I'm supposed to cart into the jungle, and a briefcase full of God knows what, and the next place *my* butt is going to be is back in El Salvador, where I'm supposed to wheel and deal with a group of armed and dangerous political insurgents, and about the only place I can guarantee my butt is *not* going to be is back on a plane to Washington, D.C., not without a courier's pouch, a flash drive, and an agreement between the CNL and Alejandro Campos."

"Unless you give me the combination and let me do it for you." The solution to all this was so simple.

But her foot was tapping.

"No," she said. One word.

And there could be only one reason for her to use that word: her sister, saintly Sister Julia Ann-Marie Bakkert. He'd done some checking on the woman, and Julia had packed quite a bit of saintliness into her twenty-one years before she'd taken the cross—starting a youth mentoring program while at a private boarding school in Europe, food bank work in Washington, D.C., chairing the fund-raising committee for a halfway house for troubled teens in Boston.

She'd dropped out of Harvard after her freshman year to marry the youngest son of Dr. Hans Bakkert, head of the Latin America Chapter of the United Health Organization. Two years later, that youngest son, Carl, had been murdered in the Hotel Langston on the island of Malanca off the coast of Honduras.

Smith had had Skeeter track down the file, including photos, and it had been a bloody mess. The miracle was that Julia hadn't died with her husband. They'd been caught in the hotel's main elevator, real close quarters for an assassination—and Honey had been in the Langston's dining room, waiting for them, when it had happened.

He'd read her statement. She'd seen the killers. They'd walked past her, three men in black balaclavas and black clothes, carrying submachine guns, pushing their way out the front doors of the hotel, and at the other end of the lobby, the elevator, with Julia collapsed in one corner, screaming, and Carl slumped in the other, silent, slaughtered by over thirty rounds of .40 S&W ammo delivered at extremely close range.

According to the file, Honey had been the first to reach the elevator. She'd gathered up her sister and barricaded herself and Julia in her suite, and she'd

gotten a three-way phone conversation going between the U.S. Embassy in Tegucigalpa, Honduras,
and the State Department in Washington, D.C.,
cobbling together an immediate departure, all before the police had even arrived on the scene.

Looking at her, it was hard to imagine.

He'd seen carnage, up close and personal. He
knew the precise terminal ballistics of every
round he used in his weapons. He knew what
she'd seen in the elevator.

And yet she was here, telling him no.

"Jenkins said you have two days in the highlands."

"Two." She nodded.

And four months ago, she'd smuggled a quarter of a million dollars into El Salvador, and then
gotten the money across San Luis in the middle
of the night, through the middle of a riot, all on
her own.

"Forty-eight hours."

"Yes," she confirmed.

"Why?"

"Garcia set the timetable. If we don't meet it,
he moves his camp, disappears into the mountains, and sells to someone else."

Fuck. He was going to do this, and not because
of the photos. There was plenty of intelligence in
the Central Intelligence Agency, but not enough

to get a treason conviction to stick to him. He'd played the game too many different ways, from too many different angles, for too many government organizations, all in the name of whatever mission they'd given him, and he could do it again, as many times as they needed him to, whenever and wherever. Those skills were the reason he'd been tagged by Grant for SDF. Those skills were what made him too goddamn useful to throw away on back-page news and a low-end payoff. So, no, the photos were no threat to him, and given her last name, they weren't a threat to Honey, either, and she had to know it, no matter how heavy-handed they'd gotten with her before they'd put her on the plane to Panama.

No, this was a flat-out opportunity, and everybody from the CIA to White Rook was using the situation to their advantage, including Honoria York-Lytton. He didn't doubt for a second that the spooks wanted their documents and data back, or that Diego Garcia had requested her as the courier for the payoff, but she was here for Julia—and because she wanted something, she'd set herself up to be used.

That's why Smith kept his damn Christmas list to himself. Nobody knew what he wanted.

Nobody.

And White Rook—hell, White Rook knew her value, down to the ounce, and that was why his ass was in Panama and outbound to El Salvador, instead of still in Peru. Brett Jenkins III had been right. This was a personal security detail, with a whole lot of freight on board for the ride.

But his job was to keep her safe.

He let his gaze slide down her again, down all those curves one more time. *Christ.* There wasn't a straight line on her—anywhere.

Yeah, he knew what he wanted. He knew what he'd been wanting for the last four months, her little steel trap of a brain working him over, her body, hot and sweet, working him hard.

Do me, Smith, she'd whispered to him that night in San Luis, and he'd done nothing but dream about it ever since, fantasize about it, get off on it, and start all over again more times than he cared to remember.

But it wasn't going to happen, not in the next forty-eight hours, and after that, her butt *would* be on a plane back to Washington, D.C.

Inside his pocket, he felt the silent vibration of his phone, and all he could think was that it was about goddamn time. A phone call was the least of what he needed before he got on a plane going anywhere, especially to El Salvador.

He pulled out his phone, checked the number—
General Grant—then checked his watch.

"You've got half an hour before we move out,"
he said, heading past her toward the door. "Don't
be late."

CHAPTER FOUR

Exaltación, Colombia

This was the last time he stole a car. Alejandro Campos swore it. He was getting too old to be hot-wiring pieces of junk in rat-infested alleys in flea-bitten border towns, and yet he kept ending up in some damn border town somewhere, usually on the verge of getting his ass kicked, and he hated to think it, but the longer he was in this particular rat-infested alley, the surer he was that he'd been in it before, staring down the same damn rats.

Mierda. Shit. He lived his life on the border, had been living it on the border for more years than was good for him. It was all getting so fucking obvious.

"Jewel, baby?" he asked.

"Yeah, boss?"

From underneath the steering wheel, he tapped a couple of wires together, and got nothing.

"Why is it again that you left me?" he asked.

Jesus. He used to be so good at this, one of the best.

True, the car was a piece of junk, a cheap-ass four-banger with rusted-out quarter panels and a hole in the floorboards—but it wasn't like they'd had a whole lot of options after the Mercedes had gone up in a flaming ball of twisted metal and smoking tires, Jewel's car, a pearl gray 380 SL, and oh, hell, yeah, he knew it was going to show up on her expense account.

The girl was ruthless.

"Because you're a head case."

A ruthless, brutally honest bitch—that was why he loved her.

He fished around for another wire.

But did he still love her like that? Hell, he'd been asking himself that question since she'd walked out of his bedroom door for the last time, two years ago, and he still didn't know. The day she'd gotten married to what's-his-name, and that would have been one year, eleven months, and two weeks ago—and yeah, that had been some kind of clue—anyway, that day, he'd thought he'd known the answer—no. Bon voyage, baby, and all that.

A short burst of gunfire pop-popped into the alley, and Jewel returned fire, precision fire, raising her pistol and squeezing off two rounds aimed toward the roofline on the south side.

A guy fell off the building and landed in a bloody pile in the alley, less than two meters from the car. One solid center-chest hit, and from the looks of what Campos could see, or rather what he couldn't see, like the back of the guy's skull, a head shot. God, she was good—but the bad guys were catching up.

He touched another set of wires, and got another big nothing.

Dammit.

Sure, bon voyage, that's what it had been on her wedding day, but when he was stretched out under a steering column, and she was in the passenger seat, arranged for maximum tactical advantage, and he could see up her skirt—well, it was times like those when he asked himself if he still loved her. And depending on how far he could see up her skirt, the answer could be either yes or no.

Today was a yes.

"Red lace panties?"

"Fuck you."

He grinned. He loved her. It was a definite yes.

"So how you doing, boss?"

"Bleeding, but not bleeding out." Not in this rat-infested alley, not in this flea-bitten town, not today. He'd gotten trimmed, that was all, a round catching him across the meaty part of his right thigh during their great escape from a lunchtime drug deal gone bad. The wound burned, but somehow not quite as badly as his brain.

Yeah, his brain was on fucking fire. Some two-bit *chingaletos* had jacked the cocaine shipment he'd been delivering to Exaltación's number-one drug lord, a player named Ray Gonzalez. They'd stolen the damn shit right out from under him and then come after him for good measure—and baby, this week, on this deal, that was a death warrant. Nobody screwed with Alejandro Campos's cocaine deals except Alejandro Campos.

Christ, the drug trade was so damned complicated these days. Too many players, too much blow, too many people with their fingers in the cocaine pie, and too many people fucking up.

The next ignition wire he tapped against the two he'd already twisted together gave him a spark—*hot damn*. The motor groaned, and whined, and finally turned over.

It was the most pitiful excuse for a getaway, and a getaway car, he'd ever been involved with—he just hoped like hell that it worked. They were a hundred miles out of Barranquilla, and if he didn't get Jewel home in one piece, what's-his-name would probably write some really crappy poem about him and have it published in some really crappy academic journal.

A poet. She'd left him for a fucking poet.

Jesus. Women.

He levered himself up into the driver's seat and ignored the fact that he was sitting in a pool of his own blood. It was only a small pool, little more than a wet smear now that most of what he'd lost had soaked into the upholstery. Yes, sir, turning his favorite silk tie into a pressure bandage had been a brilliant idea.

The car sputtered when he gave it a little gas, and he swore under his breath. "Come on, you inbred piece of shit. Don't quit on me now."

Exaltación, Colombia, wasn't that damn big, not so big that Gonzalez shouldn't have better goddamn control of the streets, and not so big that it should have been such a goddamn big deal to get the fuck out of it.

But he and Jewel were sucking air.

He tried the gas again, and when the motor kept running, he jerked the car into gear.

"Buckle up, baby, and reload."

"Buckle up?" She let out a short laugh and slammed a fresh magazine into her .45-caliber Colt. "We don't have a driver's side door, a back window, or half the dashboard, and you want me to buckle up? Christ, boss. I'm lucky to have a damn seat." She grinned. "Buckle up. God, Campos, you were always good for a laugh."

And that was probably the last damn thing a guy wanted to hear, any guy. It was only one step above the utterly demoralizing "You're finished? Already?" Which, admittedly, was a couple of dozen steps above "What's the problem? Don't you like me?"

And yes, he'd been *there* a couple of times. *Dammit.*

Once with her—but no guy got left because of an "equipment malfunction," not when a woman loved him.

So, yeah, that's probably how it had been, with him being in love and her being in something else, like in it for the thrill of the game, because baby, the thrills in the game they played were razor sharp.

"We have to stop meeting like this, boss."

Yeah, yeah, he knew it.

"I mean it, Campos. It's time for you to jump ship, cash in your chips, and say *hasta la vista*."

No, it wasn't. He'd know when it was time.

"But you won't," she said.

Christ. Was she reading his mind? He hated it when she read his mind.

He glanced over at her: "Jewel"—Joya Molara Gualterio, former U.S. Marine and Austin, Texas, high-school homecoming queen, long legs, long chestnut-colored hair, dark eyes, smart mouth, red business suit with a three-button jacket and a tight skirt.

Hell. She was fucking a poet, and he was good for a laugh. Something wasn't right with the world.

Actually, a whole lot of things weren't right with his world, beginning with these small-time hoods thinking they had something to gain by killing Alejandro Campos instead of doing the smart thing and letting him make good on his deal with Gonzalez. There was plenty of action to go around, always a way for everyone to get ahead.

But nobody got ahead by going after Alejandro Campos. That was a strictly "good way to get fucked" move. He'd spent the last twelve years building the reputation that made it so.

Twelve years, dammit.

Twelve years to go from a street corner drug thug to a major mover with an estate in the Salvadoran highlands and the kind of entourage that was supposed to keep him out of rat-infested alleys.

Not today, though. He hadn't seen this disaster

coming, and he sure as hell hadn't expected to get fucking shot and bleed all over one of his best damn suits.

Well, the street thugs had gotten all the blood they were going to get, and it was all soaked into the seat of the POS, the piece-of-shit four-banger.

Yeah, it was a hundred land miles to Barranquilla, but only two to the coast and a go-fast boat running four 250 Mercs. He'd have Jewel back in what's-his-name's good keeping and be sitting in a Beech Baron, flying home to Morazán before Gonzalez's staff finished cleaning up the mess that had started out as an elegant lunch with a little business on the side and ended with Mercedes *flambé* and a firefight in close quarters.

He had a package arriving this evening, a package with his name on it, and he'd be damned if he missed the delivery.

CHAPTER FIVE

Make it four sumo wrestlers, Smith thought, sitting next to Honey in the limo taking them to Howard Air Force Base, where they would board a C-130 to Ilopango. She wasn't giving anything away, least of all the damn combination to the briefcase she'd honest to God handcuffed to her wrist. It was the only flaw in an otherwise flawless look. He didn't know how she'd done it, honestly, he didn't, but in the half an hour she'd had to get ready, she'd managed to turn herself from a bikinied bimbette into a Park Avenue princess. All her wild curls had disappeared into a sleek French twist, and all those wild curves had disappeared inside a sleeveless canary yellow dress so simple it almost defied description. There was nothing to it: a front, a back, and a very thin black patent leather belt with a very tiny black patent leather bow in the front. That was it. And yet it looked like it cost more than his car. And it fit her like a glove. Every breath she took registered with a subtle rise and fall of canary yellow material. Every move she made, the dress was right there with her—and so was the damn briefcase.

For her own good, he was going to have to tell her the bad guys had a real quick way of dealing with wrists handcuffed to briefcases, and she didn't know it, but she would freeze her butt off inside a C-130 in a sleeveless dress. Fortunately, being cold was one problem he could fix.

"Our friend at the State Department did not give you a pair of handcuffs to wear," he said. White Rook knew as well as anyone that in this part of the world, handcuffing yourself to anything worth stealing was a real good way to lose a hand, and the bad guys wouldn't hesitate, not for a second, no matter how pretty her French manicure looked.

"No," she said, arranging the briefcase more comfortably next to her in the seat, tucking it up against her large canary yellow purse. "The cuffs are mine."

Great. Just what he wanted to hear. The woman who had written *The Sorority Girl's Guide to Self-Help Sex,* the woman who had made the covers of the tabloids with headlines about shameless sorority girl sex games, owned a pair of handcuffs—and he'd let her slip through his fingers in record time.

Yeah, about twelve hours, that's how long she'd been in his care, a real hit-and-run hookup, and wasn't that the way of it sometimes. *Hell.*

Honey turned a page in the book she was reading and let out a sigh, one of many she'd given in to since they'd left the Blake. Something was all pent up inside her, that much was obvious, and it was probably something he needed to know, like maybe the truth of why she'd let herself be roped into this mission, or maybe exactly how much and what kind of trouble Sister Julia had gotten herself into, and what in the world Honey thought she could do to get Julia out of it.

One thing Smith did know: The CIA didn't give a damn about Julia Bakkert. The station chief at the U.S. Embassy here in Panama City, William Dobbs, had made that much clear when Smith had stopped by, per General Grant's orders, and politely asked him what the fuck was going on. Covert mission gone bad, Dobbs had told him. A plane down. Time-sensitive, classified data floating around loose in the jungle. Guerrilla faction demanding money, weapons, and some woman named Honoria York-Lytton to deliver it all in forty-eight hours or less, or they were going to pack their toys and disappear, and the next time the Agency would see their documents would be on the international black market. Luckily, the Agency had enough dirt on Ms. York-Lytton to make her a malleable asset. Dirt, Dobbs had recalled, that included an unnamed covert operator under the command of General Richard Grant.

Yeah. Dobbs's opening salvo had pretty much summed up everything Honey had told him.

Regardless, the chief of station had gone on, Rydell's involvement had come from the other end of the chain, straight from someone high up at the State Department in Washington, D.C., very high up if they were overseeing the CIA's involvement in the retrieval of their own data. Dobbs had been told to support the mission, and he had, arranging transportation and personnel from Panama City to Ilopango, and from Ilopango to Morazán, and negotiating political expediency in San Salvador, a lot of very expensive political expediency, considering where the weapons were going. In return, Dobbs had been promised that Grant's operator could be counted on to deal with the rebels, retrieve the diplomatic pouch, and recover a 2GB flash drive concealed in the fuselage of the downed Cessna. The Catholic nun connection was purely peripheral and should in no way compromise Rydell's or Ms. York-Lytton's primary objective—as a matter of fact, if any part of the mission failed, Rydell's involvement would be traced back to the State Department, not the CIA, so their meeting was strictly off the books. Brett Jenkins should have briefed him. As a matter of fact, as far as Dobbs was concerned, Jenkins *had* briefed him, and thank you very much for stopping by.

To his credit, Dobbs had produced current intel on the CNL, and current imagery of northern El Salvador, specifically of Morazán Province, and most specifically of the probable plane crash sites. The analysts had pinpointed two, both within a few kilometers of the CNL's camp on the Torola River.

The pilot couldn't have picked a worse place to bury his Cessna.

Next to Smith in the limo, Honey let out another barely audible sigh, and it occurred to him she might be simply flat-out scared, and if she was, he needed to know it, and if she was, sitting next to him being closemouthed and stony-faced probably wasn't helping. Conversation might ease some of her stress, and sure, he had just the thing for openers.

"I came across the *Ocean* magazine you were talking about, the one with you on the cover." The one with her on the cover re-creating the famous photograph of Marilyn Monroe standing over a grate in the sidewalk with her skirt flying up, the back issue he'd had to buy off some Internet magazine trader in Hell-and-Gone, New Jersey, and pay an outrageous amount of money to get. Yeah, that one.

She'd told him about it the night they'd met in San Luis, and after getting home and spending the following two days thinking about her pretty much nonstop, he'd gone on a mission to find it, alone, bypassing Skeeter, who was so damn good at finding everything anyone at Steele Street wanted. Some things a guy needed to keep to himself, like chasing millionaire heiresses to ground, millionaire heiresses he didn't have a chance of landing.

But hell, it couldn't hurt to know more about her—or so he'd thought.

"The article was interesting, very well done." For a cupcake extravaganza.

Honey slanted a glance up at him from her book. "I'm glad you enjoyed it."

Yeah, enjoyed it—not quite.

"Are you still involved with a lot of charity organizations?" Her list of good deeds had taken up a good third of the interview, and he'd been impressed. Good deeds and an overwhelming net worth were a natural combination, but still commendable, even if, every now and then, those good deeds ended in arrest and front-page scandal.

It happened. He wasn't going to hold it against her, but he'd definitely started to understand why someone with newly found saintly inclinations, like her sister, preferred to keep their distance from the family.

And then, after scandalous good deeds and newspaper headlining arrests, there had been the rest of the interview, the other two thirds, the bulk of it, which had given him plenty of pause and way too much to think about, and none of it really any of his damn business.

"A few," Honey said, turning partly toward him, a note of curiosity in her voice—rightly so. Idle chitchat wasn't Smith's strong point, and if she remembered anything about him—which he had good reason to doubt—she'd remember that, but he didn't have a lot to work with here, at least nothing of substance. The article had been a fluff piece, all fluff. Apparently, she was the queen of it. There hadn't been a hard fact in it anywhere, because there were no hard facts in her life, none that he'd been able to find anyway, and that had been bugging the crap out of him, the fluff and the two thirds of the interview devoted to her famous boyfriend.

Two fricking thirds of a two-page article, more column inches than *Ocean* had given "The New State of Lingerie," which apparently was Alabama, and a "refreshingly retro" style created by a designer working out of her shop in Mobile—'Bama Mama Brassieres. The designer and her wares were all the rage, and sure, he could dig it. He liked bows on bras, especially if they untied. And 'Bama Mama's did.

"And I didn't know you'd had a job—once." Smith let the last word drop with a little more weight than he'd intended, and being a quick girl, Honey picked up on it immediately.

"Don't bother to disapprove of me, Mr. Rydell," she said, turning back to her book. "I'm simply doing the best I can with what I've got."

Tough work, but he guessed somebody had to do it.

"How many more times are you going to call me Mr. Rydell?"

"As many times as I need to." She snapped another page over in her book.

Fair enough.

He rearranged himself in his seat and wished he'd eaten a bigger damn breakfast on his last damn flight. It was a long way to El Salvador.

"Look, Mr. Rydell," she started in again, turning to face him, her tone slightly exasperated. "Being the director of fund-raising for the Kardon County Human Services Foundation was a paid position, and I held it for three years. Ergo, I had a job."

"And donated your salary back." Every year, according to the magazine.

"I made a donation commensurate with my salary. There's a difference."

Only to a tax accountant.

"The picture of you in *Midsummer Night's Dream* was an interesting part of the article. You must have been Titania."

Honey held his gaze for a second, then sat back in her seat and cleared her throat.

"We made a lot of money on our theater productions," she said, "especially Shakespeare. The Bard is a solid seller in Kardon County, and I was the one the fairy costume fit. *Ergo,* I was Titania."

"Costume?" Excuse him, but what costume? "Did I miss something in the photo?" Like an actual costume?

The picture with the article had shown her

running across an outdoor stage at night, slipping through a fantastical forest, somehow looking like she was lit from within, trailing two ribbons, three strategically placed leaves, which left her one leaf short of even the most basic modesty, and not a damn thing else, with a bunch of other scantily clad fairies flying out of the trees behind her, all of them doing their part, practically in the frickin' buff, for Shakespeare and Kardon County—and yeah, he'd probably spent way too much of the last four months looking at the photo and thinking about her naked.

"It was a theatrical production," she explained, unnecessarily, "with creative license."

"It was Shakespeare in the nude. No wonder you made so much money."

"It was for charity."

"It was outrageous." And that was the goddamn thing. Her whole life had been played out in public, laid out in gossip rags, society pages, and bad news headlines. Hell, it hadn't taken any investigative skills to build a Honey York dossier, only a couple of dozen back issues of East Coast newspapers and a few magazines. And yet, it didn't add up. The woman had graduated from Harvard *magna cum laude*, published two books, one a best-seller, spent three years running fund-raisers for half a dozen different charities, gotten arrested for indecent exposure—and then what? Become a world-class party girl for the rest of her life?

Smith wasn't buying it.

"According to the article, you played the part for three years . . . despite the reviews."

"You're working way too hard here." She didn't even look at him this time, but to his amazement, a faint blush of color washed into her cheeks.

"They were brutal, especially the *Times* critic," he said, "especially about your performance."

"Only because I have no talent other than for running around on stage half naked," she said, flipping another page in her book, the color in her cheeks deepening.

Okay. He'd buy that, even if it did seem a little harsh.

More than a little harsh.

"Well, you must have done something right for them to ask you to play the part three years in a row," he said, inexplicably coming to her defense.

Honey kept turning pages in her book, snapping them over one at a time. "Like you, Mr. Rydell, I don't live my life based on other people's opinions."

But she was still blushing. That was one nice thing about being a covert operator—things had to get completely out of hand in a very political way before anyone even knew guys like him existed, let alone what they were doing. Smith didn't just like his privacy; he depended on it for his survival.

And there she was, year after year, splashed all over the front page and the society page.

"So what did you do after leaving the Kardon County Human Services Foundation?" Honey's résumé, if it could be called a résumé, dead-ended after the Shakespeare arrest. She'd disappeared from everything except the society pages.

"I moved on to other things, some new interests." Which was no answer.

"But kept the same boyfriend all these years?"

Okay, so that didn't sound particularly professional, but too bad; given their personal history, he was curious.

More than curious.

"Boyfriend?" One perfectly arched eyebrow lifted a fraction of an inch.

"The underwear model," Smith said, getting to the heart of the other two thirds of the article. The *Ocean* writer had all but swooned on the page over the guy and packed the interview with all the juicy details.

Juicy.

Details.

Smith had marched the damn thing up to the thirteenth floor at Steele Street and shown the article and its accompanying "young stud in his underwear" photo to Skeeter, to get a girl's opinion.

Baby Bang had taken one look at Honey's boyfriend and grinned like the Cheshire cat. "Sex on a stick" had been her girlish opinion. "Something women like to lick," she'd added— which was way more opinion than he'd wanted.

So what. It was none of his business, not really, and he didn't know why in the hell it bothered him.

Yes, he did.

"Robbie MacAllister?" Honey asked.

Yes, according to *The Washington Post*'s society page the week Smith had gotten back from El Salvador. There'd been a nice picture of the two of them at some fashion gala, the guy with his arm around her, holding her close, looking very protective, which had bugged the crap out of him. Smith had been the one protecting her in El Salvador, and doing a damn good job of it under circumstances a helluva lot more threatening than a friggin' fashion show.

"He looks young." Damned young, and immature, and dissolute, especially in the picture of what was apparently his most famous underwear ad, the one included in the *Ocean* article. The young guys Smith worked with didn't have the luxury of pouting in their underwear for a living, but he couldn't see Honey York dating an Army Ranger. Never in a million years. And he couldn't see her dating a DEA agent.

Or an SDF operator.

Hell. What had happened between them had been a fluke, a point that had hit home hard when he'd seen the society page and realized it had taken her all of a day and a half to bounce back into a social whirl complete with a boyfriend—a very young, very rich, celebrity boyfriend. It was enough to make a guy wonder if he'd made any kind of an impact at all.

And then she'd made the society page again, the next week, on the arm of a French count, which had especially rankled. European royalty, in general, didn't sit well with Smith. Quasi-famous, polo-playing, race-car-driving, champagne-sipping French royalty didn't sit well at all. But hell, he wasn't the boss of her.

That job, apparently, belonged to the guy

she'd shown up with in Manhattan two weeks later, the hedge-fund king of Wall Street, a guy much older than her who looked like anything that happened between him and his underwear needed to be kept private. Very private. They'd lasted a whole weekend, and then, the next week, it had been back to the underwear model, and then back to the hedge-fund king for another fun-filled weekend of opera openings and charity fund-raisers.

The last time Smith had checked the society page, the day before he'd left for Peru, she'd been with a whole new guy who went by the unbelievable name of Kip-Woo, but whose real name apparently was Elliot Fletcher-Wooten III.

Geezus. She made his head spin.

"Well, he was young when he started in the business, and the underwear campaign took him straight to the top. Actually, the whole campaign was considered a turning point in male fashion photography," Honey said. "But why in the world are we talking about Robbie MacAllister?"

At least the guy wasn't Robert MacAllister III, and they were talking about him because the guy kept showing up in her life. The *Ocean* article was four years old, which meant Honey had held on to a boyfriend twice as long as Smith had held on to a wife, which galled the hell out of him, plus she was seeing all those other men on the side.

"I own some of that underwear."

"Well, that's very nice," she said, shifting her attention back to her book and snapping over another page. "It's very high quality, more expensive, but worth it."

And wasn't that interesting—he'd actually shocked himself with his own idiocy. Where had that come from? About the underwear?

"My girlfriend bought it for me." And that wasn't much of a save. Not really.

She snapped another page over in her book, but didn't comment.

He didn't blame her. Some things didn't deserve conversation—his underwear being a prime example.

Dammit. Smith had done nothing but think about Honey for four damn months, and now that he was sitting right next to her, the last damn place he would have ever expected to be when they'd dragged him out of his Lima hotel room in the middle of the night and given him this damn mission, the very last, he was overthinking the situation and letting his imagination get the better of him.

And he was angry.

Mostly at himself for thinking about her for

four damn months. San Luis should have been a one-night stand, not an obsession. They had nothing in common.

And yet, here they were again, off on some wild-ass adventure. *Geezus,* it felt like fate, but he wasn't buying goddamn fate. Free will, plain and simple, was the only thing he believed in. Give him free will and a .45, and he'd take care of himself, thank you.

But his free will had been usurped at three A.M., and he was stuck with Honey, and a briefcase, and a whole boatload of useless information that was none of his business.

Shakespeare in the nude. *Geezus.*

Smith shifted in his seat, and stared out the window, and let another mile roll by before he finally gave in to what had really been sticking in his craw for the last four months—dammit.

"I owe you an apology."

His admission was met with silence.

"For what?" Honey asked after a moment.

He glanced in her direction and found her watching him with a mixture of wariness and curiosity. He didn't blame her for the wariness. Anyone with any brains used at least a modicum of caution when dealing with him.

"I was a little rough on you that night in San Luis."

Her eyebrow went up again, and sure enough, the blush returned.

He almost grinned. He hadn't meant it like that.

"I mean with tossing you into my room and taking your weapon, and just generally . . . well . . ."

"Just generally bossing me around and threatening to break my neck?"

"Yeah." *Christ*. He had threatened to snap her neck. He'd kind of forgotten about that part. "I'm sorry. Sorry if I hurt you."

"I'm not," she said, shifting her attention back to her book, but without flipping any more pages. "I was in over my head, Smith, way over, and if you hadn't tossed me into your room, I probably wouldn't have made it through the night. I don't know who those men were, but I think you do, and I think they're a lot scarier than Diego Garcia."

She had that part right. Tony Royce's guys had all been handpicked from the scum of the earth, chosen for their brutality and sociopathic tendencies. She wouldn't have lasted four hours in their hands, and God forbid something should have happened to her like what had happened to Smith's friend and SDF partner, Red Dog.

The thought sent an unnerving chill down his spine.

Yeah, he'd been rough—expedient, getting the job done the best way he knew how—and yeah, she'd gotten a little knocked around in the process, but she'd survived.

And then she'd turned out to be someone he cared about more than he should. Life was so damned unexpected sometimes—most of the time.

"I'm glad you understand." Most people, especially in her social circles, didn't understand. They didn't know what it really took to make the world go round. They didn't know about guys like him, and worse, they didn't want to know.

"I'm glad I understand, too," Honey said, glancing up and meeting his gaze. "Robbie MacAllister isn't my boyfriend anymore. We just go to fashion events together."

Well, he didn't know what in the hell to make of that, not precisely, not with all those other guys literally in the picture.

"The girl who bought my underwear is long gone, too." Just a fact, nothing more, but what the hell, he'd throw it into the mix and see what happened—and he did hope something would happen, and really, he should have known better, a whole lot better. He'd thought he was smarter than that.

Apparently not.

Dammit.

What happened was a small smile, and more of the soft blush, and a sliding away of her gaze, and hell, he didn't know what to make of that, either.

CHAPTER **SIX**

Sona, Colombia

From her luncheon table on a second-story veranda, Irena Polchenko watched a black sedan drive slowly up the tree-lined lane leading to the main gate of her villa and the surrounding compound.

Good, she thought, pushing the remainder of her *pollo con arroz* aside and reaching for a fresh lime from a bowl on the table. Ari was late, Aristotle Alexandar Poulos, her chief of security, but he was finally here, and with the right news, all would be forgiven.

Or there would be hell to pay. Time would tell.

Sitting back in her chair, she rolled the fruit between her palms, then brought it close to her nose. The scent was fresh with the tang of citrus, the lime warmed by the sun and warm in her hands, the day's moment a lush and sultry reminder of why she lived in the tropics: She was a reptile at heart, cold-blooded, and she needed the heat.

With a practiced move, Irena slid a folding knife out of her pants pocket, her thumb extending the blade the instant it was clear. Two concise cuts into the fruit's green flesh got her what she wanted, a thin, perfect wedge of lime to drop into the long neck of her bottle of Corona. She pocketed the knife and waited until the amber liquid foamed up to the lip.

When it was finished, she brought the bottle to her mouth and took her first sip, still tracking the car with her gaze.

Afternoon sunlight glinted off the slow-moving sedan and threw shadows across the backdrop of the green valley below, a verdant expanse of farmland extending for miles between the hills bordering her property to the east and west. Her three-story, Spanish-style home was tucked up against the base of the western slope, four miles from the small village of Sona. Outwardly, the villa and compound looked like a typical Colombian landowner's residence.

But looks were deceiving.

The lane leading to the villa's front gate was a straight half-mile section of hand-laid paving stones lined with tall, stately trees on either side. The two rows of decorative trees had ten-meter breaks in them, spaced exactly one hundred meters apart. Should the need arise, a sniper in the villa, or on the slope above it, could use the trees as ranging markers to judge the distance of an approaching vehicle.

The black sedan was five hundred meters out and closing—an easy shot for one of her long gunners, an easier shot for her.

Irena took another short swallow of beer, her gaze sliding past the lane to the valley beyond, watching for anything unusual, anything out of place. She'd been compromised, the previous day's mission ending in near disaster, and she was on edge. The fact of the failure was bad enough, the reasons yet to be determined, but there was something else...something as yet unknown that had triggered a warning in the deepest recesses of her brain, and it made the edge she was on very sharp, very dangerous.

The car came to a stop below her in the circular drive, and she heard the doors open.

Setting the beer aside, Irena knocked a Turkish cigarette out of the pack she always kept on hand. The lighter she pulled out of her back pocket was sterling silver inlaid with gold, the Gila monster passant crest and the motto hers:

Vincit Qui Se Vincit, He conquers who conquers himself.

She held the flame to the end of the cigarette and inhaled deeply. The lighter had been a gift from an English lord for services rendered and a profit beyond his expectations. She knew her business, and she knew how to turn circumstances to her advantage. Without a doubt, yesterday's failure would be rectified.

Exhaling a long plume of smoke, waiting for Ari to make his way to the veranda, Irena let her gaze travel back along the tree-lined drive. To an aviator's eye, the carefully paved lane served another purpose. The surface of the path was dead level, rather than crowned, and the stones in the center of the lane were a distinctly lighter shade than the others. The trees were laid out precisely fifteen meters from the centerline, roughly three light aircraft wingspans. Lantern pedestals were placed between each tree-line break, dead center. Along with the lanterns, the pedestals contained ILS beacons, an instrument landing system, which could be activated by an approaching aircraft with the correct transponder codes. Day or night, the lane could be used as an all-weather, emergency landing strip.

And there were other runways on the estate. Irena's property extended almost a mile beyond the main gate, with three separate areas of buildings. The structures appeared to be single-story Colombian farm shacks with adobe siding and thatched roofs.

They were not.

Despite their ramshackle facades, the buildings were steel-frame structures containing vehicles, aircraft, maintenance facilities, warehousing, weaponry, and troop barracks. Higher up on the hill, two buildings housed her communications center. The rambling dirt roads connecting the areas were actually compacted roadbase faced with three-quarter-inch gravel, strong enough to support heavy vehicles and medium-lift aircraft. Some of the strategically placed buildings were mounted on skids, and could be rearranged to align the roads into more landing strips.

It was all hers, every last stick of it, every board, every stone, every inch, all hers, accumulated by the force of her will and a mind that did not rest or accept defeat. She'd done it by herself, alone. No man had ever given her anything of value—except once.

Irena took another long drag off the cigarette and pushed the thought aside. Sona was not the place for such thoughts.

The French doors opened behind her, and a very trim, athletic-looking man with finely chiseled

European features and blond hair stepped onto the veranda, taking care to move into her line of peripheral vision before he approached the table—with good reason. She was never unarmed, and she never missed, not with her rifle, and not with the custom Model 1911-variant .45 in a holster on her thigh.

"*Guten Tag, patrona,*" he said. *Good afternoon.*

"Hans." Irena nodded, her attention already moving toward the man coming in behind him. Ari Poulos was nearly six feet in height and weighed in at a little over two hundred pounds. Half Greek and half Guatemalan, he was forty-three years old, had served as a Guatemalan soldier in the civil war, and had been trained by Israeli military advisers in small unit tactics and weapons, including antiaircraft missiles and snipercraft.

"You've had twenty-four hours since Cuzco," she said evenly, her gaze taking in both men. "What do you know?"

Hans Klechner, her chief of operations, was a former East German intelligence officer, trained by the KGB. At one time, he'd worked for the Serbian government, heading up covert operations opposing the Albanian resistance in Kosovo.

Ari spoke first. "*Patrona,* we have received several transmissions from our remaining contact at the joint drug enforcement unit in Lima. Our two assets at the airstrip were identified, but the Peruvians have not succeeded in locating them. Presumably, they successfully entered our underground net and will contact us when they are beyond the reach of the Peruvian authorities. In any case, they are lost to us as informants within the drug enforcement structure."

Irena nodded. "Bring them here as soon as they surface," she said, flicking the ash off her cigarette into a lead crystal ashtray on the table. "We own them now, and they may be of use in deciding how to proceed with damage control in the Cuzco area. Is our remaining contact secure?"

"He has not been compromised," Ari assured her.

"You said several transmissions. What else?"

"Photographs were taken."

She stopped with the cigarette halfway to her lips, her gaze narrowing. "Photographs?"

"There was a drug enforcement surveillance team watching the Cuzco airstrip."

She'd known as much, that the *contra-narcotraficantes* had been on the hill above the landing strip. They'd been transmitting with an HF radio on the Peruvian Federal Police band, which was how she'd been able to point them out to the local *pendejos*—rather precisely, she'd thought.

"I ordered them killed," Irena said, her voice tight. "So how is it they escaped?"

Ari knew her well enough to know the question was not rhetorical.

"By helicopter, with covering fire from an A-10 close support aircraft."

"Casualties?"

"Four dead, eight wounded."

"A massacre, the fools." There would be no more *coca* coming out of Cuzco for a while, and none that she would be transporting. The Cuzco people had failed to secure the airfield as agreed, and even with intelligence assets inside the *Federales*' Joint Ops Central in Lima, they had not predicted a threat.

Ineptitude of such a high level could not be tolerated. It would not be tolerated, not when it was her life on the line. The Piper had been so low on fuel when they'd made their escape, they'd barely made it to her contingency airfield in Brazil—and now there were these photographs. With that one fact, a "near disaster" had become a total disaster.

Irena had known there was a good chance that she'd been under video surveillance, but she'd expected the agents to be caught and killed, and their damn cameras destroyed.

Her men would have gotten the job done.

"Do you know if the photographs are identifiable?" Any number of things could have gone wrong. The agents' observation position could have been at too steep of an angle for a full face shot, or her head could have been turned, or their equipment faulty.

"They've already obtained files through INTERPOL on Hans and myself."

Or everything could have worked out perfectly for the police.

"But you, *patrona*, they are unsure about," Ari said, knowing better than to in any way shade a meaning or conceal a fact. "One of the surveillance agents identified you, but his superiors in Lima believe he is mistaken, because all the information they have been able to find on Irena Polchenko says she died six years ago in Afghanistan."

The sharp, dangerous edge of warning she'd been feeling turned suddenly cold—bitterly cold. And became like a knife in her heart.

"Who is this agent?" Irena had known dozens of agents in Kabul and other places around the world. When she'd been a pilot for hire, she'd done contract work for any number of agencies in half a dozen different governments.

"There were two on the hillside yesterday, a Peruvian federal policeman named Rufio Cienfuegos, and an American named"—he consulted his notepad—"Rydell. C. Smith Rydell."

The knife in her heart twisted with a sickening lurch, stealing her breath for a moment.

"We have a file on Cienfuegos," Ari continued, "but I have no further information on the American. He doesn't seem to be DEA."

Neither was he alive.

She'd left him bound and gagged at the feet of Jamal Abdurrashid, an Afghan battle lord on the Northwest Frontier. Beaten and bloody, Rydell had fallen next to a crate of surface-to-air missiles, and for the favor of his life and the missiles, Irena had walked away with half a million dollars.

She'd heard the shot that had killed him, and been too sentimental to turn and look back—a rare and disturbing weakness, one she believed had been her last.

But this...

This was unprecedented, and could not be allowed to stand. She'd left him for dead, and that's exactly where he needed to be. He knew too much, a secret whispered in the dark of night, a precious confession of love as she'd drifted toward sleep in his arms, a secret it was too dangerous to even think.

"Where are Cienfuegos and Rydell now?" Irena asked, continuing with the movement of bringing the cigarette to her lips. Inhaling smoothly, steadily, she willed herself into a state of calmness—cold, calculating, venomous calmness. She was a reptile, a predator, and stillness was her ally.

"Cienfuegos has returned to his field post in Lima," Ari answered. "And the American . . ." He turned to Klechner, who picked up the conversation.

"Rydell was pulled off the joint drug enforcement unit during the night and boarded a plane to Panama. Our contact was able to access the change in tasking, and the American has been assigned to a personal security detail in Panama City by the U.S. State Department for a U.S. citizen, a Ms. Honoria York-Lytton from Washington, D.C."

Why? Irena wondered. There were dozens of military people and security consultants already in Panama who could have been tasked with a PSD. It didn't make sense to drag an operator off a joint mission with a foreign government and all the way out of Peru in the middle of the night to follow a woman around Panama.

Rydell was alive—a tremor ran through her hand. She hid it by stubbing the cigarette out in the ashtray.

He had survived.

"Negotiate a contract for the life of Cienfuegos. Priority immediate. I want him dead yesterday, and if you can't do that, I want him hit by tonight. We know a number of people in Lima who can accomplish the deed. Call the best we have," Irena said, and saw the quick exchange of concerned glances between Ari and Hans.

She understood. Killing a federal agent was sanctioned only rarely, and involved a fair measure of damage control in and of itself.

But if Cienfuegos had been on that hillside when Rydell had first seen her, it was all too possible Rydell had told the federal agent everything he knew about her—not out of shock, though he had probably been as shocked as she was, but because in tight situations, team members exchanged as much information as possible, talking on the run if necessary, in case one of them didn't make it.

"Yes, *patrona*," Ari replied.

"And do whatever is required to get me Rydell's mission itinerary," she said, fixing Hans with her gaze. "Activate all of our Panamanian assets. Find out what happened in the U.S.

Embassy today, who he talked with, when, and what was said. I want to know everything."

"Yes, *patrona*." Hans nodded.

"Ari, you and I are going after this American as soon as we have his location. I'll take care of preparing the Piper. You prepare field gear for the two of us, including back country supplies, the usual weapons, and a long rifle."

Ari nodded in understanding. The two of them had a history of successful assassinations to their credit. They were a good team.

"Hans, you will remain at the villa as interim director of all other ongoing operations."

"Yes, *patrona*." Hans nodded, and she made a brief gesture with her hand, dismissing the two men.

Rydell would have reported his information during the debriefing in Lima, Irena knew, but he would have been out of danger by then, and he would have had time to think things through, and with those thoughts would have come caution. The most damaging information might have been held back, considered, saved for his own government. With that in mind, it was completely possible he'd been the one to pull himself out of Peru, so he could head for the nearest home base—Panama City.

Which made the PSD and the woman at best

a ruse, and at the least negligible, or perhaps not. If there was even a grain of truth in the assignment, it could be useful.

Very useful.

"Hans," Irena said, stopping the German before he could follow Ari through the French doors. Besides being a field agent and case officer for the East Germans, Hans had been trained by the KGB in a variety of combat-oriented martial arts, hostage rescue, and in the eminently practical skill of kidnapping.

"Yes, *patrona*?"

"I want to know everything about this woman, Honoria York-Lytton . . . everything."

"*Jawohl, patrona.*"

CHAPTER SEVEN

Howard Air Force Base, Panama

Good God, Honey thought, standing next to Smith and watching wide-eyed from behind her sunglasses as eight beautiful pieces of some of the world's most expensive luggage were mushed, and smushed, and scrinched, and scrunched under a section of yellow cargo netting.

Louis Vuitton had to be rolling over in his grave.

"Does everything have to be so tight?" she asked, trying to act more nonchalant than she felt, which wasn't very damn nonchalant with the five big Vuittons getting the stuffing crushed out of them.

"Yes," Smith said, one word, very curt.

Okay. Fine. Honey repressed a sigh and

tucked a loose strand of hair back up into her twist.

It was very gloomy inside the cavernous hangar, and very hot, and she really wanted one of those little Cuban cigarillos she'd bought at the Blake, but from the smell of the hangar, and the contents of the pallet, and given her luck, she figured that's about all it would take to blow them all to hell—her lighting up.

God.

The Air Force ground crew cinched the netting one final time before securing it, and Honey told herself not to panic, it was Vuitton, it would hold—and then they were finished. There it was, the whole thing: a pallet of death and destruction topped off with haute couture, secure and ready to go to Ilopango.

Unless one of the suitcases didn't hold together and split a gut and something, anything, spilled out—oh, and then this party was going to come to a real quick end. Talk about getting "blown" to hell. What was it Smith had said that night in San Luis? Something about watching a cockroach drag half a plantain across a jail cell floor in San Salvador?

Honey had thought about that cockroach a couple of times since that night, and a couple of hundred dozen times since she'd looked in the five big suitcases that had been waiting in the garden bungalow when she'd arrived at the Blake, the ones she'd never seen before with her name written on the luggage tags. By then, Jenkins had already gone over the "coffee planta-tion tour" itinerary with her, and handed her a sealed envelope with the lading forms docu-menting the rest of the cargo she was supposed to sign off on. Gestures of goodwill for Honey to dispense at her own discretion, he'd said with a slightly put-upon air of *noblesse oblige*, tokens of the U.S. government's appreciation for the hard work of the noble Salvadoran farmers.

Not quite.

One quick read of the lading documents after Jenkins had left had made Honey wonder if it might be in her best interest to jimmy the locks on the suitcases. The "gestures of goodwill" were nothing short of a death sentence, and she doubted if there was an ounce of her discretion involved in their dispensation. They were all go-ing to the CNL rebels. God only knew what else her "handlers" in Washington were trying to pawn off on her.

Fortunately, she'd had a bit of experience in jimmying Vuitton luggage locks, and one look in-side the first suitcase had made her wonder what her chances might actually be against the treason charge, if she had a really good lawyer—or a dozen of them.

Because this was bad, very bad.

And it had already been bad enough. *Dammit.*

A beast, Smith had called the cockroach, and Honey didn't doubt it for a second. Neither did she doubt that the Panamanian cockroaches could be equally beastly, or that she was hauling enough contraband to get her locked away in a Central American prison for the rest of her life, and when that sentence ran out, they'd put her in Leavenworth for the rest of her next life.

Oh, yes. This was bad karmic energy of a cosmic nature, the kind that followed souls through countless reincarnations—and she was a Protestant.

Honey took a breath and tried to steady her nerves. She was "in" this thing. She'd made her decision before she'd ever gotten on the plane to Panama, and she was going to be "in," until she was "out," on her terms. She'd made it to the air base, and that was a good thing, even if it was all downhill and straight to hell from here. Once she got on the plane to El Salvador, there was no turning back, no escape. It was forward, into the breach, and hope for the best. Her job was clear: Deliver the Vuittons, the briefcase, and the "war in a box" detailed in the lading document to the

Campos plantation in Morazán Province. Then, that accomplished, she had to retrieve the courier's pouch, the 2GB flash drive, and do God knew what to convince the CNL not to trample Alejandro Campos's coffee bushes.

Yes. There was something wrong with the picture, like why in the hell she was in it—and yes, there were moments in a woman's life when she simply had to wonder what in the hell she'd done to get herself into so much trouble.

This was one of them.

Even if she knew very damn well what she'd done and very damn well why she'd let herself be railroaded into El Salvador.

"MRE," Honey said, reading the letters stenciled on the side of one of the cardboard containers on the pallet, while tucking another loose strand up into her hairdo. She was coming apart in the heat, and she really needed to hold together. "What does MRE stand for?"

"Meal, Ready to Eat," Smith said, and if she wasn't mistaken, he almost said it with a grin. "Three lies in one, but for all the complaining about the quality of the rations, I've never seen a hungry soldier refuse to eat one."

Okay, this is good, she thought. *Food.* She could live with that—food for the hungry guerrillas; there were a lot of cardboard containers stamped with MRE. It was the other boxes shredding her nerves. Seeing them written on a lading form was one thing. Seeing the wooden containers stacked on a pallet and knowing she was responsible for them was another. Her gaze went over the containers, reading the stenciled markings on their sides: AMMUNITION, SMALL ARMS, 5.56MM BALL, and AMMUNITION, SMALL ARMS, 9MM BALL, so yes, there was plenty of ammo headed up into the hills; PISTOL, BERETTA MODEL 92 9MM; RIFLE, M16A2, and there were plenty of those, including the ones marked RIFLE, M16A2 W/40MM LAUNCHER, M203, which she knew from the lading forms meant grenades, and yes, she could see how being able to launch a grenade from a rifle would come in real handy.

Her favorite, though, was WEAPON, ANTI-TANK, 66MM.

She doubted if there were many tanks rolling around the Torola River, but she was guessing a 66mm anti-tank weapon could blow a big hole in about anything it hit.

Guerrillas in the mountains, grenades on the pallet, trouble in the suitcases, the CIA and a very stately, white-haired man in the State Department named Mr. Cassle pulling all the strings, and not a word from Julia in four months, not a single word since she'd boarded a truck outside St.

Mary's and headed off into the Salvadoran countryside.

The truth was, Mr. Cassle and the grim-faced CIA man in his grim black suit hadn't had to threaten her even half as much to get her on board for a top-secret mission into El Salvador to parley with the rebels who had been driving the truck that had taken her sister away, especially when the government guys were supplying all the trade goods.

Damn good trade goods. Top-notch.

Did grenades and "WEAPONS, ANTI-TANK, 66MM" scare the holy crap out of her? Yes. But Honey was pretty damn sure Diego Garcia wasn't in the market for a year's supply of Estee Lauder, and Garcia was the only connection she had left to Julia. She just prayed the connection wasn't too terribly close. In a sudden turn to the right, the Catholic Church had abandoned its dissident policies in El Salvador. Most of the clergy had fallen in line, except for a small group of nuns at an isolated outpost in the hills above Cristobal who ran a school and orphanage out of a former coffee plantation. The good sisters of St. Joseph had refused to change course. According to Father Bartolo, whom Honey found alarmist at best, and deranged at worst, there were four— Sister Bettine, Sister Rose, Sister Teresa, and

Sister Julia Ann-Marie—none of whom had been seen or heard from by the St. Mary's priest in over twelve weeks.

Except for one outrageous rumor coming out of Morazán that Father Bartolo, for one, refused to believe, even for a second, and would not repeat for even a million dollars, but would apparently shout about for free until he'd worked himself into such a lather that he'd hung up in her face.

Honey hadn't been the same since.

So yes, Mr. Cassle's threats had almost been superfluous. As for the rest of it—hell, Washington, D.C., was full of strings and the people who pulled them, but only a fool thought the strings only went one way, and Honey was no fool. In the District, the strings always went both ways, and she had her fingers wrapped around more than a few—enough to see her through this mess, if push came to shove.

At least she hoped she did, and if push came to shove back and shoot—well, that was why she had C. Smith Rydell.

At least she hoped she did.

She slid a glance in his direction, which did nothing to reassure her. The man did not look happy. Neither did he look like the elegantly dressed bodyguard who had shown up at the Blake.

He'd changed his clothes immediately upon their arrival at the air base, and now looked like what she was beginning to realize he actually was: a soldier. Not some fly-by-night gun for hire who'd washed up on the shores of San Luis with a beer in one hand and a .45 in the other, just in time for a riot and to save her butt. But a real soldier who followed orders and had been trained to fight, very highly trained. It showed in the way he moved, and it showed in the way he thought—clearly, concisely, and tactically, always looking for the win. He'd had a map to a secret airstrip in his pocket the night they'd met, and an official-looking ID from an agency called IRIS, issued by the U.S. Embassy in Panama, allowing him to carry a concealed weapon throughout Central America. She'd researched the organization when she'd gotten home, and about the only thing the Institute for Regional and International Studies did, apparently, was hand out concealed carry cards—but the part about the embassy had been real.

Honey knew people, was good at reading them, and the man at State, Mr. Cassle, had recognized C. Smith Rydell when the CIA man had handed him the photographs taken at the sacristy. It had been in the almost imperceptible tightening of the older man's lips, in the long ten seconds he'd spent looking at the picture, and in the one, very brief phone call he'd made: "Get me Grant on the horn."

Honey didn't know who Grant was, yet, but she'd bet Smith did, and she couldn't help but wonder if Grant was part of the dead end of Smith's résumé at someplace notated only as SDF. It didn't seem to matter how many strings she'd jerked and pulled last night and this morning, she still didn't know what SDF meant, and the most she'd been able to find out in the last four months about 738 Steele Street, the address on his driver's license, was that it was an old garage with a shady past where people sold cars in Denver, Colorado.

Honey wasn't buying it.

Her glance slid over Smith again.

Nope. No way. There wasn't a square inch on him anywhere that said "car salesman."

CHAPTER EIGHT

Smith stood off to the side of the pallet, regarding the load with a mixture of disapproval, apprehension, and disbelief.

66mm Light Anti-tank Weapons? What the hell was he doing taking LAWs into Morazán? Rifles with 40mm grenade launchers? Just what the hell kind of war was the CIA thinking it wanted to start? And what in the hell could have gone down in the Agency's Cessna to get all this ordnance, personnel, and transportation rocketing through the system a hundred times faster than his last reimbursement check?

Smith had a feeling he was never going to know, which was fine with him. He wasn't a policy maker. He was a policy implementer. Whatever was in the courier's pouch, if they even got the damn thing back, would be encrypted; the same with the flash drive. More than likely, they both contained the same information, the hard copy being a backup in case the electronic one got zapped—standard procedure. But that was the only standard thing in the whole operation.

Smith shifted his attention from the LAWs to the suitcases on top of the pallet and almost sighed like Honey. Those things were never going to be the same. He didn't give a damn, not really, not about the suitcases, but they were as out of place in the hangar as Tweety Bird standing there next to him, and it would be all too easy for her to end up in the same mangled condition.

He gave her a quick once-over, and got stuck on her shoes. *Cripes.* They were getting ready to board a C-130, and she was wearing black patent leather peekaboo T-straps with three-inch heels.

But not for long, not if he had anything to say about it—and he did. T-straps, hell. He was guessing Prada, the spring collection, and yes, he was spending way too much time with Skeeter in her shoe closet. All he could say in his own defense was that half the Steele Street crew was spending too much time in Skeeter's shoe closet since she and Kid had put in a movie screen, a sound system, and a small section of stadium seating with leather recliners.

Yeah, it was a helluva closet, supersized, and it was exactly where Honey York needed to be: settled into a recliner, watching a movie in a shoe closet. Safest damn place for her.

The ground crew finished tying off the netting, and there it all sat, everything from designer luggage to explosive ordnance, and the longer he looked at it, the more unacceptable it became.

"Give me the briefcase and go home," he said, not even bothering to look over at her. She knew who he was talking to.

"No."

Dammit.

"Why not? And don't bother to tap your foot; I expect an answer this time."

"It's my chip," Honey said after a moment, not sounding any too happy with his ultimatum. "The only chip I've got, my bargaining chip to get into El Salvador and up into Morazán."

Yeah, he'd figured as much, and the "incriminating" photographs be damned. It probably took a helluva lot more than the CIA and the United States State Department to intimidate Honoria York-Lytton. And she was right about the briefcase. It was her bargaining chip, all hers. He'd asked Dobbs for the combination, but Dobbs hadn't known it, and the chief of station hadn't at all liked being reminded of the fact.

"Whatever is inside the briefcase isn't yours," Smith said, stating what he was sure was another unpopular fact.

"No, but the ability to *get* whatever is in it is mine, and this briefcase doesn't get opened until I get what I want."

"Which is?"

She hesitated.

"Honoria?"

"My sister," she snapped. "Face-to-face. So I can see she's safe."

Finally, the truth came out, not that it was exactly a news flash.

"Where is she?"

"She was assigned to St. Joseph Orphanage and School near Cristobal, but I've been told she spends a lot of time at the CNL camp up on the Torola River."

"Told by who?"

Honey's expression, which hadn't been happy to begin with, turned even grimmer. "Diego Garcia."

"That was the correspondence?"

"Yes," she admitted.

Well, hell.

"When was the last time you heard from her directly?"

"The last time I saw her. The morning you put me on the plane."

Well.

Hell.

Smith wiped the back of his hand across his mouth and stared at the pallet.

The damn guerrilla camp.

"What about the priest in San Luis? The one who was in the room with you, and Julia, and Garcia. Father Bartolo? Right? He must be in contact with her."

"Father Bartolo has washed his hands of the nuns at St. Joseph. They've defied the church by continuing to support the CNL. He says he can't afford to be associated with them. It's too dangerous, so he's turned them over to the priest in Cristobal."

That rankled. The guy sure hadn't had any trouble taking the money and handing it over like he'd been the one to come up with a quarter of a million dollars for the "Liberators."

"You need to let me go in alone and close the deal. I'll find Julia and bring her back to Campos's."

"That won't work."

Yes, it would. Smith was very good at finding

people and bringing them back, from wherever to wherever, clean deals, every one. He had a dozen of them to his credit.

"Why not?" he asked, which turned out to be a surprisingly difficult question to answer. After about a minute of watching her mind work without a word coming out of her mouth, he began to wonder if he was going to get an answer. Any answer.

"I have reason to believe," she started to say, then stopped for another couple of seconds, before beginning again. "It's possible Julia doesn't want to leave the CNL camp."

"Because?" She needed to help him out a bit on that one.

But she wasn't going to help him out on it. He could tell by the silence. It went on, and on, and on.

Hell. If Honey got hurt, Smith was going to have a hard time living with himself, but had anyone in Washington, D.C., thought of that when they'd gotten this ball rolling? And did they give a damn?

Finally, two questions he could answer on his own, the first with "It didn't matter," and the second with "No," no one gave a damn if Honey got hurt. Despite her net worth and family connections, he was afraid all the Park Avenue princesses in Morazán Province this week were classified as expendable assets.

Diego Garcia might trust her to deliver his payoff, but Smith didn't trust Diego Garcia, or Alejandro Campos, or the CIA, and as of two hours ago, White Rook was at the top of his "sketchy" list.

Outside the hangar, he heard the familiar drone of a C-130 approaching, which did absolutely nothing to improve his mood. The Air Force loadmaster finished checking the pallet, then walked over and pressed a switch on the hangar wall. Two twenty-foot-high doors began sliding apart on greased rails, revealing the transport aircraft with its aft end facing the hangar, and its ramp coming down. In short order, a forklift operator was moving the pallet onto the ramp.

Ready or not, he thought, and the answer to that was "not."

A serious-looking young man wearing tropical BDUs stepped off the airplane's ramp and headed inside the hangar, approaching him and Honey. The soldier's uniform was completely devoid of unit insignia or any other identification—one more sign that Smith and Honey were heading into no-man's-land.

"I'm Smith," the young soldier said with a quick wink.

"Yeah, so am I," Smith admitted, grinning in spite of himself and the whole rotten situation.

"Two to Ilopango," the soldier continued. "Transload and handoff to Salvadoran army at hangar T-195, correct?"

"That's us," Rydell confirmed. "I need a set of BDUs for my civilian package. Do you have anything that'll even come close to fitting her?"

"Yes, sir," the soldier said, his gaze flicking over Honey before returning directly to Smith. "We were warned of a civilian VIP, female, short, size four with size five shoes."

Short. Smith's grin widened. He couldn't imagine she liked that.

"We're setting up a dressing screen now." The younger man continued, pointing to the right of the doors, where another member of the aircrew was busy rigging a poncho with some suspension line. "The uniform and a pair of boots will be behind the screen."

Smith nodded, then shifted his attention back to the pallet being winched aboard the C-130. Yes, sir, he was going to be wondering for a long time what the CIA had promised the Salvadoran government in order to get their cooperation on a load of weapons being delivered to the CNL.

Talk about politics and bedfellows. That kind of information either never showed up anywhere, ever, or someday, some headline would catch his eye, and he'd think, "So that was what that was all about." It had happened to him a couple of times, but he couldn't say he'd ever gotten any satisfaction out of it. The CIA ran their own game, their own way, and anybody and everybody was grist for their mill.

"Your cargo will be secure in ten more minutes," the soldier said. "I need you on board as soon as possible after that, since we have runway priority. Wheels up in fifteen."

"We'll be ready and standing by, inside the left edge of the door," Smith said. "It would be nice if the aircrew could help us give the other passenger some visual screening between the hangar and the ramp."

The soldier gave Honey another brief glance and returned his attention to Smith, again without a single expression crossing his face—pure professional, all the way.

"Already arranged," he said. "See you in a few."

"BDUs?" she asked, as soon as the younger man had walked away.

"Battle Dress Uniform, a camouflage shirt and trousers, cotton twill. You'll be glad you're wearing them," he said, immediately launching into the hard sell in order to avoid an argument they didn't have time to have. "They'll be warmer and more comfortable on the plane, and less conspicuous—"

"Okay."

"—especially when we get to El Salvador and head up into the mountains."

Okay?

"Over there? Right?" she asked, pointing toward the poncho.

"Uh, yes, and if you could hurry it up, that would be . . . uh, great." The last few words were spoken to himself, because Honey had already started across the hangar toward the "dressing room," the briefcase still firmly in hand, locked around her right wrist.

He really needed to take care of that.

"Fifteen minutes, right?" she said over her shoulder.

"Ten would be better."

"Roger that."

Roger that?

"Five would be best," he said after her, and it couldn't take more than five. She had on one piece of clothing and was putting on two, a quick switch. He hoped.

"Then I'll do it in five," she assured him.

Well, okay, then.

She disappeared behind the poncho, and he felt an unexpected glimmer of hope. If he could get that kind of cooperation for the next forty-eight hours, they might actually have a chance of pulling this off and coming out in one piece. He'd already decided that at the first opportunity, he was "requisitioning" one of the Beretta 9mm pistols on the pallet for her personal use. A lot of guys might have chosen not to arm her, thinking it would mean there would be one less person likely to shoot them—and yeah, he appreciated that reasoning.

But she'd graduated Ivy League, *magna cum laude,* and she'd gotten a quarter of a million dollars across San Luis in the middle of the night. Those two deeds required two completely different types of intelligence. No one looking at her would think she had an ounce of street smarts, but she'd been smart on the street that night, and those had been bad streets.

Yeah, he trusted her to be smart enough to safely handle a weapon without accidentally shooting him or herself. Campos had a firing range on his estate, and hitting it was going to be the first order of the day.

In less than five minutes, she was coming out from behind the poncho—and looking good. She shouldn't have, honestly. BDUs were utilitarian, except on her. On her they were a fashion statement.

He watched her cross the hangar, somewhat dumbfounded, knowing there was a lesson to be learned here, but he'd be damned if he could figure it out. They'd given her a small tactical vest, too, and he'd be damned if he could figure that out, either. But she was loving it, opening all the pockets, looking inside, checking the straps and clips.

He supposed, to her, it might look like a portable makeup bag or something. A year from now they'd be selling them in Saks along with the rest of her "outfit."

She'd rolled the trousers up enough to expose a bit of leg, and she'd rolled the gray army-issue socks down into two small, perfect cuffs on top of her black combat boots. Her dress was folded over her arm, but she'd threaded the narrow black patent leather belt through her French twist like a headband, with the bow in front. It was the finishing touch, tying the whole outfit together—black boots, black headband. The BDU shirt was open to the waist, exposing a light brown T-shirt. He hadn't really noticed her gold chain necklace against the yellow dress, but it stood out nicely against the BDU T-shirt, and, of course, matched her gold earrings.

She didn't make sense.

Nothing about her made sense.

Him noticing every little thing about her didn't make sense.

He worked with women. He worked with Skeeter Bang Hart, who was a *fashionista* of the highest order. That girl had the clotheshorse sensibilities of a street urchin and a bottomless pocketbook to make her wildest dreams come true. But even dressed in a fuzzy pink sweater dress and pink suede go-go boots, Skeeter looked like she could kick a guy's butt—and she could.

And so could Red Dog, though she wouldn't have been caught dead in a pink anything, let alone a sweater dress or suede go-go boots. Red Dog liked black and lots of it, and enough red to earn her name. She liked supple fabrics and sleek designs. Neither one of the female SDF operators looked cute in BDUs. Skeeter always looked competent. Red Dog always looked dangerous.

Honey looked like if you shook her too hard, she'd break.

So don't let anybody shake her, Smith told himself.

Right. That was a helluva plan to take on a mission—"Don't shake my partner."

With a silent gesture, he directed her forward, toward the plane, and when they got to the top of the ramp, he wasn't at all surprised to hear her say, "Oh."

He knew exactly what she meant. The inside of a C-130 wasn't the inside of a 747.

She looked up one side of the fuselage and down the other.

"Aren't there any—"

"No, there aren't." No first-class seats, no business-class seats, no economy seats.

"Are we supposed to—" Honey made a gesture toward the inside wall and the bench seat running the length of the cabin.

"Yes, we are," Smith said, directing her forward again, past the pallet, which was secured aft, a few feet forward of the ramp.

The seats faced the center of the plane and were made out of tightly stretched red cargo netting supported by flimsy aluminum tubing. They looked and felt like cheap lawn chairs with straight backs and no armrests. They were standard troop seats, and there had been a few years in Smith's younger days when he'd practically lived in one.

It was like coming home—for one of them anyway.

Honey perched her camouflaged butt in a seat

and scooted around a bit, trying to get comfortable. He could have told her not to bother. The best thing to do was suck it up and enjoy the ride.

"The back on my seat doesn't seem right," she said, turning sideways and wiggling the frame.

"It's the way they're built."

"Wrong?"

"No," he said, coming to the venerable C-130's defense. "Don't think of this as a plane. Think of it as a sardine can designed for efficiency and maximum load."

"I'm not a sardine," she muttered, trying one more time to arrange herself in a comfortable position.

He grinned. It was going to be a long two hours to El Salvador—for her. He had his flight plan memorized and ready to go.

"Here, you're going to need these." He handed her a pair of earplugs.

When she gave them a blank look, he demonstrated, rolling another pair into thin cylinders and sticking them in his ears. The engine run-up for takeoff was deafening inside a C-130. A fact she discovered about two seconds after she got her earplugs in.

She shot him a wide-eyed look and quickly buckled her seat belt—a very good idea. Sitting at a right angle to the long axis of the airplane, with nothing to brace against, meant passengers got tossed sideways during acceleration and deceleration.

By the time they lifted off, she was holding on to anything and everything to keep her in her seat. The smell of jet fuel filled the air, and even he felt a little queasy. It would pass, but he'd been on more than one plane ride where the cabin turned into Up-chuck Central during the first few minutes after takeoff.

To his surprise, she held her own. Her mouth was tight, her nose wrinkled, her expression grim, but she didn't look like she was going to be sick.

Good, because he'd forgotten to have a barf bag handy for her.

Once they were in the air and hit their cruising altitude, the engine noise abated a bit, and a steady flow of cool, clean air purged the last of the fuel vapor from the fuselage.

"Thanks for not throwing up," he said, giving her credit where credit was due. "The takeoffs can be a little rough in one of these."

"I never throw up," she said, with enough confidence that he almost believed her.

"Never?"

"Never."

"Cast-iron stomach?"

She shook her head. "Good breeding."

He let out a short laugh. *Geezus*. Good breeding. She was something else, all right. He didn't know what, but she was definitely something else.

Proceeding with his in-flight routine, he took a thick bandanna out of one of his cargo pockets and wrapped it around his head. She went back to fidgeting, trying to get comfortable, which was not going to happen, not in a troop seat at thirty thousand feet. There was only one way to truly enjoy a C-130 flight. He secured the bandanna to the back of his seat, settled down against his seat belt, and promptly fell asleep.

Sometime later, with the drone of the engine still in his ears, he came partly awake, enough to take stock of his surroundings before returning to the best nap he'd had in days. His gaze slid through the cabin—the pallet was still secure; the aircrew was seated on the opposite side of the fuselage ... and Honey was next to him, one seat over.

An unexpected smile curved his mouth. Smart girl, she'd fallen asleep cross-legged in her seat with a long scarf wrapped around her head and secured behind her, the Gucci version of his makeshift head harness. She had a blanket tucked around her, no doubt compliments of an aircrew that was far more aware of her than they'd let on in the hangar.

He reached up and touched a loose end of the scarf. Silk. White with a lattice pattern of gold. Expensive. She looked like a kid's idea of a ninja, a slightly-older-than-Teenage Mutant Drop-dead-Beautiful Ninja.

He liked gorgeous women. Every woman he'd ever been with had been gorgeous for as long as he'd been with her. Sometimes the luster faded after a breakup, and a couple of times, after a couple of particularly bad breakups, a woman he'd once thought beautiful had taken on the features of a hound from hell.

So yeah, he'd known his share of beautiful women, maybe more than his share, and Honoria York-Lytton still disconcerted the hell out of him. Maybe it was because she was always so out of place.

San Luis? Hell. She'd had no business being in San Luis. And rumbling along at thirty thousand feet in the belly of a C-130? She had no business being here, either. So what was it with her? Some aberrant get-your-ass-in-a-sling gene? She was obviously good at the Park Avenue thing, so why didn't she stay on Park Avenue?

Maybe it was a family trait. Julia Ann-Marie sure knew how to drown in hot water. Two of Honey's brothers, the oldest and one out of the middle of the four-pack, had actually made names for themselves in the adventure trade—the middle one, Haydon, with his grand, ecoenvironmental, media-extravaganzas-to-the-ends-of-the-earth expeditions, and the oldest, Avaldamon Thomas York-Lytton, for his oceanic research in faraway places, especially places with no oceans, at least that seemed to be the gist of the intensely academic articles Smith had found.

Avaldamon—now there was a first name to rival Smith's. It had to be a family name, one passed down through the generations. He knew what that was like, too, and figured a lot of bad ideas happened that way. He'd always wondered what in the world his mother had been thinking, and why in the world his father had let her get away with it.

Love, he guessed. Jack Rydell had loved his Melinda Jo, and when she'd died after giving him two sons in nine years of marriage, he'd enshrined her in his heart as a saint.

Smith shifted in his seat. He didn't think of his mother much. She hadn't been in his life very long—and he didn't know why he was thinking of her now.

He let his gaze go over Honey again, noting the scarf tied around her head, holding her in place. For as little time as they'd actually spent together, she was racking up a fair-sized list of good choices in the middle of all her bad decisions. If she kept it up, he might have to reevaluate his knee-jerk, testosterone-driven opinions of Park Avenue princesses—at least this one, the one he'd had in his bed in San Luis.

God, she'd been sweet that night, hot, and silky, and willing. More than willing. And then she'd gone, and even though he'd been the one hustling her out of town and shoving her on a plane as fast as he could, he was still angry about . . . hell, he didn't know, maybe about only having her once.

His gaze fell to her hand, the one closest to the briefcase, and his anger gave way to a quick grin. *Sonuvagun*. The handcuff had slipped off her hand and was lying in her lap. Slipped off— not been unlocked and removed. Smart girl, all right; she wasn't worried about rebel bandits and mountain guerrillas taking the briefcase, oh, hell, no. She wasn't worried about Salvadoran troops absconding with it, or rogue government officials impounding it. The only person she was worried about stealing Zorro's briefcase from her was him.

Fair enough, he thought, settling back into his seat. At least now he knew he didn't have to worry about the handcuffs.

The next time he woke it was to a light touch on his shoulder and the sensation of the airplane throttling back. The young man in BDUs leaned down and spoke over the roar of the engines.

"Twelve minutes out, sir."

Smith nodded, stretched, and untied his bandanna. Even with all the noise and turbulence, Honey was still asleep, a skill he would have bet a hundred dollars she didn't have.

The aircraft banked sharply left, leveled out, and throttled back still more. She started to stir as the plane began its final approach to the main runway on Ilopango's military complex. Outside his window, he saw the familiar FAS—*Fuerza Aerea Salvadoreña*—insignia of the Salvadoran Air Force on immaculately maintained fighters, transports, and helicopters. El Salvador had one of the strongest and most professional military traditions in Central America, and Smith strongly suspected that every round of ammunition and every explosive device he was bringing into the country was going to be used against Salvadoran soldiers. Government shenanigans and backdoor deals aside, he knew if the troops on the ground in Morazán found out who had delivered LAWs and M203 grenade launchers to the CNL, they were going to take it damned personally.

CHAPTER NINE

Sona, Colombia

Inside one of the hangars on her estate, Irena stepped down off the skid pad of her Piper Seneca and did a visual check of the underside of the plane. Everything was prepared, the aircraft loaded with her and Ari's field gear. All they needed was a location for C. Smith Rydell, and they'd be in the air in minutes.

It was gnawing at her, the whole notion of Rydell being alive. She should have looked back that day in Afghanistan. She should never have walked away in the first place, but oddly, she had not wanted to see him die. He'd been a favorite among her lovers, something she wouldn't have admitted then, and barely chose to acknowledge now. But faced with his existence, and the need to kill him as quickly as possible, she supposed the memories were inevitable—and important. The more she remembered about him, the better her chances of success when she and Ari found him.

Under the circumstance, it seemed ironic, but she'd bought the villa with his blood, with the money from Abdurrashid, or so she'd always thought. Now she wondered if it had been Abdurrashid's blood that had been spilled that day. Back then, she wouldn't have cared. She'd just been starting out. The deals had come fast, and her partners had usually been short-term, and always expendable.

Not so, now. She built relationships and worked them to her advantage. There were only so many people at the top, and she knew them all, like the English lord, and the heads of the Cali cartel. By working with the best, she had increased her profit margin tenfold in the last six years. By faking her death, she'd bought a measure of safety for herself and for what she held most dear: a five-year-old girl who lived in luxury and security on the Rue de Bois-Guilbert in Paris.

The child, Anastasia, was not Rydell's, but he'd been the lover she'd taken after Rutger Dolk, another contract aviator for the DEA, had left Afghanistan. Rydell had been the lover who had noticed the changes in her body. He'd been the lover she'd stupidly confided in one night during a moment of weakness.

Therefore, he'd been the lover who'd died. Or should have.

But even if he hadn't, as long as he'd thought her dead, there had been no danger, because in his mind, there never would have been a child. Even now, he might not be sure. Women miscarried. Children were stillborn. A hundred things could have happened to have kept her from being a mother—but they had not. Anastasia was hers, but not in Sona, not where anyone connected with the drug business could find her.

"*Patrona.*"

She whirled at the sound of the voice, the pistol in her thigh holster drawn and instantly aimed, her finger on the trigger, the slack taken up.

"My apologies," Hans said, with a slight bow, the color drained from his face. "I thought you heard me enter the hangar."

She should have. He was ten meters inside the doors, the concrete surface crossed in hard-soled shoes. That she hadn't heard him was indicative of a disturbing mind-set she needed to bring under control. Inattention got people killed. Inattention caused mistakes to be made, mistakes she couldn't afford.

"What have you found?" she asked, holstering the gun with no apology of her own for bringing him within a split second of death. He knew better.

"The intelligence you requested." He lifted the folder in his hand. "Rydell was briefed by the CIA chief of station at the U.S. Embassy in Panama City, and a request was made for current imagery of northern El Salvador to support that briefing. Immediately after the meeting, Rydell and the woman were taken by limousine to Howard Air Base."

"Heading to El Salvador?"

"I don't have that information yet, *patrona*. I have alerted a contact at Ilopango, and if they land in San Salvador, we will know shortly. The flight time between Howard and Ilopango is two hours, and they've had that since leaving Panama."

"Northern El Salvador," she said, extending her hand for the folder, which Hans immediately relinquished. "The Cuerpo Nacional de Libertad has started up strong there again, in Morazán Province, haven't they?" Her sources of news were wider and more varied than the legitimate media, but no one had to look further than the San Salvador newspapers to keep track of the CNL. Guerrilla warfare on the borders was always news in Central and South America, and keeping track of it was part of her business.

"Yes. According to our friend in Cali, a group of the CNL based near the Torola River has been stirring up a lot of trouble in the area, with the guerrillas under the control of a new leader, Diego Garcia. He's been able to bring a fresh infusion of cash to the resistance."

She smiled. Cash meant drugs.

"Who is he doing business with?"

"Our friend in Cali, for one," Hans said.

Her smile grew even more satisfied.

"Does our friend know how unhappy I am about the quality of the arrangements in Cuzco? Does he know we've lost the use of one of our most important airstrips because of the inadequate security provided by his people?"

"Yes, *patrona*. I made your displeasure very clear to him."

"Then tell him to give me Diego Garcia. I want to know everything the CNL is doing in Morazán, and who they're doing it with."

"It has been done," Hans said. "We have been promised a full report."

"Immediately." She needed that clear to the Cali contingent. There was no time for delay.

"*Inmediatamente*, yes, *patrona*."

"Good." She snapped open the folder and

glanced at the top page. It was a poor copy of a satellite image. "Can this be enhanced?"

"Yes, *patrona*."

"Then do it." She flipped to the next page, another satellite map, also in need of enhancing, but she never had to tell Hans anything twice. He got paid to solve her problems before they became problems, and he got paid for his loyalty, which was absolute.

The subdued ringing of a phone had him proffering another short bow. He pulled the cell out of his pocket and brought it to his ear.

"*Ja.*" It took him no more than thirty seconds to receive the news. After he hung up, he met her gaze again. "A C-130 has landed at Ilopango, on the military side of the installation, arriving from Panama. There were two passengers among the crew."

"Americans?"

"Our contact cannot confirm, but he did get a visual, and one of the passengers is a woman, not very tall, blond."

"And this Honoria York-Lytton, what have you found out about her?" she asked.

"Thirty-two years old, unmarried, very wealthy. Her father was the American ambassador to Denmark through two administrations. The family lives in Washington, D.C. She went to

Harvard, but has no apparent employment. She arrived in Panama City shortly after midnight last night. I put a photograph of her near the back of the folder."

Irena flipped to the back, took one look, and made up her mind. Honoria York-Lytton was very beautiful, very short, and very blond.

"Find Ari. Tell him we're leaving. I want everyone we do business with in El Salvador put on alert." She paged through the folder until she found the expected map section. The maps were in chronological order: Peru, Panama, El Salvador, and if Hans received any information regarding Rydell connecting him to another country, another map would be added to the folder. It was their standard tracking procedure for building a file on a target.

"San Miguel is the closest large town to Morazán Province," Hans said.

"Yes." She saw it in the southeast part of the country. "Who do we know in San Miguel? Anybody?"

"Federico Perez."

"Is in San Salvador, not San Miguel."

"But he was born in San Miguel. His mother is still there, aunts, uncles, two sisters."

And she paid Hans to remember the thousand details they needed to always stay one step ahead of the hundreds of people who wanted what was hers. They were out there, constantly circling her territory, her connections, her deals, her sources, and they were always looking for a weakness, always ready to swoop in for the kill.

"Call him. I want a Hughes 500 helicopter ready for me when I land, and I'll need a vehicle waiting for me in Morazán, its destination to be determined by you. I want the closest landing zone to wherever you find Rydell, but not in Diego Garcia's backyard, unless making contact with him is to our advantage. This is a hit, not a party."

"Yes, *patrona*."

"And I'll expect the report on Garcia before I get to El Salvador. Something is going on in Morazán, something unusual. We've got a rich American woman showing up in Panama City at almost exactly the same time that Rydell is getting on a plane out of Peru. He visits the U.S. Embassy on the Avenida Balboa, and then the two of them meet and are driven out to Howard Air Base to board a C-130 headed to San Salvador."

"Yes, *patrona*."

"Why?" She didn't ask rhetorical questions. Hans knew it as well as Ari.

"I will discover the reason."

"A C-130 is a transport aircraft," she said.

He nodded.

"I want to know what was on the one that landed at Ilopango."

"Yes, *patrona*."

CHAPTER **TEN**

Campos Plantation, Morazán Province, El Salvador

"What's this?" Campos asked, picking a letter up off the silver salver offered by his manservant, Maximiliano. "Ouch, Doc, watch that."

"If you'd stop getting shot, I wouldn't have to watch anything," Dr. Sofia Cristiani said, putting the last suture in the top of his thigh. Dark eyes, dark hair, almost as round as she was tall, Sofia Cristiani ran her clinic like a Gestapo, charged a small fortune for home visits, and was completely immune to his charm.

From the corner by the hearth, he heard his cook, Isidora, shushing her children, admonishing them to be quiet while *el patrón* had his surgery. Yes, just another night at the old homestead, he thought, sitting in the kitchen of his Spanish-style villa, surrounded by the warmth of terra-cotta tiles, weathered wood, the smells of good food cooking, and getting stuck with a needle—repeatedly.

He'd gotten skinned, that was all, but for someone who had only gotten skinned, he'd bled a helluva lot, and he wanted sympathy and plenty of it, not attitude.

Not really so much blood loss; not the way she was reading the wound, the doc had said, but what did she know? Sofia hadn't seen the seat of the four-banger. Sure, his blood pressure was fine and his color was good, but he'd bled like hell. He should call Jewel. She could tell the doc how bad it had been.

Then again, maybe not. Jewel had already called him a head case once today.

"Where did this come from, Max?" The envelope looked like it had been dragged behind a donkey cart for two days.

"The back door, *patrón,* some *campesino* passing through." Maximiliano was on the wrong side of seventy, a hundred and thirty-five pounds on a good day, white-haired, and absolutely, completely in charge of the mail. If it had a stamp, it went through Max. He always dressed in black trousers and a pressed white shirt.

Campos looked at the envelope again. The chicken scratching on the front looked faintly familiar through the mud stains. Holding it up better into the light, he could read his name; but there was no return address and the stamp had not been canceled.

"The *campesino* said it was from your sister," Max added.

Well, that would be a good trick. Campos didn't have a sister.

Then it came to him: Sister Julia, formerly of St. Mary's parish in San Luis, the angelic nun who'd passed through Morazán with Diego Garcia and his thugs four months ago on her way to St. Joseph. She'd written him twice since then, once to thank him for his hospitality and to solicit a donation for the St. Joseph orphanage, and the second time to request his help in procuring a generator, and to solicit a donation for the St. Joseph orphanage.

He'd sent her a generator, and both times he'd sent her money for her orphanage. She wasn't the only nun up in the hills trying to keep St. Joseph up and running as a school and orphanage. Two other recent arrivals, Sister Rose and Sister Teresa, were doing their best to hold the place together. The headmistress, Sister Bettine, had been up there, mostly on her own, for the last twenty-odd years, and he was being generous. Battle-ax Bettine, the less generous called her, ruling the motherless and abandoned with a palsied, iron hand. For his money, Campos had thought Sister Julia was a huge improvement and exactly what the old place had needed. Other than that, and the occasional solicitation, he had never given the nuns in the hills much thought.

Until yesterday, when he'd been contacted about a Cessna that had crashed into the Salvadoran hills the day before—into his neck of the woods. During the twelve hours before he learned of the disaster, he had left Morazán to work the Gonzalez deal in Colombia, and the plane had been found by the CNL and stripped. So now they had a full-blown "incident" on their hands, complete with extortion, politicians, rebel forces, the U.S. State Department, and a few secret squirrels from the CIA. It had been the Agency's plane, and they wanted their stuff back—and they wanted him to grease the wheels that would get their people in and out of Morazán with their mission accomplished.

It was his specialty—greasing wheels, moving people, contraband, money, influence, whatever the job required, and lately it had required a lot.

Tonight and tomorrow, it was going to require even more. Sister Julia had a sister, and for reasons that completely escaped Campos no matter how many times he ran the plan through his brain, Diego Garcia wanted Sister Julia's sister to deliver the money that would buy back the Agency's diplomatic pouch. To their credit, the State Department had at least given the woman a bodyguard, a PSD specialist they'd pulled out of Lima, Peru, named C. Smith Rydell, and according to the last fax to come over his secure line this evening, the two of them had arrived in San Salvador and were on their way north into Morazán.

The second page of the fax had been the load manifest of the duo's cargo, and every time he thought about it, all he could do was shake his head.

"*La vida es tan loca, Sofia,*" he said, leaning over in his chair to pick his pants up off the floor. *Life is so crazy.*

"You are what's crazy, Alejandro." She pulled the last suture tight as she finished it off, and he figured she did it on purpose to make him wince.

He obliged with appropriate theatrics. "You are a mean, mean woman, *chiquita,*" he said, rummaging through his pants pockets until he found his folding knife. He took it out and used it to slit open the envelope.

"I'm not mean. I'm honest."

"Mean and honest" was the most he could

concede. He snapped open the letter and read the date written at the top. It was a month old.

"More honest than mean," she said, taking hold of the top of the letter and pulling it down. She met his gaze squarely over the piece of paper. "And it is time for you to go home, *alférez*." *Ensign*.

He hardened his gaze. She knew better than to call him that out loud.

But she wasn't having any of it.

"Your luck has run out, Zorro." And she had no business calling him that, either. That was the damn thing with doctors. Sometimes a person got sick, and they'd end up in some doctor's evil clutches, and if the sick person had some godawful jungle fever that made them spill out their life history with all the damned delirious details, well, then the doctor had them by the balls.

Sofia's not-so-gentle talons had been around his *cojónes* for the last eight years, which was a helluva thing to be thinking when he was sitting at the kitchen table in his boxers.

"It's going to run out a lot faster if you keep talking." He wasn't having any of it, either.

"This is the third time this year you've gotten hurt badly enough to need me."

"I *always* need you, *chica*." He tried to tease her out of the stony look she was giving him.

But she didn't relent.

"You're going to need me to sign your death certificate, if you don't stop now, and leave, while you're still ahead of the game."

"I'm always ahead of the game," he said, and she poked him next to his new stitches. *"Dammit."*

"I love you." She poked him again.

"You're old enough to be my mother."

"You never knew your mother."

He grabbed her hand before she could poke him again. "And how long have you known that?"

"Since the fever."

He was impressed. She'd actually kept something from him.

"Sofia, Sofia—" He started to sweet-talk her, but fifty-five-year-old Salvadoran doctors with five kids, twelve grandkids, and one very macho husband had all the sweet talk they needed without his meager offering.

"Jewel and I talked," she said.

Not what he wanted to hear. He let go of her hand and leaned back in his chair. If Sofia and Jewel had been ganging up on him, he wished he was wearing his pants.

"Jewel doesn't live here anymore." She lived with what's-his-name in Barranquilla.

"She left you because she loves you."

Yes. He remembered hearing words to that effect and wondering what in the hell they meant—*I love you so much, I can't bear to be with you.*

Tricky statements like that were the heart and soul of the war between the sexes.

"She didn't want to be here when you died."

Coming from a guy's doctor, those were fairly alarming words.

"It's a flesh wound, Sofia. You said so yourself. Eight stitches."

"Don't make light of this, Alejandro."

Not very damn likely, not with her practically putting the juju of doom on him.

"I have to leave," she said, turning aside to pack her medical kit. "I want to get home before the storm hits. But I want you to think about what I've said."

Not if he could help it.

"What storm?"

"Rain's coming again tonight, in about an hour. I'm going to leave you some pain medication."

"Thank you." It was always nice to have legal narcotics in the house.

Pain meds. *Christ.* Sofia knew what he did.

"Max," he said loudly, and waved the letter

through the air, hoping to catch the old man's attention.

When Max looked up, he directed him toward the door.

"See Dr. Cristiani out, *por favor*. Isidora," he called to his cook. "Bring me food."

Yes, he was the badass Alejandro Campos, eating soup at his kitchen table in his underwear, and reading a letter that did nothing but demoralize the hell out of him and make him lose a little bit more faith in the world. Which was a crying shame, because he didn't have much faith left in anything, and that was why he needed to leave Morazán. Not because he'd gotten hurt a few times in the last year, but because he was having a hard time believing in what he was doing—and Sofia was right, that would get him killed.

He folded the letter, put it back in its envelope, and stuck them both in his shirt pocket.

Hell. Nuns and guerrillas. Now he'd heard everything—except why in the hell Diego Garcia had chosen Honoria York-Lytton to be his designated gofer for tomorrow's exchange, and why in the world she had agreed. From what he'd been told about the woman, and from the brief dossier he'd been sent, he had not understood why, sister or no sister, the honorable Honoria had allowed herself to be dragged into this mess. Society divas usually avoided jungle guerrillas. They usually chose not to risk their lives in Third World country backwaters. They did not go out of their way to rub shoulders with AK-47–toting gunslingers who could easily choose to hold them for ransom rather than close their deal. For sheer financial gain, she was probably worth more than the documents she'd been sent to retrieve.

The same, of course, could be said about the surprising Sister Julia Ann-Marie, the surprisingly wealthy Sister Julia Ann-Marie—and to think he'd been giving her money.

He shifted his attention to the windows overlooking the fountain in his courtyard, his gaze drawn by the fast-moving black clouds closing in on the moon. *Perfecto.* Eight brand-new stitches, a pregnant nun, two hundred and fifty kilos of jacked cocaine he needed to find, and two welcome, but undeniably troublesome visitors and a deluge on their way.

Make that one deluge arrived, he thought as the sky opened up with a blast of wind and dropped untold buckets of rain in one fell swoosh guaranteed to last for hours.

Now the night was perfect. The villa was glorious, everything the brochure had promised: hardwood floors, five fireplaces, built-in pizza oven, hot tub, lap pool, seven bathrooms, twenty-two rooms in all, French doors everywhere, and enough elevations on the tile roof to rival Notre Dame—five of which leaked.

"Buckets," he hollered, and three of Isidora's preschool-aged brood took off like shots, laughing and scrambling to get the buckets out of the pantry.

"Campos." A dark-haired man in a gray T-shirt and a pair of camo pants came out of the office, carrying a sheet of paper. Jake Williams was a Wyoming cowboy who had opted for a life of adventure and a chance to be all he could be. Campos had been happy to oblige. He always had use for another "security consultant" contracted and paid for by the U.S. government for his convenience, especially one with Jake's skills. "Panama wants us to pass this intel along to Rydell when he gets here."

Campos took the paper and read down the page. Fortunately, he didn't mind mysteries. He took them as challenges. Obtuse bits of information flying into his life were not avoided. They were accumulated, and without fail, eventually, they made a whole—a whole idea, a whole plan, a whole revelation about how much crap he was seriously sinking into, like a lot.

Normally, cocaine cartel hits were not his

number-one concern. There were simply too many of them to prioritize in a reasonable manner. A lot of people died in his business, usually badly, never in their sleep.

Normally, a federal policeman in Lima, Peru, getting waxed by a contract killer was not news in Morazán Province, El Salvador. But, when the dead guy's partner was scheduled to arrive at his villa within the hour, well, Campos figured there was something at stake. He stayed alive by making sure it was never his ass.

A drop of water hit the fax, and then another one, and another one.

He swore softly and gave the piece of paper a shake, getting the water off. "Jake, can you ... uh"—it was a stream now, splashing onto the table—"get a bucket?"

CHAPTER ELEVEN

Morazán Province, El Salvador

The rain, when it hit, caught Lily Robbins off guard. After a week of it, darn near nonstop, she should have been better prepared, but "Be prepared" was a motto she'd lost the option on the day she'd landed in San Salvador with her laptop, her new digital video camera, a rucksack, and enough naïveté to have sunk the *Titanic* twice.

Good God, there ought to be a law against people like her, especially against letting them out into the world on their own.

A gust of wind caught her car broadside and almost blew it off the road—in a manner of speaking. In truth, what she was driving on in no way resembled a road, and it wasn't her car.

Lily was on what was euphemistically referred

to as a "track," or possibly a "trail." Fortunately, the car she'd stolen was often referred to as a "Jeep," or a "four-wheel drive." Even more fortunately, the "Jeep" she'd stolen just happened to have a gun in it. The gun—which she couldn't see well enough in the dark to determine what it was, exactly, other than a "handgun"—was holstered on a belt that had been buckled around the passenger seat in a manner to provide quick and easy access for the driver, should said driver need to defend him- or herself.

Lily was thinking that was a distinct possibility.

She had a knack, only one: for orienteering, for reading maps and for knowing where she was on the planet, almost anywhere on the planet, give or take a second of latitude or longitude here and there. She was good in European subways. Train stations held no fear for her. Mountain trails were her best friends. As long as there was a road, Lily Robbins was not lost, and tonight, even without a road, she wasn't lost. She had a map, and she knew exactly where she was: hell-bent-and-gone from St. Joseph School and Orphanage, and please-dear-God-more-than-halfway to the Campos plantation.

Alejandro Campos was her only hope—and given that he was the biggest drug dealer in Morazán, Lily figured she was in way more trouble than she'd ever bargained for when she'd decided a sabbatical and a few months abroad in the world were a good idea.

Take a trip, she'd thought.

See Central America.

Bring home real-life experiences to share in your classroom.

Make that intensely compassionate documentary film you've been secretly dreaming about for years, the one that wins you an Academy Award for "Most Intensely Compassionate Documentary Film of the Year."

She was so full of it.

Her compassion had taken a hike two days ago, approximately five minutes after the Cuerpo Nacional de Libertad had burst into St. Joseph School and Orphanage. They'd had a man with them, an American, and he'd been badly hurt.

And then they'd asked the American some questions, which he hadn't precisely answered.

And then he'd died.

End of story.

Except she'd be damned if she let them get ahold of her and ask her any questions. Though God only knew what she might know that could possibly be of interest to a group of Central American guerrillas.

Can you explain the difference between cen-

trifugal and centripetal forces in human geography?

Yes. Yes, she could.

Give us the names of the three most important cultural groups in Nigeria.

Hausa, Yoruba, and Ibo.

What's the official language of the southern region of Belgium?

French.

No doubt about it. She was ready to be interrogated by anyone. Unless they were Third World rebels, and unless they asked her for her camera.

The left front tire of the Jeep slipped into a muddy rut, giving her a quick tossing-about, and for the next few seconds, she kept her foot off the gas and let the wheel slide through her hands while the car jostled from side to side. When the rut played out, she pressed her foot down and grasped the wheel more firmly, and continued fighting to keep the vehicle on the track.

She was going too fast. She knew it. She'd jammed the Jeep into fourth gear and had the pedal back to the metal. A couple of times, she'd out-and-out careened around a turn or over a bump, but she wasn't slowing down.

She didn't dare.

There were lights behind her, flashing through

the rain. Sometimes she lost them, but never for long.

Today was Thursday.

She had arrived at St. Joseph the previous Friday, camera and notebook in hand, to begin documenting the work of a small group of nuns standing strong against an oppressive government buckling under the demands of capitalist corporations out to monopolize the Salvadoran coffee industry. The good sisters' own church had abandoned their cause, but they were undaunted, fighting side by side with the CNL for the independent farmer and the future of those farmers' children. Or so they believed.

So that was Friday, an acclimation to the situation and the gathering of preliminary data.

Saturday had gone pretty well. Lily had gotten some good footage and conducted two interviews.

On Sunday, Sister Bettine had died, and quite unexpectedly Lily had gotten her last words, a prayer for the faithful, on film.

On Monday, during matins, Sister Teresa had broken down and confessed to carnal knowledge of a CNL rebel soldier and that she was pregnant. Everyone present, including Lily, who had been filming, had been terribly relieved that Sister Bettine had been spared both the confession and the sordid details, which they had all listened to verily on the edge of their pews.

The American had died on Tuesday, on the altar, at Jesus' feet, and Lily, from the safety and secrecy of the sacristy, had gotten it on film.

On Wednesday, it had been revealed that Sister Teresa's carnal knowledge had included more than one rebel soldier, but the child, she swore, could only be the *Capitán*'s, an older man named Diego Garcia. Another nun, Sister Julia, swore also that this was true, having been Teresa's sole confidante during the love affair— the initial love affair. Sister Julia had been as shocked and dismayed as the rest of them about the other, younger rebel soldier.

At that point, with the CNL still in residence, and a sworn bride of Christ committing adultery and then cheating on her boyfriend, things had really gone downhill, and Lily, discreetly, had been getting it all on film. She'd kept rolling, capturing real life, thinking it was going to beat the hell out of all the intensely compassionate documentaries it would be up against at Cannes.

She had actually seen the headlines in her mind: *Move Over, Indiana Jones. Albuquerque Lily Steals Show*.

It had taken subterfuge and stealth, and hiding out in the nooks and crannies of the old church and convent—all parties concerned feeling that once the CNL had commandeered the church, and the poor American had died, it was better for Ms. Robbins to leave St. Joseph, or at least appear to have left.

And then, four hours ago, Diego Garcia himself had shown up, a man who did not take anything at face value, let alone the idea of an American woman's convenient disappearance from St. Joseph, after an American pilot had so inconveniently died on St. Joseph's altar. A pilot, the information had come out, whose plane had been shot down over Morazán, the operative words being "shot down." Lily had also, unexpectedly, captured *his* dying words on tape. Far from a prayer for the faithful, he'd had only two: "Fuck you."

She'd heard them very clearly, even from the sacristy. The soldiers gathered around him, asking questions, had also heard him very clearly, and if he hadn't chosen that moment to die, she was certain they'd have killed him on the spot.

And she had it all in her camera.

When Diego Garcia had ordered a full-scale search of the church and orphanage—after he'd beaten Teresa and shot her young lover dead, two events that Lily had also gotten on film, but had sworn, so help her God, to never, ever, ever look at again—she hadn't hesitated for a moment. She'd turned tail and headed out the back door. Sister Julia had caught her in the kitchen and given her a map, one of Sister Bettine's habits, and an escape plan: Alejandro Campos, a friend to the church, especially the orphanage, who despite having pushed a few thousand kilos of cocaine through Morazán in the last year, was a good man.

Lily doubted it.

Go to him, Julia had said. *Campos is the only one who can protect you from Garcia.*

Lily didn't doubt that, and in the rush of escape and the heat of the moment, she had obeyed, trusting Sister Julia not to send her to someone who would as soon slit her throat as let her in on a dark and stormy night.

Now all she had to do was get to him.

A flash of light in her rearview mirror sent a cold trickle of dread down her spine. She glanced at the pistol holstered on the side of the passenger seat and hoped two things with all her heart: that it was a .45, and that it had an extended magazine.

CHAPTER TWELVE

"I like the rain."

Rain? Smith looked at Honey sitting across from him in one of the two Land Cruisers they'd acquired at Ilopango along with a two-and-a-half-ton cargo truck. This wasn't rain. It was a torrent.

"We're practically underwater," he said. The world on the other side of the windshield was a solid sheet of gray night sky melding into wet pavement. He had the wipers on light speed and still couldn't see a damn thing—a fact proven when he skidded onto the shoulder going around the next curve, the same way he'd skidded onto the shoulder going around the last curve.

Honey grabbed for the dash and cleared her

throat, the same way she had the last time, but this time she didn't let go of the dash. She did use her free hand to take her cigarillo from her lips so she could blow a small cloud of fragrant smoke into the cab—cherry with a hint of whiskey—most of which found its way out the small open crack at the top of her window.

Smith tightened his grip on the steering wheel and checked his rearview to make sure the deuce-and-a-half behind them stayed on the road. The last thing they needed was for their pallet of weapons and luggage to end up at the bottom of some damn gorge.

"Do you want me to drive?" Honey asked, before taking another hit off the small Cuban cigar.

He looked at her—once, sharply, briefly.

"I'm an excellent driver," she said, resting the hand with the cigar back along the seat.

"No." Smith kept his eyes on the road. One word to say it all, that was his motto. The fewer words the better. Keep it short. Keep it simple.

Or say something he was bound to regret, something cold and true about misplaced do-gooders and self-sacrificing nuns.

"And I'm rested. You were up all night and—"

"I'm driving."

And if it took more than two words to get his point across, he was losing his touch.

"I drove at Talladega."

"You did not."

Another mile passed in silence and a small puff of cigar smoke.

"Did too."

Smith let out a breath, a heavy breath. It was not a sigh. He did not sigh.

"I almost graduated from their training school." The end of the cigarillo glowed momentarily in the dark cab as she inhaled.

No way. Not even almost.

"Did not." A person had to actually be good to graduate from a Busch Series training school or a NASCAR school. They didn't hand out diplomas simply for paying the money.

"Did too . . . almost."

Well, this was a definite deterioration of the lovely silence they'd been sharing, a juvenile squabbling match.

"When we get to the Campos plantation, it's going to be my rules, all the way. Anything I tell you, do it. Any questions may or may not be entertained later. Don't expect me to explain myself, especially not in front of anyone else."

"Talladega was the second driving school I went to," Honey said, which was not the confirmation he'd expected. The words "yes, sir" would have been more appropriate.

"If we end up in the CNL camp tomorrow, which I'm going to do my best to ensure we don't, then, more than likely, I won't be speaking to you at all, except when absolutely necessary. Just follow my lead." The last damn thing Smith was inclined to do, under any circumstances, was drag Little Miss Cigar-Smoking Sparkle Toes into an insurgents' camp in the mountains, but it was a possibility. It was also his definitive definition of insane. So insane, he was considering resorting to serious intimidation to get the combination out of her—very serious. The kind she wouldn't forget for a long time, if ever, and then he'd take *his* handcuffs and lock her to something immovable at Campos's, while he and the plantation owner went and retrieved the CIA's merchandise and the saintly Sister Julia.

Sure, he could do it. He didn't need Honey on his side. Once this deal was over, they'd go their separate ways, and she'd be nothing but a nagging, niggling, confusing piece of unfinished business that would probably drive him nuts for the next twenty years.

"The first driving school I went to was DDD in

Los Angeles." Honey knocked her ash into the Land Cruiser's ashtray.

Smith shot her another glance. "Dandridge Dynamic Driving?" In the circles where driving skills could mean the difference between life and death, Dandridge's was considered to be the finest school in the States, if not the world. Every tactical driving school had their theories and a track. DDD had a proven track record.

"Yes." She was sitting sideways in the seat, facing him. "My brother Thomas sent me a few years ago, and I did graduate from their course. I still can't parallel park worth a damn, but I can do a ninety-degree controlled slide and a reverse one-eighty."

Okay. He was impressed—and Thomas, he remembered, was the brother stuck with "Avaldamon."

"I've been to Dandridge's," he said. It had been part of his training for SDF.

"When?"

"Recently" was all he said. Smith didn't give the actual details of his life away, ever, not even the fairly innocuous details, if there even were such things, which he doubted.

"Did you meet Steve Thornton?"

"Steve? Yeah. He was doing a two-day defensive course for a group of L.A. limo drivers while we were there." And wasn't that unexpected. They had something in common besides one wild night in San Luis. Nothing could have surprised him more. They even had an acquaintance in common, someone besides Brett Jenkins III, who was probably a foreign agent. There had been times when Smith had thought half the State Department comprised alien nationals, and he meant cosmic, not political.

"Steve was my personal instructor."

Yeah. He believed it. Any guy with some pull would have picked Honey out of the crowd and taken her under his wing, just for the fun of having her around. She was beautiful, friendly, warm, liked bourbon, and actually wasn't too spoiled.

That last thought brought him up short.

Sure, she was dripping in money, confidence, money, designer clothes, looks, and more money, but when he thought about it, she wasn't at all like Natalie.

Natalie had been spoiled R.O.T.T.E.N.

He'd actually liked it the first couple of weeks of their liaison. He'd liked all the hair-tossing and coyly sly smiles, all the breathless conversation about all the breathlessly fascinating moments that made up the life of Natalie. He'd liked the underlying sexuality and overt sensuality of every move she'd made, every touch, every step, of every time she'd slid into a chair, of every cup she'd lifted. He had personally watched her performance scramble men's brains. It had scrambled his for a while.

Na-ta-lie.

Natalie de Salignac. She'd been half French, and all, all, all about Natalie, but he'd loved her for two solid, trying months, until she'd beaten his initial fascination into the ground, and then she'd turned into a bitch, one of the hellhounds. His crime, as he recalled, had been in not listening to yet another "Day in the Life" pout about a rude *barista* at her favorite coffee shop. Rude, apparently, because the new coffee guy had charged her for her latte. Natalie de Salignac did not pay for lattes. They were gifts from the corporate coffee world in payment for her presence in their shop.

No kidding.

She'd even had a name for it: the Princess Discount. She got it all over town, just for showing up and being Natalie.

Smith glanced over at Honey, whose French twist was doing a little of that coming-undone thing, enough to put a few loose curls around her face. The black patent leather bow was still perfectly in place, a sleek and shiny band across the top of her head, proclaiming her Queen for a Day, or Audrey Hepburn, or something, he guessed. It made him grin. Who wore headbands besides teenage girls and women in magazines?

Oh, right. She had been in a magazine, and it was easy to see why, even with her BDUs rumpled and her tactical vest filling up with all sorts of odds and ends. He'd watched her put her lipstick and a small brush in one ammo pouch, and some cash and a credit card in another. Her cell phone had fit neatly in a pouch usually reserved for a spare pistol magazine. Tissues, some gum, a pen, a small notebook, granola bars, perfume—it had all disappeared into her vest.

But somehow, she was still missing something from the mix. With the cigarillo clamped between her teeth, she was back to searching through her big canary yellow purse.

"Thomas was planning a research trip to Nepal and wanted me along for company," she was saying. "But it was the kind of trip where there was very limited access to the sites he needed to visit." She took the cigarillo from between her teeth, blew out, and then held the small cigar in the fingers of one hand while she continued searching through her stuff with the other. "Everybody had to pull their weight and be approved by the Nepalese, so he wrote me down as one of the expedition's drivers and sent me to Dandridge's."

She probably got Princess Discounts all over the world, but every time Smith had been with Honey, it had been all about Julia, and getting into trouble, and going boldly, fearlessly, and stupidly where no Park Avenue princess had gone before. It had never been about Honoria York-Lytton, unless he'd pried the information out of her, or come up with it on his own.

San Luis, El Salvador? Give him a break. She'd had no business being there. And buying a gun off the street in front of the old Hotel Palacio? He'd never really had a chance to ask her how that piece of idiocy had come about.

But she wasn't stupid. He'd gone and gotten her other book, *Women's Sexuality Under the Yoke of Twenty-first Century Political Tyranny*, and man, that had been a real slog. Avaldamon Thomas wasn't the only York-Lytton capable of writing nearly indecipherable academic treatises.

Smith was a smart guy, but that thing had beat him cold.

"My brother Haydon got the plum assignment, though." Honey was still talking and still searching through her purse. "He ended up in

·muleteer school, so he could help with the mule train on the trek up the valley. The gist of which is, the roads in Nepal are much worse than this, even with the rain tonight, so if you'd like to relax, maybe take a nap, and let me drive, you'd be in good hands. I really did pay attention at Dandridge's, and Steve, as you know, is an excellent teacher."

Honey finally found what she was looking for, and pulled a small case out of her purse.

"He taught me how to feel where the weight is in a car," she said, "especially on an SUV, which we used a lot in the class, and I can brake accordingly, and control where the vehicle is at all times, and I can, uh, keep it off the shoulder and from going over the side"—she blew out another cloud of smoke—"... no offense intended."

Flipping open the case, she flashed a pair of glasses at him.

"Driving glasses," she said. "A slight prescription with yellow lens for night. It'll keep lights from haloing and sharpen everything up a bit."

Smith grinned. Piece of work—she thought she could drive better than him? Not on Dandridge's best day, glasses or no glasses. Still, he actually considered her proposition for a moment, which gave him pause. He was always in the driver's seat, physically, intellectually, and emotionally. He controlled his immediate environment absolutely, and his broader environment to the best of his ability, and he had some very precise, exacting, and extremely well practiced abilities—especially when it came to control.

"Thank you," he said. "But we're only an hour out from Campos's. It's best to keep the convoy rolling, rather than risk a driver change."

She let out a sigh, and sat back in her seat, and he felt like a jerk.

She had that effect on him, a lot.

"So what kind of research was Thomas doing in Nepal?" He'd read something about Nepal lately, but he couldn't quite remember where.

"Giant ammonites of the upper Kali Gandaki River. It's kind of an obscure branch of study."

Yeah. He bet it was.

"They really are giant, as big as tires, some of them," she said. "I was along for the luxury portion of the trip, from Kathmandu to Pokhara. Thomas knows I'm only good for as long as the hotel rooms and the hot water hold out, but in Nepal the roads run out with the hotel rooms, so he didn't need an official driver after that anyway. Beyond Pokhara, it's all mule trains and yaks and frozen plateaus, but we bounded around a bit in the lower river valleys, seeing what had washed down from Tibet, if anything, and visiting shrines. Thomas is big on taking samples and organizing data and extrapolating theories. He's the scientist in the family."

"And Julia's the saint," Smith said. A misplaced do-gooding saint. "And Haydon is the big-time adventurer, so where does that leave you and your other two brothers, Gerald and William?"

Honey turned to look at him again, a quizzical expression on her face. "Have you been investigating me? More than accidentally stumbling over the article in *Ocean* magazine?"

"A little," he admitted. Hell, he investigated everybody who bumped into his world, especially if they'd made a dent—and she had.

"So what did you find out?"

"Besides Shakespeare in the nude?"

"I had leaves on."

"And underwear-modeling boyfriends?"

"The romance in that romantic relationship was very brief, no pun intended, and a very long time ago. We truly are friends—and no, I never think of my friends as 'just friends,' even if they were former boyfriends. I like to keep the people I care about a little closer than that."

Touché, and ouch. Any woman he'd ever been done with had been done with him. Really done.

Natalie was probably still sticking pins in a voodoo doll with his name on it, and she probably wasn't the only one. The only woman he'd never been done with had been his first full-blown love affair, a lush and lovely thirty-year-old tax accountant named Caroline, who had taken his nineteen-year-old ideas about sex and turned them inside out. He still kept in touch with Caroline.

"How about hedge-fund kings of Wall Street?"

"Strictly a professional association. We're both on the board of directors of Century Opera. Raising funds and attending openings are part of the position."

"And French counts?"

"Distant relative, the Norman side of the Lytton side. Not very popular with my father, but some of us do try to stay in touch."

"And Kip-Woo?"

Honey took a long draw off her cigarillo, all the while giving Smith a very considering look from across the darkened cab of the Land Cruiser.

"You've been reading the society page," she said, after blowing out a long stream of smoke.

"Current events."

"My ass." She let out a laugh. "You didn't forget about me after you put me on that plane."

Not hardly.

"As a matter of fact, Mr. Rydell, from the fashion week galas I attended with Robbie to the publishing party I went to with Kip-Woo was about four months exactly. I'd say you've been reading about me every week since San Luis."

"Not quite," he said, adjusting his grip on the wheel and settling into the road. He'd been out of the country a couple of times in the last four months and missed the weekend sections of *The Washington Post* and *The New York Times'* society pages.

"I'd say you've got a crush on me."

Smith gave her a quick, quelling glance, and went back to watching the road. A crush. He didn't think so.

They drove along in silence for a long while, with the windshield wipers slapping back and forth, the heater blowing hot, and the scent of her cigarillo, cherry whiskey, teasing the air. And with every passing, silent mile, the atmosphere inside the cab became more laden, riper, heavier. He was watching the road, but she was watching him. He could feel her awareness washing up against him, feel her gaze sliding over him. It was a distinctive, unusually compelling sensation, and he liked it.

He liked it a lot.

"There hasn't been anyone since you," she said, her voice very soft, the words carefully spoken.

And he liked that even better.

CHAPTER **THIRTEEN**

Campos Plantation, Morazán Province, El Salvador

This was amazing.

Amazingly dangerous.

Alejandro Campos looked down at the pistol in his hand and was nearly flabbergasted at its appearance in his home. It was one of a matched set of Colt .45s, with the owner's name engraved on the slide.

The last time he'd seen the pistol had been two weeks ago up on the Torola River. It had also been the last time he'd seen the pistol's owner—Diego Garcia.

"What is Diego Garcia's pistol doing at my villa?" he asked, looking up from the gun and meeting Max's gaze.

"A nun brought it, *patrón*. Señor Jake has her

in the foyer. One of the guards found the *pistola* hidden under her robes."

He looked at the old man for a moment.

"Under her robes?" he repeated, because he couldn't possibly have heard Max correctly.

"*Sí, patrón.* Under her robes."

And wasn't that the most perfectly awful news he'd had in the last five minutes?

Oh, hell, yes.

No wonder the nuns in Morazán were ending up pregnant, if the men of Morazán were frisking them under their robes.

"Bring the *religiosa* to me, *inmediatamente.*" The flip side of the bad news was even the idea, let alone the reality, of a pistol-carrying nun. The guard on duty deserved a bonus for reaching a level of sharp-eyed suspicion that would have eluded a hundred lesser men.

Under her robes. *Good God.*

Instead of moving to get the good sister, Max's gaze dropped to his employer's lap.

Campos immediately understood.

"Isidora!" he called out. "*Pantalónes, por favor.*"

He had barely gotten himself decently clothed and reorganized before Max returned to the kitchen, with Jake and the woman close behind.

Woman, not nun.

He knew the difference.

Nuns did not have cleavage.

This woman did, a fascinating phenomenon created by a habit twelve sizes too big that was falling off, and an intriguing array of somewhat unbuttoned multibutton T-shirts underneath— and maybe a push-up bra.

Nuns, typically, did not have Spyderco knives in their pockets, or cinch up their habits with gun belts.

This woman had, with a hand-tooled, elaborately scrolled, leather gun belt with an engraved silver belt buckle and a hand-tooled leather holster with the initials *DG* on it. Half her habit was caught up in the belt and bloused over the top, revealing the other set of clothing she had on under her robes, which made the frisking business a whole lot easier to buy.

Nobody would mistake this woman for a nun— except Maximiliano, who thought all women were saints.

But even Max had to have wondered about the earrings. Nuns did not wear multiple earrings.

This woman did, three on one side and two on the other, a matched set of pearls and tiny, square-cut sapphires, plus a small gold cross dangling from her left ear.

Nuns did not have canvas messenger bags bandoliered across their chests, macramé bracelets on their wrists, rings on their fingers, and button-fly jeans lying low on their hips—and most importantly of all, nuns did not get him hot.

This woman did, standing in Campos's kitchen, soaking wet, with somebody else's clothes falling off her, and her own clothes clinging like plastic wrap to five feet eight inches of lanky curves—with cleavage.

Not even the gloriously lovely Sister Julia got him hot, not in any sense of the word. Sister Julia was one hundred percent pure nun. She looked like an angel.

This woman looked like an angel, too, one of the Victoria's Secret angels. Dark, shoulder-length, sable-colored hair, wet and slicked back off her face, pale skin sprinkled with freckles across her nose, eyes to match her sapphire earrings, and a face that said she was more trouble than she was worth.

Which was probably why she wasn't wearing a wedding ring. Yes, he'd checked. He always checked. In Campos's experience, and he had quite a lot, beautiful women with bad disguises and stolen .45s actually were nothing but trouble. Actually, in his experience, beautiful women with good disguises and their own custom .45s were nothing but trouble—take Jewel, for example.

But this woman was not Joya Molara Gualterio,

not by any stretch of the imagination. She was scared, for one thing, and Jewel baby did not get scared. She got even.

"What's your name?" Campos asked.

"Robbins. L-Lily Robbins of Albuquerque. Albuquerque, New Mexico, that is. I'm a teacher, a high school teacher—social studies, geography, sometimes reading. I'm on sabbatical. Here, I mean, in El Salvador. But I'm going back to . . . to, uh, Albuquerque. I hope."

One of his eyebrows shot up, and he glanced at Jake.

Good Lord, the woman was a fountain of information, all of it tumbling and blurting out of her, and wasn't that sweet of her to clarify about Albuquerque.

Jake shrugged, the slightest lift of his shoulder, but he'd recognized it, too. Unvarnished truth with no holding back. How odd.

"And how did you come by Diego Garcia's pistol?"

Her pale face grew even paler.

"The p-pistol is Garcia's?"

And how odd that she didn't know whose pistol she'd taken.

Campos released the magazine out of the gun with a practiced move and checked the chamber before presenting her with the side of the slide engraved with the owner's name.

Diego Garcia, it said in flowing script.

"*Sí, señorita*. It is Garcia's, and you have it. Why?"

"It . . . it was in the Jeep." She looked a little stunned, a little wide-eyed, and was a shade breathless, but under the circumstances, whatever they turned out to be, he didn't blame her. It was a wild night.

Campos looked at Jake.

"She drove up in a black Jeep. The guards are checking it out now."

They didn't need to check it out. A black Jeep with Diego Garcia's pistol in it was undoubtedly Diego Garcia's black Jeep. Campos had ridden in it two weeks ago.

"Was she alone?"

"Yes."

Well, then, that was it. All hell was going to break loose. Diego Garcia did not loan his Jeep to anyone, especially not American women, and Lily Robbins had Made In U.S.A., Albuquerque, New Mexico, stamped all over her. Campos looked to the guard standing by the kitchen door and made a brief gesture, touching the inside edge of his hand to his neck.

The guard turned on his heel and left.

"Take off the habit," he ordered her, then checked the magazine before seating it back in the pistol. He did not chamber a round. When she didn't immediately obey, he called for Isidora again. *"Isidora, venga. Ayude a esta mujer para quitar las vestimentas de monja."* Come help this woman take off her habit.

In moments, the cook was there, with two children underfoot, chattering away while stripping the woman out of the offending attire.

Lily Robbins resisted for a second, but then seemed to understand and started helping, beginning with lifting the messenger bag off over the top of her head. But she didn't let go of it. She didn't put it on the floor or the table. She kept the strap over her shoulder, kept it close.

He'd planned on searching it anyway, but now he was truly curious.

"It's a terrible costume. No one in this room believes you are one of the sisters from up in the hills," he said, taking the gun belt from her when it came off. He slipped the Colt back in its holster.

"I had it more buttoned up and on a little better before. In the car, I was . . . I was trying to get out of it, in case I had to leave the Jeep and run. I'm b-being followed."

"Of course you are." She had Diego Garcia's

hand-engraved pistol and his late-model Jeep Cherokee. He could guarantee the CNL captain would follow her to the ends of the earth to get them back. He was that kind of guy.

"By soldiers, armed soldiers."

"Soldiers are always armed." Campos didn't mind stating the obvious, especially to women whose nerves were straddling the edge. It could help anchor them a bit. "You were at St. Joseph, correct?"

"Yes, but h-how do you know that?"

She was wearing a habit, and Diego Garcia spent a lot of time at St. Joseph. After reading Sister Julia's letter, Campos now knew why the CNL captain was spending so much time on his knees.

It hadn't been quite the reason he'd thought.

"I know everything, Ms. Robbins, except why you are here, why you're wearing one of Sister Bettine's habits, and why you stole Diego Garcia's Jeep."

"The Jeep is his, too?" she asked with appropriate dismay. She was in trouble, and it was good for her to know it.

"Sí."

If he wasn't mistaken, she swore under her breath—another thing nuns did not do.

"It was Sister Julia who told me to come here,"

she said, struggling to get out of the sodden, heavy habit, a difficult proposition, even with Isidora's help. "She gave me a map and said you could help me."

"Help you do what?"

"Just . . . just get through this, this awful night," she said, working down a row of buttons.

Which wasn't much of an answer. Getting through the night was considerably less than what most people asked of him, and probably considerably less than what she really needed. No matter, he'd find out everything soon enough.

"Garcia, and his men," she continued, "they . . . It's been . . . been a bad week at the orphanage. People dying. It's been . . ." Her voice trailed off, maybe on a sob, or possibly a catch of her breath.

"Who has died?"

She stopped in her undressing for a moment and met his gaze. "Sister Bettine died on Sunday."

Well, he hadn't known that.

"*Dei gratia*," Campos murmured, making the sign of the cross. Isidora and Max did the same. "What happened?"

"She started feeling poorly shortly after supper on Saturday night, and on Sunday afternoon, she slipped away." The woman stepped out of the habit as Isidora worked it down to her feet. "Sister Julia said Sister Bettine was r-ready to go, called by God. She was very, very old."

"Eighty-eight her last birthday, but still robust the last time I saw her." Very robust, about a hundred pounds more robust and four inches taller than Lily Robbins. She'd been the largest nun in Morazán—Battle-ax Bettine. "She will be missed." Campos turned to his cook. "Isidora, we'll launder the habit and have it returned to the sisters."

"*Sí, patrón.*" The woman gathered up the habit and her children and trundled off to the laundry room. Max began wiping up the floor where Lily had dripped rain.

"You said people dying; has someone else died at St. Joseph?"

"A man," she said. "He—"

"*Patrón.*" A guard entered the kitchen. "The CNL is here; one troop truck and a pickup truck have been stopped at the gate."

Por Dios.

"Has our patrol returned?"

"Not yet, *patrón.*"

"I want their report immediately when they get back."

"*Sí, patrón.*"

"Jake," Campos said, handing over the holstered pistol. "If Garcia himself is here, we'll talk. If it's one of his lieutenants, give them the Jeep and the pistol, and send them on their way. Tell the lieutenant this incident tonight is of no consequence. The *Capitán* and I will deal with it during our meeting tomorrow."

Jake gave him a quick nod and took Garcia's weapon, before heading for the front door. The man knew the drill, knew how to maintain domination of the field while allowing everyone to save face—unless domination by brute force became the only choice.

And Jake knew how to do that, too, as did all of Campos's men. With tomorrow's negotiations and money on the line, Campos was counting on the CNL soldiers to be content with the return of the *Capitán*'s vehicle and sidearm, and to back off.

Campos turned to Lily. "Come with me."

He directed her to an open stairway leading up to a balcony and loft overlooking the kitchen and dining area.

"Where are we going?" she asked, without budging an inch in the right direction, which was simply unacceptable.

"Ms. Robbins, you came to me," Campos said clearly. "I'm assuming because of the men now parked on the road to my villa. If you want to go back with them to St. Joseph, by all means, stand there and ask questions. If you want to get back to Albuquerque, New Mexico, you will do as I say."

He gestured once more to the broad, curving stairs, and this time, she started forward.

At the top of the stairs, he opened one of a set of double doors and directed her into a room.

"This is my office. You may have a seat by the fireplace."

Max had laid a good fire, and with the strike of a match, Campos had it lit.

It took some effort for him to rise from the hearth, effort attached to pain, and when she was still standing by the door, he rephrased his statement.

"You *will* have a seat by the fireplace, and you *will not* move, until I say you may. Are we clear?"

She hesitated for another moment, before moving into place and sinking into one of the overstuffed leather club chairs flanking the stone hearth. There were two T-shirts plastered to her lovely bosom, a sleeveless tangerine one with little buttons, and over it a dark turquoise one that was unbuttoned to her waist. They were both cotton, both wet.

She was shivering, a tremor running through her, so Campos limped over to the bathroom, and tried not to think about how much his leg was starting to hurt, and how much he wished he could just go the hell to bed with a couple of Sofia's Vicodins in his system—and, if he was honest, with Lily Robbins, or someone very much like her, curled up next to him.

But that wasn't going to happen. Not tonight. *Dammit.*

He pulled two large towels out of the linen closet in the bathroom and limped his sorry ass back to the fireplace.

"One for your hair, and one to wrap around your shoulders," he said, handing them over before he dropped into the chair opposite hers. After he got the rest of her story, he would decide what to do with her.

Pulling his phone out of his pocket, he pressed a button to make a call.

"Contact our convoy," he said, when Jake answered. "Route them through Tilomonte. Have them hold up there until they're directed to proceed."

There were a lot of things Campos didn't need tonight, and Garcia's men meeting up with the Agency's LAWs and his briefcase was real close to the top of his list.

He let his gaze fall back on the woman.

He could toss her back out into the rain, but

he had a feeling he wasn't going to, not tonight, a decision based somewhat on her looks and the fear in her eyes. It was a crappy strategy, completely unprofessional, and yet, there it was— she was a beautiful damsel in distress, who had somehow ended up in the middle of one of his problems. So he'd keep her at least through the night, unless she proved to be more trouble than she was worth, or not worth the trouble of keeping her.

Then all bets were off. Campos could have her delivered to a hotel in San Miguel and be done with her before midnight. But Sister Julia had sent her to him, and Sister Julia's sister was expected shortly this evening, and somehow Campos thought he could serve himself best by keeping unexpected guests well within his grasp. After he got the CIA's documents and data back, things could sort themselves out. People could run around and steal whatever they wanted at that point. For now, he needed to be in charge.

"Tell me about this man who died at St. Joseph."

She stopped toweling her hair and met his gaze across the short distance separating them. "There have been two this week. Garcia, he... he shot a soldier, a young soldier. He shot him dead, tonight, in the chapel. That's why I ran. It was awful, worse than awful, the screaming, and the uproar, and . . . and the blood, and I knew I needed to get out of there as fast as I could."

This was not good.

"You saw this?"

She nodded, her face pale.

Poor thing. Violence was such a shock to the uninitiated and the unprepared.

"One of his own soldiers?" He hadn't heard of any Salvadoran troops near Cristobal in the last couple of weeks.

"Yes. There's a nun, a Sister Teresa—"

Oh, yes, Campos thought, as she went on to tell the story he'd read in Sister Julia's letter, but with the addition of another lover, which didn't work well anyplace, but which really didn't work in Latin American countries. The whole part about Garcia killing the young man in the chapel was especially distressing.

And again, not for the first time in the last few months, he wondered if it was time for him to cut his ties and go home. Blood, death, religion, drugs, guerrilla warfare—and him in the middle of it for too damn long.

In her letter, Sister Julia had been afraid the breaking of Teresa's vows would bring the wrath of God down on St. Joseph, and Campos figured that was a pretty fair description of Diego Garcia, especially a cuckolded Diego Garcia.

Under normal circumstances, and Campos had a very broad definition of "normal," Garcia could be as businesslike as a Brazilian banker—cutthroat but predictable. But with the woman carrying his child getting hot and heavy with another man, especially some young stud out of his own CNL troop, and the woman being a nun, well, yes, Campos could see where it would be both the wrath of God *and* the work of the devil, and at least one guaranteed death. It was a wonder Teresa was still alive—if in fact she was. From St. Joseph to Campos's villa was at most an hour's drive, even on a bad night. Anything could have happened up there in an hour.

Jesus, what a mess.

"Sister Julia apparently knew about Garcia and Sister Teresa," Lily Robbins was still talking, "and of course had been counseling Teresa and trying to bring her back into the fold, if that's even possible after breaking a vow of celibacy, I don't know, but—"

Diego Garcia and a nun. How in the hell did stuff like that even happen? Campos wondered. The man was a Catholic, a murdering rebel bastard of a Catholic, but Campos hadn't met a criminal or guerrilla in Central or South America yet who didn't take his religion seriously.

And he had to negotiate with Garcia tomorrow, with a socialite and her bodyguard in tow.

"—I think the penance would last a lifetime. The only good thing, the *only* good thing, was that the children weren't anywhere near the chapel. Julia confined them to the orphanage the minute the CNL arrived on Tuesday."

The woman kept talking, and he didn't mind. He just wished she'd had the foresight to grab Sister Teresa on her way out the door. If Garcia got it in his head to avenge his honor by killing the nun, too, well, there really was going to be hell to pay.

Mierda. A grief-stricken, guilt-ridden, and doomed-to-everlasting-fire-and-damnation adversary who had nothing left to lose put Campos in a ridiculously poor bargaining position.

He was going to have to be good tomorrow. Damn good. He hoped York-Lytton and Rydell had brought the cash he'd been promised. Two million U.S. dollars fresh out of Langley, and Garcia needed it, no matter what he did tonight, or his slice of the rebel pie was going to disappear. Things had been a little lean for the CNL these last couple of months—Campos had made sure of it, cutting into Garcia's drug trade and doing his best to dry up a lucrative source of funds for the CNL. He was going to press the fact home very hard to get what he wanted—to close the deal on the courier's pouch for one mil and call it good. The 2GB flash drive hidden in the plane was a different story. If it had survived the crash, and if Garcia's men hadn't accidentally tripped the destruct trigger, Rydell and York-Lytton were the ones tasked with its retrieval. No one else was to touch the flash drive. Washington didn't want any of Campos's local crew to get their hands on it. His job was to run the negotiations and to find the damn plane for Rydell and York-Lytton, and with the satellite imagery he'd been sent, he didn't have a doubt about his patrol getting the job done.

One million free and clear, that's what he needed tomorrow. If he couldn't track down the bastards who had jacked his load to Gonzalez, he was going to have to replace it in order to restore his very damaged reputation and get him back in the international game he and Jewel were trying to play. Cash that had already been accounted for was a good place to start—and it was all the kind of loose and easy, think on your feet, don't call us, we'll call you administration of his little bailiwick in Morazán that the Agency counted on.

Anytime they sent him two million dollars,

they could rest assured he was going to milk it for all it was worth to their benefit, not his. That's what he got paid to do, and he didn't get paid anywhere near as much as the *pendejos* he dealt with on a regular basis, day in and day out.

Loose and easy, yeah, that was him, all right—him and the ulcer he was sure he was working on. He had more loose ends than a fringed coat. He was juggling balls, and connections, and deals, and merchandise, and every other thing he could think of, trying to keep it all in the air—and the gods of war and rain had dropped a peach into his pond.

He looked her over again, carefully, while she finished up her sordid tale of nuns and murder.

"*Triángulo de amor,*" he said with a note of sadness in his voice, when she was done. "These things always end badly." And very often violently.

She was still shivering, even worse than before, and he wished he'd thought to have Isidora make something hot for her to drink. He would, in a moment.

"So now, *señorita,* tell me about the other man who died at St. Joseph this week."

"He was American, a pilot. He died right on the altar, right at Jesus' feet, and I . . . I got it all on film."

And with those words, she won herself a week's free lodging, gourmet meals included, personal bodyguard, limo service, unlimited use of the villa's spa facilities, including Isidora's massages, and a free ticket home, first class, anything she wanted.

Good God. She'd gotten the Cessna pilot's death on film. He hadn't died at the crash site.

Neither Diego Garcia nor San Miguel would be getting Ms. Lily Robbins tonight.

CHAPTER FOURTEEN

San Miguel, El Salvador

Federico Perez defined the word "obsequious," coming damn close to actually groveling at Irena's feet where he and she stood next to her Piper— the slight dip of his shoulder in her direction, the clasping of his hands, the smile fading in and out depending on her reaction to his nonstop stream of flattery and chatter.

She approved.

All was as it should be. She'd made Perez a rich man, and she could just as easily strip him to the bone.

Next to Federico, the aircraft company representative who had flown the Hughes 500 to San Miguel was standing by with the helicopter's logbook. The Hughes was parked near a hangar on the other side of the airstrip.

Irena held out her hand for the book, ignoring Federico and letting him chatter on to Ari. The company rep, an older pilot with a strong build and dark hair sprinkled with gray, had a very orderly appearance, his uniform neat, his boots shined.

"Has there been any deferred maintenance on the aircraft?" she asked, flipping the logbook open when the pilot handed it over.

"None," the man said.

"And how many flight hours since its last scheduled maintenance?" The night was cool and smelled of the rain moving across Morazán farther to the north, the direction they were heading. According to her latest weather report, the storm was supposed to worsen for the next hour, but then wear itself out to an intermittent drizzle.

"Twelve."

Irena ran her gaze across the page in the logbook and confirmed his answer. Good. She didn't like dealing with people who didn't know their business.

"Any unusual flight characteristics for this particular aircraft?"

"No," the man said. "And I had the fuel topped off when I got here."

She gave him a more careful look, impressed.

"Thank you." She liked efficiency. "We'll take it from here."

It was a dismissal, and the pilot took it as such, with a short formal nod of his head. She would let Federico know when she was finished with the helicopter, and he could arrange with the aircraft company for its return to San Salvador.

While she'd been talking with the company rep, and with Federico chattering at him non-stop, Ari had unloaded the gear he'd packed for the business at hand: the assassination of C. Smith Rydell. With luck, they'd find Rydell in a matter of hours, not days. The hit itself would be quick and clean, with no luck involved. All they needed was the target.

"Did you bring drum magazines for the G36?" she asked, when Ari had pulled the last rucksack out of the plane. The H&K 5.56mm assault rifle was selectable for semi or fully automatic fire, with its own integral bipod. The hundred-round drums turned the weapon into a light machine gun, and were a relatively easy way to take a lot of firepower to a party.

"Yes, *patrona*," he said, handing the rucksack to her.

Good, she thought, and lifted the pack onto her back, shrugging into it. There was no sure way to know what they were going to run into up in Morazán, not with CNL rebels involved.

After Ari closed the hatch, they grabbed the rest of their gear and cased weapons and started across the airstrip with Federico in tow, still talking. Irena's weapon for the mission was an ACOG-sighted M4. Ari carried the G36 in one hand and had the case for their long rifle, a Steyer bolt action .308 with a fixed 20-power Zeiss daylight scope, in the other. The night optics for the rifle were in their kit.

They were each easily hauling over eighty pounds of gear from where they'd parked the Piper to where the Hughes 500 awaited them. Perez was only hauling himself, and was barely keeping up.

"You need to work out, Federico," she told him.

"Yes, yes. *Sí*. This is very true."

"And not over a plate of *pupusas*."

Federico's taste for fried food was one of his more benign addictions.

"*Sí, patrona, es verdad.*"

"And not over that stable of whores you keep in San Salvador."

"*No, no, patrona, no con mis mujeres.*"

"You don't feed them my cocaine on the side, do you? A little off the top here and there?"

"*No, patrona.*" He was vehement. "No. Never."
He was lying.

She said nothing, striding the last few yards to
the helicopter. She and Ari loaded their gear into
the back, and she started her preflight check, beginning with a walk around the outside of the
craft.

Moving clockwise and popping access hatches
as she went, she checked fuel lines and reser-
voirs, and looked for any visible damage on the
fuselage.

"The Hughes is good, *mi amigo,*" she said to
Federico, pleased with the condition of the helicopter. He'd obviously dealt with a first-class
company, which was as she expected. "You did
very well to get it here on such short notice."

"For you, *patrona,* anything." He stayed by her
side all the way to the tail rotor, where she
checked to make sure the bearings were greased.

"I'm glad to hear you say so." She kept moving,
doing a visual check of the main rotor. "This will
wipe the slate clean between us, Federico, unless..." She stopped and met his gaze, letting
the statement hang in the air, unfinished.

"*A menos que, patrona?*" he repeated, his smile
turning unsure.

"Unless another one of my loads out of San
Salvador comes up short. Klechner is watching

you, *mi amigo,* and you know how unpleasant he can get."

Federico's smile disappeared completely, and the color drained from his face.

"There will be no shortages, *patrona*. I will check every kilo myself. Please, *por favor,* tell Señor Klechner that nothing will get by me and my men. If there is a *problema,* we will take care of it, before it touches the *coca.*"

She looked at him for a long time, holding his gaze, her face expressionless, her eyes giving away nothing. At the exact moment when he started to physically squirm, she released him with a short nod. The shortages had been minor, and had actually proven quite useful. Better to put Federico on his guard, than to let him think she was in his debt for the Hughes. She'd paid cash for its use. Nothing else was being offered.

Yet she'd seen it in his eyes, his clever little mind trying to figure out how to extract some kind of concession from her, some extra favor, or even better, to add a layer of intimacy between them—all in return for a job simply well done.

Federico Perez should thank her for keeping him in his place, which was far from her. For all his machismo, he did not have the heart or the stomach for the level at which she played the game—and he certainly didn't have the brains.

"I will call and warn you when we are headed back to San Miguel. Have the Piper serviced and fueled in my absence."

"*Sí, patrona.*" He took a step back, and when she turned to climb into the helicopter, she heard him break into a trot.

Inside the Hughes, Ari was grinning.

She smiled back. "Some things are too easy, aren't they?"

"For you, Irena, yes. But you have nothing you haven't earned, including your reputation." In Sona, she was *patrona*, always. But in the field, or when they were alone, the two of them reverted to the familiarity of years of friendship.

"What have you got for us?" she asked, noticing the SAT phone in his hand.

The base station in Sona was only one satellite hop away from anywhere in El Salvador. Any information Hans acquired was being fed to them via the SAT phone, be it voice, text, or images, and he had been acquiring intelligence in a constant stream since before she and Ari had left Colombia. It was Hans's specialty, finding people, making connections, putting on pressure, calling in debts, and offering incentives or threats, the latter of which everyone in their underworld knew to be promises. Nothing less allowed them the means to accomplish their missions with the speed and efficiency that was her trademark, and considering the stakes, she was demanding his best for the job at hand.

"Our Lima contact at the joint drug enforcement unit has reported the death of the federal policeman."

"Good." At least part of the problem had been taken care of satisfactorily.

"And Cali sent the report on Garcia and the CNL," Ari continued. "The information is guaranteed correct up to noon today and does a good job of tying the current sequence of events together."

She gave him a questioning glance.

"Garcia's men shot down a plane two days ago," he said. "A Cessna in transit from Panama to Washington, D.C."

"The cargo?" She buckled into the restraints in the pilot's seat.

"No confirmation yet, but something's got everybody from Washington to Lima jumping through hoops."

"Whose plane?" she asked. "CIA? DEA? DOS? Or military?"

"The CIA briefed Rydell, pulling him off a DEA mission, but the woman was run through State, DOS. It was the embassy who made her reservation in Panama City."

"So we don't know."

"We don't know who was making the run, and we don't know exactly what was on the plane, but we do know what makes the world go round."

She let out a short laugh. Ari was right. They did know what made the world go round.

"Guns, drugs, and other people's secrets," she said, and his smile broadened.

"One of those is creating a lot of excitement in Morazán."

"Or maybe all three," she said, opening the logbook to the preflight checklist.

"Or maybe all three," he agreed. "Which means something, possibly a lot of money, is going to change hands, and soon, given the timing of Rydell's arrival in San Salvador."

"The Americans aren't going to let him walk into a CNL camp cold. They'll use a broker, find a local negotiator, a go-between to set things up. There's always somebody on the ground. Who is that going to be?"

"In Morazán, according to our Cali friend, there is only one man. Nobody trusts him, but everybody uses him, including the Americans, when they need somebody. His name is Alejandro Campos."

Campos. Alejandro. She'd heard the name before, but she couldn't remember where.

"Alejandro Campos sounds familiar," she said. "Why?"

"He's been on the edge of a couple of big deals originating in Exaltación, Colombia, over the last few months. Ray Gonzalez's deals."

"Ah, Gonzalez." He was a definite up-and-comer, one of those men who thought he should have what was hers. "Call Hans. Have him find this Campos for us. Then get Federico back on the horn and tell him I need a name, some farmer in Morazán, close to wherever Campos is, who wants to get rich tonight. And ask Hans if he found out what was on the C-130 that delivered Rydell and this York-Lytton woman to San Salvador." She reached forward and started flipping switches and checking dials on the instrument panel. "Somebody at Ilopango got a look at that cargo, and I want to know what they saw."

CHAPTER FIFTEEN

Morazán Province, El Salvador

It was a dark and stormy night—the words went through Honey's mind and stuck. Very dark, she silently added, very stormy. They'd gone beyond rain in the last half hour, way beyond, straight into a tropical deluge—most of it, as far as she could tell, dropping right on top of the Land Cruiser.

Unless Smith had accidentally driven them straight into a waterfall.

Which she wouldn't put past him.

"We're lost." The words slipped out of her. She hadn't meant to say them out loud, but there they were, lying in the air between them now, the truth.

Just as well. He needed to know.

"No, we're not," he said.

Yes, they were.

"I have a GPS and a map, and we're on a road," he said calmly.

No, they weren't.

"This isn't a road." It was a streambed, or a river, or a flooded rut. She could hear the water rushing by the tires, and yes, she could see the GPS in his hand, and the map in his lap, and the flashlight in his other hand, and even with all that, they were still lost. The radio was out and the phone didn't work, basically, she knew, because they were stopped under a waterfall, in the middle of nowhere, in the middle of the night, with not a damn thing anywhere in sight.

"We have a break in contact with the convoy," Smith conceded, "but we are not lost."

Yes, they were, with the nose of their vehicle noticeably lower than the tail end of their vehicle, which meant they were headed downhill—which pretty much summed up her take on the situation as well.

Great. She and the Land Cruiser were in agreement. Only Smith was in denial.

Honey liked adventure, to a point. She loved traveling with Thomas, had loved the trip to Nepal, and had been to Antarctica and the Sahara with him, exploring and investigating all sorts of scientific phenomena—without ever getting lost. She'd gone adventuring with Haydon and his inevitable film crews to Alaska, the Amazon, and Borneo, documenting environmental disasters—without ever getting lost. With Gerald and William, she'd survived countless clubs from Saint-Tropez to Monte Carlo, and with her mother, she'd personally conquered the rarefied shopping districts of Dupont Circle, Georgetown, and Upper Northwest near Friendship Heights, not to mention Fifth Avenue and every boutique in Manhattan.

Never lost.

She let out a sigh.

"Do you need another granola bar, or a drink of water?" he asked, calm as a rock, which was starting to get under her skin. Panic was in the air, and he was clueless.

"Suck eggs." If he could get them lost, she could sigh.

Smith held the GPS back up and muttered something under his breath—she thought it was "Eggs, *geezus*."

Ditto, as far as she was concerned. She started to sigh again, then held it back, which probably wasn't healthy.

Damn, it was dark out there.

And Julia was in trouble. Honey knew it down to her bones, and for all the other adventures she'd had, this was the worst, because her sister's safety, maybe even her life, was at stake. If Julia was pregnant, as Father Bartolo had suggested with all his ranting and threatened recriminations, then something terrible and awful had happened to her, and Honey needed to find her. Julia would never have willingly had sexual relations with a man, not after having taken her vows, and Honey wasn't buying into immaculate conception, not with her baby sister involved.

She needed to find damn Diego Garcia and probably shoot him, and Smith had lost the convoy. She didn't know how. But from the looks of where Smith had stopped to try and get reorganized, he didn't have a clue where the other Land Cruiser and the cargo truck had gone. They'd simply disappeared in the darkness and the deluge.

They'd gotten a call—their last call—informing them of a detour they needed to make on their way to the Campos plantation, and between one curve and the next, the other two vehicles had disappeared.

Smith had obviously missed a turn, or made a turn he wasn't supposed to make. She was guessing the latter, because no one would have detoured them into a waterfall.

No, she thought, looking out the windshield

and giving her head a shake. This situation had "mistake" written all over it.

And dammit, those were her trade goods on that truck. If Julia was with the rebels, the anti-tank missiles and grenades were Honey's ticket into their camp, along with the briefcase at her feet—of course, the briefcase she was sure contained money, lots of money. That thing would probably get her into anywhere she wanted, especially into trouble.

"We're not that far from St. Joseph," she said. "Maybe we should go there first and get our bearings."

"I thought you said we were lost."

"We are," she said. "We're just lost not that far from the St. Joseph School and Orphanage." She'd been studying the map of El Salvador for weeks before she'd been shanghaied into this disaster, and she knew that no matter how far off track he'd gotten them, St. Joseph was between where they'd been and where they were going.

He muttered something noncommittal, which she was sure was not an admission of his deficient navigation skills.

Honey looked back out the windshield and tried to control a shiver. This was not rain, not unless it was End of the World rain, apocalyptic rain, forty days' worth jammed into one night, either that or it really was a freaking waterfall. There was no other explanation for the sheer amount of water pouring over the SUV. If they weren't already in a river, they would be in about five more minutes.

"Do you have a plan for when we start to float away?" she asked, working to keep any stray, strident note out of her voice. There was no reason for him to know she was on edge. But the question was real. She wanted to know about the floating-away problem, and she wanted to know right now, and Mr. I'm in Charge, Get Used to It had better have an answer, because she was getting nervous, and she didn't like to get nervous, especially when she was practically trapped underwater.

Oh, hell, what a terrible thought to have.

"We are not going to float away."

"Bull," she whispered under her breath, way under.

"If you've got something to say, go ahead and say it," he said. "God forbid you should hold anything back."

She was holding plenty back, like that last sigh.

"Bull," she repeated a little louder, and a gust of wind caught them, rocking the Land Cruiser back and forth, a huge gust, and then another, buffeting them around. She clutched the door handle, and felt an edge of fear slide down her spine. She couldn't say for certain, but between the headlights and the occasional flash of lightning, she thought they were on one of those roads that had been dug out of the hillside, the kind with one real side made out of dirt and rocks and vegetation, and one drop-off side made out of thin air.

And now there was buffeting wind.

Damn, oh, damn.

When the wind passed, Honey took hold of her purse, dragged it into her lap, and started searching. She'd had it. Panic was going to win, unless she wrestled it down and drowned it.

"What are you doing?" he asked, as if it was any of his business.

"Looking for something." As if that wasn't obvious.

"If it's another granola bar, I've changed my mind. I think you're already on sugar overload. You need to switch to protein."

"I don't have any protein."

"Then get an MRE out of my ruck."

"I don't want an MRE, I want a drink." What the hell else could she possibly need right now? She couldn't think of a thing—other than maybe a driver who knew where in the hell they were.

But she wasn't going to be telling him that now, was she?

"What kind of drink?" he asked, sounding skeptical.

She threw him an incredulous glance, and he swore under his breath.

"I heard that," she said, digging back into her purse, and boy, did he have a lot of nerve. If she'd been driving, they'd still be with the convoy.

"Don't get so drunk that I have to carry you out of here," Smith said coolly. "I don't need the aggravation."

Fat chance. She only had two tiny bottles, both strictly for medicinal purposes.

"And I don't need you yelling at me." Smith had been his father's mother's maiden name, and coming from a long line of hyphens, she personally understood how names could get a little out of hand. But that didn't explain his first name. Nothing did.

"I'm not yelling."

"Bull," she whispered again. She was scared, and when she was scared, sometimes a little bourbon helped brace her. Not enough to get drunk. Honoria York-Lytton hadn't been drunk since she'd been eighteen, and that was a fact. But she had been known to brace herself a bit now and then with a shot of bourbon during a difficult situation—her current situation being a case in point. And despite all the natural drama, it wasn't the wind, and the rain, or the being lost that scared her the most.

It was the being lost, and being late, and not making it to Julia before the forty-eight hours were up. Garcia had promised to disappear if his timetable wasn't met, and if by some awful set of circumstances, Julia really was carrying his child, he might very well take her with him— again, *goddammit*.

Honey hated him.

She'd only written him those nice, chatty, embossed notes because deep in her heart she'd been afraid she would need him someday for the exact damned reason she did need him. And she knew he'd only written her back because he hoped to get more money out of her.

It was called business, and networking.

Well, she didn't have a problem doing business, and she was networked from the Hudson to the Potomac, inside track all the way. She did have a problem with her sister living by a value system that at best seemed painfully naïve, and at worst was dangerous. If the pope had decided against the Salvadoran guerrillas, didn't that mean the nuns followed suit?

Apparently not at St. Joseph.

Somebody needed to read them the riot act, at least one of them, and Honey was the girl to do it. The other three misguided saints could do what they wanted, but it was time for Julia to come home.

She found one of the bottles and screwed off the lid.

"You know we're on a schedule here," she said, in case he'd forgotten. "A tight schedule."

Smith didn't answer, but she was pretty sure she'd gotten her point across.

The next few long moments passed in silence, with the rustle of his map and the glare of his flashlight the only activity in the cab of the Land Cruiser—and her, slowly sipping her bourbon, letting each small drink sit in her mouth, clear her sinuses, and sharpen her senses before she swallowed.

"Okay, I think I've found the problem," he said, putting his finger on the map.

Good.

"We're in a slight depression."

Honey slanted him a disbelieving glance. What a brilliant piece of insight. She was definitely in a slight depression, and no, the bourbon wasn't helping.

She took another swallow.

"If we move forward about . . . fifty meters, we

should be on high enough ground to get our communications up and running."

"Move?" She didn't think so. "We can't see our hands in front of our faces."

"This isn't supposed to last the night. I checked the weather report at Ilopango, before we left. When it lightens up, we'll inch down the road. It'll be fine."

She didn't think so.

"There will be no inching." No inching themselves right off a cliff.

"I thought you were worried about your tight schedule?"

And I thought you knew what you were doing, she thought, but again, she kept the news flash to herself.

"I offered to drive," she said instead. That wasn't a news flash, that was a fact, a very succinct, heartfelt, I-told-you-so fact, and she had no problem whatsoever sharing it with him.

"You're pushing your luck, Ms. York," he said, and went back to checking his map and his damn GPS.

Ms. York? This man had slept with her, and he was calling her Ms. York? What gall.

"I know your name," she said.

"No, you don't."

Yes, she did.

She took another small sip of bourbon, sitting quietly and looking out the windshield as Mother Nature and all hell broke loose on the world and sent sheets of water driving into the Land Cruiser.

"Cats hate rain," she said.

The rustling stopped. Then he gave the map a good snap and spread it out over the steering wheel.

"Dogs don't mind it," she added, and took another sip of bourbon.

"Why don't you stop while you're ahead." It was an order, not a question.

"You were crabby in San Luis, too," she said. "You're always crabby, probably the crabbiest person I know. You get crabby in the heat, and you get crabby in the rain, and—"

"And you become unreasonable and lose all capability for thinking logically when you're scared."

She was struck speechless . . . almost. "That is the most *untrue*—"

"*Christ*, I'd have been dead twenty years ago, if that happened to me. Thinking clearly in a crisis is a skill you might want to spend some time developing, for your own sake . . . let alone mine." The last was muttered under his breath, but she heard it loud and clear.

She sat back in her seat, her jaw clamped shut. She wasn't speaking to him...right after she told him this last thing.

"I only have enough bourbon for one, two shots, and I won't be sharing, so you'll have to go someplace else to vent your repressed anger at your mother for giving you such a weird name and have your...your...and have your crabby little breakdown."

CHAPTER SIXTEEN

Someplace else?

Smith didn't think so.

And his crabby little breakdown?

Right.

Like that was going to happen.

Like it had ever happened.

God, like he even knew what in the hell a crabby little breakdown was—unless it was one of those things Natalie had done a few times.

Fuck.

Like he could even begin to get himself that worked up over anything—anything at all. He didn't have that much emotion in him on a good day, and on a bad day, he tended to have even less.

Lost? Not really.

The GPS coordinates, sporadic though they'd been, had allowed him to track their progress precisely on his map. He'd stopped the Land Cruiser when he'd noticed their path was diverging ever farther from the road he thought he'd turned onto, and realized they were following a trail that snaked through the hills above a stream.

When he'd first broken visual contact with the other vehicles, he'd increased his speed to catch up with the lead Land Cruiser. When that hadn't worked, he'd slowed down to allow the truck to catch up to him, but that hadn't worked, either, and now he was certain neither vehicle was on this track.

Even if the radio had been working, which it wasn't, linking up with the convoy under the present circumstances would have been difficult. The track was too narrow for him to turn their vehicle around. His plan was to keep going forward when they could, get to higher ground, and get on the cell phone when the rain let up.

Except for the goddamn torrential rain, and being stuck in a car with a woman on the verge of a meltdown, tonight actually wasn't so bad. As long as nobody was shooting at him, he usually figured he was in pretty good shape, and nobody was shooting. Hell, the bad guys could be twenty feet away and they wouldn't know which way to point their weapons. The weather was wild out there.

But from Honey's point of view, he could see where the night could be looking a little scary. They were definitely off track. But not lost, not even in the ballpark of lost. True, the rain was amazing, completely biblical. It had gone beyond being a pain in the ass into some weirdly cool territory. He had never seen anything like it, but the storm wasn't slated to last much longer, and he didn't think they were going to float away before it ran itself out.

If he did, he'd be taking precautions. That's what he did. Anticipate problems and deal with them before they had a chance to come about.

She, on the other hand, had gone from enjoying the rain to thinking the worst, and her idea of a precaution was a minibottle of bourbon. When actually, the situation was fine, far from disaster. They had food, water, shelter—and the potential ingredients for sex. Him. Her.

Yeah, he was thinking it. He'd been thinking it ever since her little whisper in the dark about him being the last guy she'd had. Any guy would be thinking it, no matter how much rain was coming down.

At least he'd been thinking it up until she'd started unraveling.

"I don't have any repressed anger at my mother," he said. "She was a saint."

Honey didn't say a word on her side of the cab, just sat there, looking out the windshield, looking angry, and looking worried—and he felt a pang of guilt, not his first of the night, *dammit*, and probably not his last.

She'd been the one to drag him into this, no matter how many other people had their hands in the cookie jar. Grant, and Dobbs, and White Rook, and those damn photos were merely the aftereffects of Smith showing up at St. Mary's in San Luis, and he'd only been there because of her.

And he'd only gotten that far because for whatever reason, when he'd seen her standing out in front of the damn Hotel Palacio, he had not been able to leave well enough alone.

"Her name was Melinda Jo," he said, and then wondered for a moment if he was really going to talk about his mother. *Geezus*. The last woman he'd talked with about his mother had been the one he'd married, and she'd stolen his socks when she'd left him, every single pair.

He'd never understood that.

"Melinda Jo Rydell," he elaborated, "and she

died in a car accident when I was nine." Hell, he was going to do it.

"Oh." The word was soft. She didn't budge, not an inch. There was only the word.

But he'd gotten her attention, and the more she focused on his mother, the less she'd be focusing on herself and whatever dire doom she was imagining, and that's all she needed, a little break to get her through the storm.

Her two-shots-of-bourbon method might do the trick. He wasn't really worried about Honey getting drunk, despite her size. She'd had two shots that night in San Luis with no noticeable effect, and she'd had plenty to eat since they'd landed in San Salvador, a late lunch at Ilopango, and numerous snacks on the road. She was actually kind of an eating machine, always nibbling on something.

But, hell, he was talking anyway.

"She wasn't as old as you are now," he continued. "Blond hair, brown eyes, not very tall." No taller than Honey. "My dad married her young, seventeen. She didn't quite make it out of high school, and at twenty-six, she was in a head-on collision with a drunk driver. He lived, she died." History as far as he was concerned, old news, but here he was, dragging it out and sharing it with a woman he hadn't spent so much as twenty-four consecutive hours with, using his dark family secret to calm her down.

It was working. Honey had turned to face him, being all but perched on the edge of her seat now, her face still a little drawn, but curiosity starting to win.

"Her maiden name was Hill, and they were one hundred percent pure Arkansas redneck. My grandpa, Walter Hill, was a mean son of a bitch until the day he died, so I always figured Mom might not have had it so good at home, growing up."

She was nodding, her expression intent.

Women were so sweet that way, always trying to help a guy out with his conversation.

"I know, well, I know how difficult those situations can be," she said.

He doubted it.

"My York-Lytton grandfather was mean, too," she went on. "But it was always from a distance, barked orders and edicts coming down from on high to stay off the banisters, and don't slam the doors, and no running in the upstairs halls. We hardly ever saw him. He didn't like children in the house. A fifty-room estate, and there wasn't enough room for me and my brothers to be there without bugging him."

Fifty rooms?

He'd grown up in seven, and now he lived in one—one huge open loft in a building in Denver's lower downtown at 738 Steele Street. His place was kind of commando central, with Creed and Cody's jungle across the hall, Skeeter's abandoned spaceship and Superman's art gallery one floor up, and the Steele Street armory and firing range one floor down.

He'd done all right for himself, sure, especially since coming on board with Special Defense Force, but Honey still didn't have any business being in this Land Cruiser with him. Under normal circumstances, their paths would not have come within a hundred miles of each other, let alone crossed.

"I can guarantee you that redneck Arkansas fathers don't hand out too many of their edicts from a distance," he said, reaching over and taking the small bottle out of her hand.

Honey was a quick girl, and she didn't miss his implication.

"He hurt her?" Her voice was even softer than before.

Smith finished the bourbon, all five drops of it, and thought that someday he should take her out for a real drink, something with a mixer in it, or at least ice—and maybe dinner, something that didn't come out of her purse.

He handed the bottle back. There wasn't much of his life he could talk about, nothing he'd done professionally. Most of his missions were going to the grave with him, shared only with the men and women who'd been there.

But in the dark, in the rain, with a woman he liked far more than he should, he could talk about sweet Melinda Jo.

"My father remarried years ago, but he keeps a picture of my mother on a bookshelf in the family room. I remember she always wore jeans or slacks of some sort, but the day the picture was taken, she was wearing a dress. I was fifteen when my cousin pointed something out to me I'd never noticed. It was strange—I'd looked at the photograph hundreds of times, and yet I'd never seen the scar on her leg. I thought it was a shadow, a trick of the light or something, but my cousin had the story, and in the way of every family's dirty laundry, he'd decided it was time to air it out and put me in the know."

She was very still, waiting, her mouth set, her gaze unwavering. With such a buildup, she had to know what was coming, and Smith wished like hell he could disappoint her. But the only disappointment in the story was its truth.

"It was a burn scar, almost a brand. My grandpa laid into her with a hot poker one night and deliberately held it on her leg to mark her. She was only thirteen at the time."

Honey's hand came to the base of her throat, the concern on her face turning to unmistakable shock.

"I'm—I'm so sorry."

"I'd never really liked the old bastard," he said. "But after I found out what he'd done, I hated him. That he had scarred her. That he'd hurt my mom."

He stopped and shifted his attention out the windshield, waiting for a moment.

Okay. Maybe he had a little more emotion in him than he'd thought. He still hated the old bastard, and Walter Hill had been dead for twenty years—and it had probably been six years since he'd given the son of a bitch a thought.

Well, hell. "It was a long time ago."

He dragged his hand back through his hair, then draped his arm over the steering wheel.

"Her life, and the old shack where they lived, it was way below the poverty line. Nothing but squalor, abuse, too much liquor, and never enough education."

"Until you."

"I got the education," he agreed. "And thanks to my dad, I managed to skip the squalor and abuse, but make no mistake, I'm still a good fifty percent redneck, no apologies and no regrets. Some of the people I've worked for, I think they test for it in the blood."

"Because it makes you tough."

A small grin curved his mouth. Yeah, that was it, but he was surprised a blue-blooded socialite knew it.

"Damn near indestructible. It really does take a bullet to kill us, and sometimes even that won't do the trick."

"Us," she said, saying the word with a surprising thoughtfulness. "You mean guys like you."

"Yes."

"I didn't think there were any other guys like you."

His grin broadened.

Maybe he was in love.

He hated to think so, really he did. Love had not been his strong suit in life, and the truth was, black patent leather hair bows and gold jewelry aside, he liked Honey too much to want to ruin it with another screwed-up relationship. There were thousands of guys like him in the world. He'd worked with them, bled with them, killed a few—okay, more than a few—and gone up against them, but he honestly didn't think there were too many Park Avenue princesses knocking around the backwaters of the borderlands in any other Third World country, looking for a sister who should have been the responsibility of the Catholic Church.

"There's a couple of other guys out there like me," he admitted. "But you wouldn't like either one of them."

"Bull," she said, letting out a short laugh. "I'd probably adore both of them." Her mouth curved into an easy smile, and another emotion went through him, hot and sweet.

God, she was gorgeous.

He remembered what it had been like to kiss her.

He remembered what it had been like to be inside her, and how she'd felt, naked in his arms— so freaking soft, and so incredibly hot. The whole night in San Luis was permanently hardwired into his memory banks—and there she was, not three feet away, smelling like Paradise perfume in a lingering cloud of cherry whiskey cigar smoke, with her hair coming undone.

She was so unexpected. Her eyes clear and guileless and such a pure ocean green, her skin so satiny, her hair those hundred subtle shades of blond, everything about her so polished and just so, and then there were the cigarillos and the bourbon, and those hot, soft words she'd spoken in his ear: *Do me, Smith.*

Geezus. Those words and the sound of them had truly been seared into his brain.

What would it take, he wondered, to "do her" again tonight? Complete abandonment of common sense? Total disregard for mission protocol? Or simply giving in to what he wanted—her.

Dammit. He knew better, but he didn't think knowing better was going to be much of a deterrent. Not when they were trapped in the middle of nowhere, alone in the dark, with nothing but time on their hands.

The last guy she'd been with had been him, four months ago in San Luis? He didn't even want to analyze the huge sense of relief those words had given him. Nobody got exclusive rights off a one-night stand, and if he'd been able to in any way, shape, or form put her out of his mind, none of it would have mattered. But every time he'd seen her picture in the paper, it had mattered. A lot. And driven him a little bit closer to an edge he knew better than to go over for a woman, any woman, but especially a woman he was probably never going to see again the rest of his life.

But life had thrown him a curve, a whole set of them in extra-small BDUs, and they were sitting next to him in the dark, in the middle of a rainstorm.

"So the point of all this is about that name you're thinking."

"Yes?" She tilted her head to one side, giving him her full attention.

"My mother didn't give me that name. I dreamed it up myself at fifteen, and my dad let me make it legal."

She stared at him for a second, then asked the inevitable question. "Why?" Which he always considered one step better than "What in the world were you thinking?"

"Because I thought it was cool, and I refused to be Walter Smith Rydell for even one more minute after I knew what that old man had done to my mom. My dad never called me Walter anyway. I'd always been Smith to him, after his mom's side of the family."

She still looked slightly incredulous. "And out of all the names in the world, you picked—"

"Cougar." He gave in to a grin. "Cougar Rydell. It didn't get any cooler than that at fifteen. My little brother wanted to change his name to Soaring Eagle, but Dad put his foot down and told him we only had room for one idiot in the family."

"You're nuts."

"It was the last wild thing I ever did. Scout's

honor." He held up three fingers in the age-old salute.

"Liar."

"Well, there was this one night in San Luis," he admitted, "at the Hotel Palacio, I did a 'wild thing' that night."

Even in the low light, he saw a blush race across her cheeks.

"You . . . you're, you are such a jerk to say it like . . . to bring it up like that."

Probably, but it was the truth.

Honey crossed her arms and gave him a hard look, or as hard as she could get it.

"I am so not a wild thing," she said indignantly. "It was just . . . that night was just . . . just—"

While she tried to figure it out, he sat back and enjoyed the view—green eyes holding his own despite the blush, blond hair, soft mouth, and a tactical vest full of her survival gear—perfume, lipstick, granola bars, a credit card, and a little cash.

Smith supposed he'd seen worse tac rigs.

On second thought, no, he hadn't. No commando was ever going to find comfort by spritzing on perfume. Honey did on a regular basis.

"—just crazy," she said, finishing the thought by tightening her arms across her chest with her chin tilted up, silently daring him to discount her version of events.

Not on a bet.

"Riots. Explosives. Car bombs. A quarter of a million in U.S. cash. Yeah," he agreed, leaning forward. "It was pretty crazy."

Like what he was thinking.

Oh, hell. He was more than thinking.

Reaching out, he slid his hand around the back of her neck and rubbed his thumb across her nape.

"You are not going to get anywhere with this," she said, her tone quite firm.

But she didn't pull away.

"I know," he said, and drew her closer.

"You are such a jerk." They were really close now, with her eyes all flinty and no-nonsense, and her Audrey Hepburn updo coming undone, and her mouth looking like the first step to salvation.

"I know." He'd been told quite a few times, but never by anyone who looked like her. Nobody looked like her, so perfect, and yet not quite. Being with her all day, he'd noticed a few intriguing flaws. "Two of your bottom teeth are crooked."

"You are *such* a jerk," she said, and he grinned. "I stopped wearing my retainer when I was twenty-one, which of course is none of your business, no matter what my teeth look like, you jerk."

They were both sitting sideways in their seats, meeting halfway over the console.

"And you have really dark eyebrows for a green-eyed blonde."

"I never said I was a *natural* blonde, and you never even called me, not once, Cougar Rydell."

Cougar. God, what she must have thought of that when she'd first heard it. He grinned again and lowered his head, brushing his mouth across her ear and down the side of her neck—and he loved it, just because her skin was so soft and she smelled so good, and because she let him.

Sure, he needed to be thinking about the mission, and what he was doing, and put it all in the big-picture scheme of things. He needed to be thinking about a truck full of LAWs careening around the mountains in a deluge without him riding shotgun on it. He needed to be thinking about what might be in the briefcase, and how he was going to use it.

Yeah, he needed to think about all those things, and he was going to—in a minute, or two, or thirty, or sixty, depending on how lucky he got.

"I had you tracked after I put you on the plane that morning out of San Luis," he said, his lips barely touching her skin. "I knew where you were every step of the way, and I knew the minute you got home. And the next thing I knew, you were dating the underwear model again." And that had been the end of it, he'd thought. "So I backed off. I figured your life was back to normal, and you wouldn't want to be reminded of how out of hand things had gotten in El Salvador."

"Completely out of hand," she said, leaning in to him a little, her hand coming to rest on his chest, which he loved. "I've never been involved with anything so . . . so out of hand."

He believed it. Shakespeare in the nude didn't come close to what had been going on in the streets of San Luis that night, or in his bed in the Hotel Palacio.

"I wrote you a letter," he said.

"I never got it."

"I never sent it."

He kissed her cheek, and she tilted her head ever so slightly, granting him a little more access to the soft skin on the side of her neck.

He lightly grazed her with his teeth, and a small shiver went through her.

Yeah. He needed to be thinking about rifles, grenade launchers, and crates of ammunition, not sex.

Right.

But if this got going, it wasn't going to stop.

"I wrote you a letter, too," she said.

"I didn't get it." But he was damned intrigued, wondering if it had been the same sort of carefully worded, "gee, I really, really like you, and even though we have absolutely nothing in common, the next time I'm in Washington, D.C., I could give you a call, if you'd like" type letter.

"That's because when I read it over, I had second thoughts."

Damn. The same thing had happened to him.

"What were your second thoughts?" Not that he couldn't imagine them. They'd probably run pretty much along the same lines as his—long-distance relationship; his job was hard for a lot of women to understand, let alone accept; she was one of the wealthiest women in America—stuff like that.

"Well, I knew how much I'd paid for my dress, so that was easy, but I didn't know how much to charge you for the panties. They were a birthday present."

He stopped kissing her neck. She'd almost sent him a bill for the clothes she'd left in his room at the Hotel Palacio?

"You were going to send me a bill?"

"Itemized," she whispered, tunneling her hand

up into his hair. "Including my gun and the bullet I bought."

Goddamn. He grinned. She'd written him out a damn bill.

He laughed against her skin and bit her neck, just hard enough to make her giggle.

"Who gave you the panties?" They were shameless, so sheer they could only be called "see-through," and if anything, she owed him for taking that damn gun off her hands.

"My mother."

"I thought mothers gave chastity belts to their daughters, not see-through underwear."

"They were on sale, in Paris, buy one, get one free, and she couldn't resist—all that luscious silk for half price."

He grinned again. Luscious was right.

"Go ahead and send me the bill. I'm keeping them." He wasn't a trophy kind of guy, but those panties were amazing—and he'd gotten them off her.

"Smith?" she said, moving against him, lifting herself even closer to him.

"Yes?"

"I'm wearing the other pair now."

And that set the game. Sex won out over common sense, hands down.

It was all so simple.

Opening his mouth over hers, he took her in a drugging kiss, cupping her face in one hand, and sliding his other hand up under her shirt. When he reached her lacy, satiny bra, she made a soft sound in the back of her throat. She was so lush and full, and hearing her groan and feeling her nipple harden was enough to send a flood of heat to his groin.

He shifted in his seat, trying to get closer to her, wanting more.

God, she was sweet, such a visceral addiction, all heat, the taste, and feel, and scent of her imprinted on every fantasy he'd had in the last four months, which had done nothing but drive him goddamn crazy. He'd wanted to forget, not remember. But every time sex had crossed his mind, Honey had been hot on its tail.

Today had been such a tease, to be with her and meet the challenge of keeping his memories and his imagination in check. He'd done a pretty damn poor job of it. Every inch of bare skin had made him want to run his tongue over her to make a connection, to get her wet and mark her as his—the side of her neck, the tender inside of her wrist, the short expanse of bare leg between her rolled-up BDU trousers and her rolled-down socks. He wanted his mouth on her everywhere.

It was a conquest thing, meeting the challenge,

and she was such an exquisite challenge. Yeah, he knew the goal. He understood what was happening between them.

Except for the part about practically wanting to eat her, so gently, so carefully; to somehow bring her inside of himself without leaving a mark or taking a bite. It was like he wanted to meld with her, but he wasn't a guy who "melded." He was a guy who conquered.

Okay, it was a little crazy how much he'd thought about her, how much he wanted her, and there was nothing about the fact that had made him happy. His life was all about control, and wanting something he couldn't have did not fit the paradigm.

But here she was—in his arms, and he'd gotten hard by simply touching her breast, holding her in his palm, feeling the weight and softness of her. And he knew she'd gotten wet, because as close as he was trying to get to her, she was trying to get to him—something they were going to have a damn hard time doing in bucket seats.

He kissed her deeper, and unsnapped her bra, and wished they were in a bed for one simple reason: access.

That's what he wanted. That's what he needed.

"I don't think—"

"I don't, either." *Geezus*. How could he think

with one of her hands sliding up his thigh and the other one sliding under his shirt?

"We need to—"

"Yes." They needed to bail out of this impossible front seat into the back cargo area.

"Oh," she breathed softly, when the hand she had between his legs finally slid those last few inches home.

Yeah.

Oh.

Suddenly, bailing into the cargo area dropped a few rungs on his priority list.

Staying put had hit the number-one slot.

Staying put and getting his pants off.

"Oh," she said again, running her hand up the length of him, but it was even more of a breath, less of a word.

Their mouths were touching, but the only movement between them was her hands unbuttoning his pants.

God, he loved a girl who knew what she wanted, especially if she wanted him. Every move she made kept him riveted in place with anticipation. Every breath she took he felt on his lips.

"In San Luis, we didn't really get the chance to—"

"I know." But in his fantasies, they did it all, every time.

"I like . . ." She let her words trail off, finishing it with the slow glide of her fingers up his cock and then down.

"Yes." *Yes. Yes.* He closed the kiss between them and sucked on her tongue, letting her know exactly what he liked, and he lifted his hips to push his pants down—and he kept kissing her, again and again, while she drove him a little bit crazy with the softness of her palm and the sweet teasing of her fingers going over the top of him, circling him, priming him for a release he didn't want to happen too quickly.

This was a game he wanted to play with her all night long.

Moving his hands to her shoulders, he started taking her clothes off, dropping the tac vest into the seat, tossing the BDU shirt into the cargo area. Her T-shirt came off over her head, and her pants went down next, and then his hand was there, between her legs, his fingers sliding into her soft folds.

Wet. Silky. His.

He lowered his head, parting her with his fingers and taking her with his mouth, and she melted against him, her soft, hot body molding itself to him, her hands tunneling through his hair, holding him to her.

"Smith, *oh, Smith* . . ."

God, it was incredible, and totally impossible to get enough with her half dragged over the console and him doing his Cirque de Soleil impression in the front seat with the steering wheel jabbing him in the hip.

Kissing her softly, he worked his way back up to her mouth.

"Last one into the back gets to take the rest of the other one's clothes off," he murmured against her lips, then bodily lifted her toward the cargo area. "You first, sweetheart."

The back seats in the Land Cruiser had all been put down to make room for his rucksack, a case holding a submachine gun, one of her small suitcases, and the black briefcase marked with a Z. The rest of their gear had gone on the deuce-and-a-half with the pallet. But even with all the cargo stacked around, the back of the Cruiser beat the hell out of the front.

Shoes went one way, socks went another, and when he finally got her right where he wanted her, naked and on top of him, he started feeling, for the first time in months, maybe years, like everything was right with the world for a change.

It didn't happen very often in his line of business. Guys like him thrived on conflict—and on having beautiful women they liked more than they should sliding down between their legs and taking them in their mouths.

A thousand pounds of tension lifted off him with the first glide of her tongue.

He closed his eyes, and threaded his hand through her hair, and drifted with the pleasure.

Yeah. She liked it, he could tell, and he loved it. The wet heat of her mouth surrounding him, her hand stroking him, her body a warm and lovely weight on his.

He wanted it to go on forever—right up until he wanted her to finish him off. She'd hit a rhythm it was impossible to resist, but whatever he wanted, he needed something else more.

"Honey," he said her name, reaching for her. "Come here, baby."

She lifted her head, and he pulled her up his body, angling himself over her, and he kissed her, taking her mouth again and again, his fingers finding the soft, hot center of her arousal and playing with her.

Her response went straight to his head, and his heart, and his groin. God, she felt so perfect in his arms, and the longer he played with her, the more ready she felt to give him what he wanted. She had one hand in his hair, holding him close, and the other wrapped around his biceps, holding him tight, telegraphing her need for him not to stop, not yet, not until . . . until—

Her groan echoed in his mouth, her body stiffening. Moment after endless moment, she gave it up for him with soft kisses, and softer bites, and his name on her lips.

"Smith," she sighed, her body pulsing and moving against him, needing to be closer, and closer. "Oh, Smith."

He knew.

He knew exactly what she needed.

Fitting himself to her, he thrust, and this time, when the rhythm became irresistible, pulling him on harder and harder, he gave in to it, entering her again and again, until he felt so damn "melded" he came apart inside her.

Geezus. Yes. Always, always, yes.

CHAPTER SEVENTEEN

Campos Plantation, Morazán Province, El Salvador

From where she sat in her chair by the fireplace, Lily Robbins watched the biggest drug dealer in all of Morazán Province talk on the phone and pace his office.

"Bring the convoy in the east gate and take them to the warehouse," he was saying. "They can unload there. I'll send Jake over as soon as he gets rid of the CNL."

Yes, please, she prayed. Let Jake get rid of the CNL—*Señor* Jake, the guy from the good old U.S. of A. The man's accent and the way he looked were unmistakably American.

Campos was more of a mystery. She'd hardly taken her eyes off him since the moment she'd walked into his kitchen and still hadn't figured

him out. Quite literally, she had never seen anyone like him.

Never.

"Ask the commander to keep them contained,
Tomás," he continued. "Tell him I'm trying to
avoid a confrontation with the CNL just now,
and not to let anyone wander away from the
building. I'll get there as soon as possible."

Long dark hair sweeping back off his face,
deep-set, forest green eyes, his features finely
chiseled, high cheekbones, firm mouth, elegant
nose, a faint shadow of beard stubble along his
jaw—he could have been ridiculously beautiful
for a man.

Three things saved him from such a vacuous
fate.

The dangerous grace of his movements—and
it wasn't just the shoulder holster he'd quietly
shrugged into, or the semiautomatic 1911 he'd
smoothly holstered under his left arm. He em-
bodied economy of movement. He paced with
languid purpose, his long strides taking him from
his weapons safe, to the cell phone he'd picked
up from a row of phones on his desk, to the bank
of televisions he was turning on, one at a time,
between two floor-to-ceiling bookcases housing
the works of Shakespeare and Milton, Blake,
Rilke, and Whitman.

The biggest drug dealer in Morazán was a highly educated man, or possibly, he merely owned a lot of very good books. Lily wondered if she would ever really know.

The intensity of his gaze saved him from vacuous beauty. In the short hour of their acquaintance, he had been both charming and commanding, the difference between the two so slight as to be almost nonexistent and noticeable only by the subtlest of shifts in his gaze, from direct and forceful, to merely unavoidably direct. He truly was nearly impossible not to watch. Not because of his strikingly handsome looks, but because, like everyone else around him, how would she know what to do, if she didn't watch him?

Everybody watched him—his servants, the guards, the other man who had been in the kitchen, the one named Jake. They watched his eyes for questions, and his hands for gestures. The questions were theirs to answer. The gestures were theirs to obey. Since the minute she'd driven into his compound, every glance, every action, every word, had swirled around him, the center of the universe, Alejandro Campos.

The absolute fact of his absolute sovereignty kept her firmly in her chair, waiting and reminding herself that Sister Julia believed in this man, believed he would save Lily from Garcia without throwing her to some as yet unknown, even more vicious wolf.

But there were rebel soldiers at his gate. Lily could see them on one of the television screens, along with CNN on another, and views of other parts of his compound on the others, and she wasn't at all sure how much of a bargaining chip she might become in order for him to get the rebel soldiers away from his gate. Or worse, he'd mentioned a meeting with Garcia tomorrow. She had to get out of here by then, somehow, some way. If Campos didn't sell her out tonight, she swore she'd figure out some kind of plan for tomorrow.

Or, no doubt, as she had walked into the lion's den, the lion would figure something out for her.

She wondered, fleetingly, if Sister Julia suffered from some sort of saintly dementia where everyone was seen in a good light, even Salvadoran drug lords with green eyes who did not look particularly Hispanic.

He stepped back to his desk and entered a few keystrokes on his computer's keyboard, then closed the cell phone and slipped it into his pants pocket.

He did look particularly exotic in a black silk shirt, cream-colored linen slacks, and a pair of expensive black leather dress boots. His belt was black, narrow, and adorned with an ornate silver buckle. He was tall, elegant, assured, and undoubtedly dangerous, and only one last thing saved him from vacuous beauty. Not only saved him, but destroyed any illusion or potential claims of perfection: the scar. For all that she was staring at him, she was trying very hard not to stare at his scar.

It ran along the left side of his face, from above his temple, down to his jaw, a troubled line of white—an old scar, long healed, that looked as if someone had meant business. It followed his hairline too closely for it to have been the result of an accident.

No. He'd purposely been cut, and she didn't even want to imagine the circumstances under which the deed had been done. He was a drug dealer. She'd read horrible things about drug dealers in the newspapers and news magazines, things everybody heard and hoped would never happen to them or anyone they loved.

Take a sabbatical, she'd told herself. *See the world.*

Well, here she was, all right, seeing the inside of a drug lord's private office, and he owned Rilke. Whether Campos read the poet or not, she was impressed, and probably not nearly as frightened as she should be.

The scar alone was a warning of violence, but Lily's capacity for panic appeared to have a limit, and she'd used almost all of it in the last two days, hiding from the CNL in St. Joseph, taking the risks of filming, pushing herself to be a witness to the violence of Teresa's beating and the young soldier's wrenching death, and to the death of the pilot.

A bone-deep shiver went through her and had nothing to do with being wet and cold. It was pure emotion.

There was no Academy Award in her future, and no more naïveté. The illusory veil of security had been lifted. Possibly, the only safe place for her tonight was right where she was sitting. Campos's office felt safe. Against her better judgment, he felt safe, if only because he was so calm in the midst of all the chaos and what was, without a doubt, the wildest rainstorm she'd ever seen.

Rain slashed against the windows, making the panes shake. Lightning flashed far away in the dark sky, revealing towering levels of clouds and the wild swaying of trees in the wind.

Yes, she felt safer inside, but she still wished she'd tried a little harder to hold on to Garcia's .45, hidden it better in Sister Bettine's habit, maybe hidden it in her canvas bag. She'd let herself get backed into a corner, where a stranger held the key to her safety, and that was a colossally huge mistake, one she needed to learn from and make sure never happened again. If she died from this ill-advised escapade, she was only going to have herself to blame, which wasn't much comfort.

"Ms. Robbins," Campos said, turning away from his computer and the bank of television sets and walking toward her, "your camera, please."

The other thing she needed to learn was how to keep her mouth shut. Babbling a little bit in Albuquerque had never gotten her in trouble. Babbling in El Salvador was a very bad idea.

She reached in her canvas bag and pulled out her brand-new video camera, a gift to herself on the first year anniversary of her divorce, and handed it over.

The pilot's death, that's what he wanted to see. He'd gone very still when she'd said she'd gotten it on film. Perhaps the pilot had been working for Campos when he'd been shot down, some rough-and-tumble mercenary down on his luck, running drugs for a Salvadoran kingpin. The American, Jake, was definitely rough-and-tumble. He looked hard, like a soldier for hire. Of all the hundreds of mistakes she'd made in the last week, she wouldn't make the one of thinking she could count on him for anything other than what his boss commanded. A shared nationality was the only thing the two of them had in common.

It took Campos a few minutes to figure out a connection between her camera and his television, with the final configuration including his computer. Once he had it up and running, he picked up a remote and came back to sit by the fire.

One thing became immediately clear. She was an idiot.

He watched the beginning of her rough footage in silence, her whole heartfelt introduction of herself, including a ridiculous stream of educational honors, and the even more heartfelt, and under the circumstances, even more painfully ridiculous introduction of her film and the vital importance of bringing "The Struggle for St. Joseph's Children" onto the world stage.

Yes. She'd actually said "world stage."

A lesser woman would have expired on the spot.

Lily endured.

"Sister Bettine would have appreciated your sincerity," Campos said, casting her a quick glance as the introduction wound to an end.

Well, she didn't know what to think of that. Kindness wasn't exactly what she'd expected.

He fast-forwarded through the initial interviews, then slowed the film for Sister Bettine's death, watching it in real time.

"She was a strong woman," he said, without taking his gaze off the television screen.

"Yes. I wish I could have gotten to know her better."

He let out a soft laugh. "If you knew Bettine for five minutes, you knew everything. You knew she loved her church, and her school, and her orphans, and you knew she would always stand firm against anyone or anything who tried to bring them harm."

Yes. Lily had known what the good sister had loved.

At Bettine's prayer, her last words, he crossed himself, the gesture fluid with years of practice, appearing almost unconscious.

He fast-forwarded again to the pilot's death and ran it over and over and over again. *Fuck you. Fuck you. Fuck you.*

The words had been a challenge, a final assertion of self from a man who knew he had reached the end. They were the only clear words in the scene, even when Campos increased the volume.

"Do you know what the soldiers are saying?" he asked. "Could you hear them?"

"No." Their voices had been low with menace.

He ran the scene again.

"Did you talk with the pilot before he died?"

"No. Not exactly. I asked him if I could get him anything, but he didn't answer. He just . . . just held my hand."

"He held your hand?" Those dark, forest green eyes slid a glance in her direction.

"Yes. The sisters and I were in the chapel when the soldiers brought him in. I . . . I went over to him, while Sister Rose ran for her medical kit."

The scene had been chaos. She and Sister Teresa had rushed to help the injured man— but the soldiers had been having none of it. Brandishing weapons and shouting orders, they had frightened Sister Teresa into a near faint. Lily had been a little harder to get rid of, if only because the moment she'd dropped to her knees next to the pilot, he'd grabbed ahold of her hand with both of his—fiercely, with more strength than she would ever have thought possible for someone who was so horribly scraped up and bloody.

Her hand still hurt, he'd held it so tightly—

until one of the soldiers had broken his grip with the butt end of an AK-47.

She'd heard him groan.

Another shiver went through her and curled in her gut.

In those few moments when she'd been by his side, the pilot had given her something, passed it off his wrist and onto hers with his right hand while he'd held her hand with his left. The pass had been smooth, the macramé bracelet of a dying man coming to rest around her right wrist within seconds of when she'd first reached him. She'd hardly been aware of the transfer, he'd moved so quickly, so surely. The soldiers had not noticed, and then they'd torn her away from his side.

Her hand went around her wrist, covering the bracelet, feeling the thick, rough knots of hemp.

"They wouldn't let us help him," she said. "So we hid in the sacristy, and I . . . I got out my camera." She'd filmed through a small pane of glass in the sacristy's door, catching the scene and the man's dying words. "Did you know him?"

"Yes," he said simply.

"What was his name?" It had bothered her, not knowing his name, after being the last kind face he'd seen.

In answer, Campos merely shook his head.

Lily understood. In the world of drug kingpins and crashing pilots, names were secrets, not social tender.

She let out a breath and looked back at the television. He was running the scene again.

"What are you looking for?"

"Whatever is there," he said. "You're sure this man said nothing to you?"

"Nothing." Not a word. There had only been the look in his eyes, pain and resolve, utter, determined resolve. To what end, she didn't know. But he'd given her his bracelet, and she'd watched him die, and she was loath to part with it.

A subdued ring tone sounded, and Campos pulled his phone out of his pocket. "Campos," he said, and listened.

The bracelet had no value, she was sure. It was knotted string, nothing more, but she wouldn't keep it long, just until she got home. Once she was safely back in Albuquerque, she'd be able to take the bracelet off—until then, it was her talisman, her good luck charm.

"Good work, Jake," he said after a few moments. "Our convoy is in the main warehouse. I'll meet you there."

He hung up the phone and gestured at the far screen.

"The CNL is leaving."

She looked up, and sheer relief flooded through her, making her weak. She sank back into the chair, the towels he'd given her clutched to her chest. The trucks were turning away from the gate.

Thank God.

Sister Julia had been right. Alejandro Campos had not only been able to save her from Diego Garcia, he'd been willing.

"You will be safe here in my home, Ms. Robbins, for as long as you care to stay, and when you are ready to leave, I'll arrange for a flight back to Albuquerque, my compliments."

She stared at him, taken aback by his generosity.

"Your compliments?" She wasn't sure she quite understood.

"The tape out of your camera, of course, will not be going with you," he said, rising from his chair and walking back over to his desk. "Other than that, you may avail yourself of the amenities, and by this time tomorrow night, you will be back in New Mexico, if you wish."

If she wished. New Mexico. Oh, God, she was so ready to go home. The week had been bizarrely wild, so totally unexpected, and completely out of her control. She swore to God, if she could just get home, she would never, ever . . . ever . . .

Except that was her film on that tape, her Cannes entry.

"Don't overthink it, Ms. Robbins. Go home," Campos said, popping the tape out of her camera and dropping it into his pocket. "And now if you'll excuse me."

She was going to overthink it, she thought, watching him leave. She overthought everything.

He walked out the door and was back on the phone before he reached the stairs. She heard him talking to someone in the kitchen, and within minutes of his departure, the woman, Isidora, brought a tray holding hot coffee, hot soup, and a small basket of hot bread smelling fresh out of the oven.

She took a bite of a soft, buttery slice, then dipped it in the soup and took another bite—and she wondered, could she be bought off with incredible food and safe passage?

The smart answer was an unequivocal yes.

So why was she equivocating?

CHAPTER EIGHTEEN

Standing in the middle of his main warehouse, Campos looked down at the pallet full of weapons and the suitcases his men had unloaded from the Salvadoran army's deuce-and-a-half.

"What do you mean Honoria York-Lytton and her bodyguard are missing?"

"They didn't show up with the convoy," Jake repeated, smoothing his hand over the map he had laid out on top of one of the rifle crates. "I went over every inch of the route with the Salvadoran captain, and he thinks York-Lytton and Rydell wound up here." He put his finger on a section of tight turns on the map.

"And what in the hell are they doing there?" Campos asked, putting his finger on the map

three inches below Jake's. "When they are supposed to be here?"

"The captain thinks they missed the turn we
called in for the detour. There are two side roads
coming off the main road in that area. In the
kind of rain we're having tonight, it would be
easy to take the first turn instead of the second.
The turns are less than twenty meters apart."

Campos knew that. He knew everything about
Morazán Province, especially the roads. The
track above the streambed was dangerous, even
in dry weather. Rydell would be lucky not to end
up at the bottom of a ravine.

Goddammit.

York-Lytton and her bodyguard had disappeared—with his goddamn briefcase. It was the
first thing he'd asked for, and the only thing no
one had been able to produce.

"What about all this?" he asked, gesturing at
the Louis Vuitton luggage piled off to one side of
the pallet. "What in the hell is all this?"

The whole damn pallet was nothing short of
alarming, the last kind of cargo anyone wanted
showing up in their backyard—but he'd expected
LAWs and cases of ammunition. He had not expected five extra-large Louis Vuitton suitcases.

"They all have Honoria York-Lytton's name on
them," Jake said.

"They weren't on the manifest." And unless the woman was moving her whole damn household to Morazán, he didn't know what in the hell could be in them, and that was unacceptable.

"Open them up."

"They're locked," Jake said. "And she's here as an agent of the U.S. State Department, not some tourist."

"I don't give a damn."

"Then they're open," Jake said, pulling a small set of bolt cutters out of his pocket.

Which was as it should be. Jake had known exactly what they were going to do with any locked suitcases. The only concession the State Department connection had bought Ms. York-Lytton was the care Jake was taking to get into the damn things. If she'd been a tourist, he'd have taken a knife to Vuitton's finest, before he let any damned mystery luggage lie around in one of his buildings.

While Jake cut locks down the line, Campos unzipped the first suitcase.

And then he stood back and stared.

Holy shit.

The night had been full of amazing things: Sister Julia's letter, Diego Garcia's pistol, Lily Robbins's camera, Honoria York-Lytton and her bodyguard's disappearance off the face of the earth with his two million dollars, and Ms. York-Lytton's suitcases.

Good God.

"It's cocaine," he said.

"It sure as hell is," Jake confirmed, zipping open the second suitcase. "Here, too."

Campos was looking down at fifty kilos of cocaine carefully packed in a large piece of luggage—his cocaine— It was a miracle, a god-blessed miracle on a night full of amazing things.

"The others?" he asked Jake, who was opening suitcases as quickly as he cut the locks off.

"Fifty keys apiece, boss, for the full load of two hundred and fifty not-so-jacked kilos of coke. We're back in business."

Now if he only had his frigging two million dollars, life would be good.

"So what do you think happened here?" It wasn't often that goods stolen in Colombia were hand-delivered to his front door in Morazán by the Salvadoran army, especially illegal stolen goods.

"I think Dobbs's guys jumped the gun and had this load intercepted ahead of schedule. Dobbs got wind of it and was smart enough to know he needed to get it back in the pipeline ASAP, before Langley found out he'd fucked up, and there was this York-Lytton woman with a C-130 authorized out of State, coming through Panama with a load of weapons with just enough room left on the pallet to top it off with two hundred and fifty keys of cocaine."

Yes, that's what Campos figured, too. None of the cocaine he dealt with ever actually made it to the streets of the United States, but the Agency usually let it get a helluva lot farther away from him than Exaltación, before things went wrong. That's how he stayed alive.

"We're having a lucky day, Campos."

Lucky, lucky day. Eight stitches, fricasseed Mercedes, dead pilot, lost briefcase, and epic rain stacked up against the return of his load and the unexpected arrival of Lily Robbins—he thought Jake was being overly optimistic.

"We're still missing two million dollars."

"The night's young."

Not that young.

Campos checked his watch. It was ten o'clock. If his two million dollars showed up before sunrise, he'd have to start believing in miracles, and that was really going to go against the grain.

CHAPTER NINETEEN

Carolina, Morazán Province, El Salvador

"I hate the fucking rain."

Irena glanced over at Ari where he was standing by the window of their room in the Hotel Grande and silently agreed. They'd barely made it to the small town closest to Campos's plantation before a literal wall of water had dropped out of the sky and forced them to halt.

If they'd been caught in flight, it could have been a disaster. The storm was freakish, much worse than Hans had predicted with his weather report.

An hour earlier, from Sona, Hans had given them a confirmation on Rydell's destination: Alejandro Campos's plantation south of the Torola River. She and Ari both had the location locked into their GPS devices, along with maps of their objective area. Hans had found a landing site for the Hughes near the town of Carolina, and the farmer who owned the field had brought them into town. Ari and she had planned on picking up their rental car at the hotel and immediately leaving again.

The rain had changed everything, and she was not pleased. She'd come all this way for the shot, one shot, only to be stopped cold short of her objective.

She stubbed her cigarette out in the ashtray and threaded another oiled patch through her cleaning rod. She'd finished going over her M4 and set it back in its case. Her 1911 was perfectly clean and maintained as well, but the familiar routine of running patches kept her focused on the job, kept her thoughts from straying too far, kept her fears at bay.

Anastasia.

Irena spoiled the child. Ari said so, the only one who dared, the only one who knew, other than Anastasia's caretakers. But Ari spoiled her as well.

"It's time to go to Paris," she said.

After a moment of silence, she looked up and found him watching her, his gaze considering, his posture very quiet where he stood by the window, very still.

"Is that what this is all about?" he asked. "Is Rydell her father?"

She shook her head and went back to cleaning her pistol.

"I knew him at the time, after Anastasia's father left Afghanistan. Rydell knew I was pregnant. It is enough reason to kill him."

"Maybe," Ari said, the ambivalence in his tone drawing her attention.

He was looking back out the window.

"We're a long way from home, Irena, calling in every favor we have, spending tens of thousands of dollars and the goodwill of our partners for one unimportant American to die?"

"He's important to me."

"Precisely my point," he said, turning and meeting her gaze again. "Your involvement with this man is clouding your objectivity."

"No, Ari," she said sharply. "You're wrong."

One shot, one kill—that's the only reason she was here. No question.

She could see it in her mind, Rydell's head in her scope, her reticle superimposed on his face or the back of his neck—her breath softening, then stopping for the length of a heartbeat, the pad of her trigger finger pressing against the small, sweet curve of metal, then her breath continuing, and Rydell's stopping for all time, his medulla severed by her shot, resulting in instant destruction of his central nervous system.

He would drop like a stone, and her secret would be safe.

Maybe.

Her only surety had been stolen the moment he'd escaped off the mountain in Peru. But his death still served a purpose, closure if nothing else, and probably more. No one else except Ari had known her as well since their time together in Afghanistan. No one other than Ari had even the slightest knowledge of even the possibility of her having a child. She'd gone underground in Paris, after selling Rydell out to the warlord and faking her death by sabotaging her own plane. The pilot she'd sold the Piper to had thought he'd gotten such a good deal, and so he had, up until his maiden flight.

She'd left Afghanistan with money, connections, and a bright future in the underworld. Her months in Paris had been spent alone, hidden in plain sight, living on the Left Bank. A childless couple named Deschamps had befriended her, dear people, never knowing she had been the one to choose them after weeks of investigation. Educated, middle-class, she had elevated them to a life of luxury in return for their loyalty to her. Their love for Anastasia had been natural and was without question. Perhaps such love would become a problem someday. For their sake, she hoped not.

"Call Hans again," she said to Ari. "I want to know when this storm will pass."

She held the barrel of her 1911 into the light and looked down the bore—so clean it gleamed. With a new patch, she wiped the guide rod, did a final check on the slide and frame, and brushed a coat of oil on the weapon's components.

"We're drowning here, Hans," she heard Ari say into the satellite phone. "How much longer is this going to last?"

She slid the barrel into place.

"Another hour," Ari said into the phone, looking at his watch. "I hope to hell you're right."

Piece by piece, she put her pistol back together, staying quiet, remaining self-contained.

Possibly, they would be in place by midnight, if the weather broke. Carolina was only twenty minutes from Campos's estate. She and Ari planned on parking a couple of kilometers away and going in on foot, carrying their gear.

Logistics were the heart and soul of smooth operations. For a lightning-quick hit across international borders, there was no room for errors. Ari was correct, to a point. The assassination of C. Smith Rydell was putting all her years of experience, all her communication lines, and all her assets in Central America to the test, and so far, every phase of the mission had been performed to the expected standard—excellence.

All she needed was Rydell's head on a platter.

"Sixty-six millimeter light anti-tank weapons?" Ari said, and she looked up from pressing the barrel bushing into place.

Finishing the assembly, she rose to her feet and crossed the room to the window.

"Rifles," he said, lifting an eyebrow in her direction. "Grenade launchers, small arms, ammunition, MREs, and a lot of very big suitcases . . . yes . . . yes, that's very interesting . . . yes, I'll tell her."

He signed off and met her gaze.

"The C-130 cargo," she said, and he nodded.

"One of Federico's men leaned on a soldier who was at Ilopango when the transport aircraft arrived from Howard Air Force Base this afternoon."

"Weapons."

"A full pallet of them from the U.S. government going into El Salvador and heading into the mountains of Morazán. I'd say we've got some sort of very international incident brewing here."

"And some very strange bedfellows." She performed a quick function check on her pistol, running the slide, checking the safety, and releasing the trigger, before loading a magazine.

"The woman, Honoria York-Lytton, had a black briefcase handcuffed to her wrist."

Irena glanced up again, a smile curving her mouth.

"*Perfecto.*" She chambered a round, then flipped on the safety and holstered the pistol. "We've got guns and money."

"All we need are drugs and secrets."

"There weren't any drugs on the Cessna." A Cessna full of cocaine didn't get anybody other than the seller, the buyer, and maybe a few policemen excited.

"No," Ari agreed. "So that leaves secrets." He was grinning, too. "Very expensive secrets to get all this going in less than two days."

"Politically vital secrets," Irena said. "The U.S. State Department, the CIA chief of station in Panama, ex-DEA agents getting pulled off missions, and a rich *gringa* in the middle of it, cuffed to a black briefcase."

"We don't change our mission."

"No." She shook her head. "But we can do our Cali friend a favor and let him know he needs to shorten his leash on Diego Garcia and the CNL. Raise Hans again. Tell him to relay all the information we've gotten today to Miguel Carranza. If the cartel wants to tighten its hold on northern El Salvador, today is a good day to do it."

CHAPTER **TWENTY**

Morazán Province, El Salvador

Sex was not love.

Honey knew it, and she was pretty darn sure Smith knew it—and yet there they were, tangled up together in the cargo area of the Land Cruiser like two people in love, with him backed up against a gun case, and her draped against a rucksack with a corner of her suitcase digging into her butt.

Goodness' sakes, he'd come twice.

But that was sex, not love. Motivated, inspired, dedicated sex, for which she took full, lovely credit—but it was not love.

She'd come twice.

And that was wonderfully, lusciously lovely, and she gave him full credit for all his mad, lovely skills—but it wasn't necessarily love.

He hadn't taken his hands off her, not once. He was molding her with his palm, seeming to memorize her size and shape, his strokes even and smooth, one continuous touch from her shoulder to her thigh, with slow and easy forays over her breasts and belly, down over her hip, and up her back.

Still, no one would ever mistake tender touches for love.

But there was one other thing, a nearly indefinable something that made her want to put her mouth on him just to taste his skin again—and someone might mistake that for love.

She was on the verge of that mistake. She could tell. And it worried the hell out of her, but even with the risk, she didn't have it in her to resist.

Snuggling up closer, she rested her head on his arm, and her cheek on his chest, and breathed him in, the warm, erotic scent of man and sex. God, she'd wanted this for so long, to be with him again. Nothing about longing for him had made sense, and yet she'd longed for him. Thousands of miles away, more than likely, without a clue where he was, or what he was doing, or even if he was still alive, he'd invaded almost her every waking thought.

He smelled so good.

She yawned, and kissed him, and felt more at peace and at home than she had in a long, long time.

"Do you know Darcy Delamere?" Smith asked, completely out of the blue, and about startled her into next week.

Her eyes came open.

Darcy Delamere? Good Lord.

"I think everyone in Washington, D.C., knows Darcy Delamere," she said, amazingly calmly. "She writes a weekly column in *The Washington Post,* for the society section." What in the world was he thinking, to be asking her about Darcy Delamere?

She didn't even want to know.

"Yes. I've been reading her for the last few months, since I've been...uh, looking through the weekend society pages. Her column usually runs on the front page."

Oh, dear, Honey thought, and wondered if she could possibly interest him in another "go" to get his mind off the society pages.

And for the record, Darcy Delamere's column *always* ran on the front page of the society section.

"Well, then you know as much as I do," she said, and hoped they'd reached the end of the conversation.

No such luck.

"She's funny, but in a very sharp, biting way, very insightful. She skewers everybody, the Right, and the Left. She even goes after the Centrists."

"Politics is easy satire. Everybody knows that." At least Darcy Delamere made it look easy. In truth, Honey knew it was a helluva lot of work to be scathing when it was called for, ruthless with the truth, to wrap it all in the fluff of Washington's social whirl, and still make people laugh—and who better to do that than an A-list, Harvard-educated sorority girl?

"People on the Hill credit her with breaking the Lundt-Creasy scandal," he said, smoothing his hand up her thigh and hip, until he came to rest with his palm on the side of her breast.

She almost purred, his hands were so warm. His whole body was warm, putting out heat like a furnace. She loved it.

"Sex and politics is the easiest satire of all," she said, scooting even closer. "Everybody looks foolish and culpable, and at least a little perverted, if not out-and-out bent, and it's always there, somewhere." And those were the bare naked facts. Darcy Delamere's particular genius was in finding the worst of the culprits, the venal ones, the ones peddling their influence for sexual favors, and in the case of the Lundt-Creasy affair, the hypocritical ones pounding political pulpits to hide their own sexual quirks and hi-jinks. She didn't care what people did in their private lives, unless it threatened to affect every-one else's private life.

"She also exposed the Pittsburgh-Cayman Brac-Potomac connection between government contractors banking offshore and funneling their money through the rust belt."

So she had. Rather brilliantly, Honey had thought. The whole exposé had come about through an offhand comment overheard in the ladies' room of the upscale District Lounge, a ci-gar and martini bar on the Hill and a personal favorite of Honey's. There were no secrets in Washington, only items of interest people were too afraid to shout in public. The society pages of *The Washington Post* made a great mega-phone.

"Scandal and double-dealing are also very easy to find and blow the whistle on in Washington," she said around another small yawn, "if you're not afraid of losing your job or stepping on toes that can step back hard."

"Apparently, she isn't."

"She's not." Darcy Delamere wasn't afraid of anything. She didn't need to be. Nobody knew who she was; no one knew her real name. Plenty of people had their suspicions, but too many people in Washington fit Darcy's profile for anyone to nail the pseudonym on her.

Actually, one person did know the truth.

Okay, two: Kurt Miller, Darcy's editor, who had first approached Honey four years ago, and had actually come up with the name Darcy Delamere; and the man who had gotten Honey into El Salvador so fast it had made her head spin, Mr. Cassle, the white-haired gentleman with an office in a little-used corridor far up in the highest reaches of the Department of State. He'd known everything, including Honey's social calendar for the next six months and the last two years, and how she'd become Darcy Delamere.

"She dated an underwear model once," Smith said.

She slanted him a wary glance.

"How in the world do you know that?"

Honestly. She wanted to know. How in the ever-loving world did he know Darcy Delamere had dated an underwear model?

"She mentioned it once in a column."

About a thousand years ago, maybe.

"Well." What could she say? "Underwear models are very popular guys."

"And she went to Nepal."

Her eyebrows rose nearly into her hairline.

"How long did you say you've been reading the society pages?"

The Nepal column had run eighteen months ago, but it had been six years since the giant ammonite adventure. No one had made a connection between the two—until now.

"Not very long," he said. "But I looked through her archives."

Oh, dear.

"I hope she had as nice a time as I did. The mountains, the Himalayas, are so—"

"Elemental?"

"Yes," she said, lifting her head and giving him a quizzical look. "Exactly. Profoundly elemental."

"You use that word a lot in your writing— 'Elemental Female Orgasm: Privilege or Right? A Primer for Men.'"

A small laugh escaped her. "You read the rest of *Sorority Girl*."

"The whole thing," he admitted. "And then I toughed it out through that *Yoke of Political Tyranny* thing you wrote with Dr. Barstow, although I might have slept through a few of those middle chapters, and I noticed you used 'elemental' a few times in there, too."

"How amazing." And how darn near unbelievable. Very few people outside of feminist studies academia had ever gotten through *Women's Sexuality Under the Yoke of Twenty-first Century Political Tyranny*, asleep or awake. She could probably count them on one hand.

"And then I remembered the chapter in *Sorority Girl* titled 'Postorgasmic Mind State: Getting There Is Half the Fun—Enlightenment through Bliss,'" he said, turning his head to better see her. He'd flipped the flashlight on to find his shirt to cover her with, and left it propped in a manner to cast a faint glow over the darkened back seat. "You write a lot about orgasm."

"Well, you know what they say," she said, leaning down to whisper in his ear. *"Write what you know."*

He laughed, and kissed her, and gathered her close.

And he kissed her again.

Outside the Land Cruiser, the rain was still falling, but in bucketfuls instead of a continuous sheet. The weather was lightening up.

"And then one Sunday, I was reading Darcy Delamere," he picked up where he'd left off, "and she was drawing blood through the Right and the Left over something she called EBM."

Oh, crap.

"And I kept wondering, what in the hell is EBM? And I wondered right up until the end of her column, where she spelled it out in big capital letters—ELEMENTAL BELTWAY MIND STATE—and something clicked in my brain. But it wasn't a big click. The lightbulb didn't really go on until a few minutes ago, after you mentioned Nepal earlier. I couldn't get it out of my mind. Nepal. I haven't met many people who have been to Nepal."

Lying by means of omission was not considered a sin north of the Potomac, so she decided to keep her mouth shut.

He was quiet, too, for a long time, while the rain poured down and the lightning flashed and the wind barely buffeted them at all.

"So," he finally said. "You've got a job."

She wasn't admitting anything.

"You're notorious, you know that, right?" he said.

Yes.

"And you know you're right about the EBM."

Okay, she couldn't resist. She gave her head a small nod.

And he swore.

"*Goddamn*. I knew it. I'm on a top-secret intelligence mission with a damn newspaper reporter."

Yes, he was.

"*Unfu . . . unbe*—this is . . . this is unbelievable."

He was stammering, which simply fascinated her. "Didn't they check you out, before they sent you down here with a damn briefcase belonging to the fricking CIA? I mean, *geezus,* don't you have to have 'Journalist' tattooed on your passport or something?"

"I write a column for the society page."

"Bull," he said. "You are a highly political animal, have been ever since that damn sorority girl book. That thing is pure political feminism, and dammit, I read where Darcy Delamere is the first thing the Secretary of Defense reads on Sunday mornings."

She couldn't help herself; she smiled and settled in closer to him. She'd *loved* being mentioned by the SECDEF. Miller had given her a raise and grinned like a fool for a week.

"But, dammit, the thing you said about EBM being a blind way to conduct a country's business, putting politics and power ahead of common sense or the truth," he continued, "and it being dangerous, except to the people doing the conducting, the politicians—that was dead-on. It works out great for them, keeps them in office, gives them the power they want. And you were right when you said the people actually doing the country's business, guys like me, the ones on the ground implementing the government's policies, that we can get burned real badly by the Elemental Beltway Mind State. I've seen it happen more than once, oblivious politicians expecting incredibly daunting missions to be accomplished at the drop of a hat. Too many of them don't have a clue about how the real world works, where men bleed, and men die." He slid his leg between hers and moved his hand down and wrapped it around her thigh. "*Dammit*. Darcy Delamere." He let out a soft laugh. "I'll be a sonuvabitch...a damned impressed sonuvabitch."

Okay. Maybe it was love. Every word he said turned her to mush. But she couldn't take full credit for the column he liked. Her research assistant, Mindy Brighton, came from a military family and had married a Special Forces soldier. She knew about the men on the ground, the guys doing the job, and the risks they were tasked with taking. Honey hadn't spent much time with any "men on the ground," until one of them had chased her down in San Luis and locked her in a hotel room.

Nothing in her life had been the same since.

She wasn't complaining.

"Are we doing this again, Cougar?" she murmured in his ear, getting comfortable on top of him, loving the feel of him, his broad chest a wall of hard muscle and soft hair, his arms iron-bound, and yet so gentle with her.

"Cougar, hell." He let out another soft chuckle. "Not yet, *Darcy*, baby. I need to get some sleep, that's all, and I want you close."

Darcy, baby. She grinned and kissed his mouth, and then she kissed his jaw. She kissed his cheek, running her fingers back through his hair, and by the time she kissed his temple, he was asleep, out like a light, gone.

She sighed and relaxed into him.

She'd been in love twice, and it had not worked out very well for her. The first time had been during her literary period, between the publication of *Sorority Girl* and the publication of *The Yoke of Tyranny*. The second time had been between Shakespeare in the nude and Calvin Klein underwear models, between not-quite-misspent youth and getting a real job, one that gave her the kind of connections she could have used to keep her out of the cargo area of a Land Cruiser on a back road in El Salvador.

She wasn't sure she was ready for love a third time. It could hurt so badly—but she wouldn't have missed this, not for the world.

The flashlight cast him in harsh shadows, made the angles of his face even more stark, and still he was so beautiful.

She pressed her lips to his shoulder, then reached over and turned the flashlight off, and with his heart beating next to hers, with his breath in her ear and his arm so strong around her, she drifted off to the sound of the rain.

CHAPTER TWENTY-ONE

Campos Plantation, Morazán Province, El Salvador

Dawn was not Campos's favorite time of day. For his money, dawn could have been done away with completely, and days would start about ten-nish or so, after coffee and pastries and sex, a civilized hour, with civilized pastimes, for a civilized life.

Dawn was the hour of barbarians. Literally.

All he had to do was look out his second-floor bedroom window at his front gate to prove it. Diego Garcia had arrived for their meeting, far, far too early, and in far, far too great force.

Garcia had brought half of his whole damn army, half of the CNL soldiers in Morazán. The contingencies of his job aside, Campos tended to follow the party line when it came to the politics of Central America, and his party, the United

States government party, was in support of the Salvadoran government, not the ragtag band of rebels blowing up coffee plantations, rallying landless villagers behind a populist front, and, in some part at least, creating a cover for a lucrative, if not yet world-class, drug trafficking business.

After three years of unqualified support, the Catholic Church had changed course and thrown in with the government as well—except for the three *religiosas* standing at the gate with Diego Garcia.

Sister Teresa, and Campos used the term lightly, looked very much the worse for wear. Her *vestimentas de monja* had been taken from her, and Garcia had put her in a modest skirt and peasant blouse accessorized with a hefty length of rope. Her wrists were loosely bound, a statement, Campos supposed, if not exactly a restraint, and her hair had been chopped off.

Campos was not shocked at the sight. He'd watched the styling session on Lily Robbins's tape last night, seen the tears and recriminations and the beating. It could have been worse. Teresa was standing and walking unaided.

She wasn't dead, and for her crime, death was not uncommon. Her young lover had certainly paid the ultimate price. Campos had watched his death as well and been deeply disturbed by all of it, the act itself, the location—Garcia had gunned him down in the chapel for God's sake— and the reason behind the rage, an unfaithful woman. The CNL captain was out of control, a true murdering bastard who needed to be dealt with, before he ran amok over the whole damn province.

So, of course, Campos would be giving the guy light anti-tank weapons this morning. Some days, in his dictionary, the words "irony" and "insanity" were listed as synonyms for "politics."

Today was one of those days.

Of the other nuns, Sister Rose, despite her youth, had visibly taken up the mantle of Bettine's authority. Even in the company of thugs, she exuded an air of calm control, as if she knew, truly, that God was on her side.

Campos didn't doubt it for a second.

No less could be said of Sister Julia. She was undaunted. But the thing with Julia, the odd thing he never failed to notice and be somewhat unnerved by, was her aura.

Yes, the woman had one, and it was golden, as pure as sunlight on a clear day.

He'd grown up on the streets of America, stealing and cheating, lying and scamming, and skating the edge of felonies, until he'd skated over the edge. He'd stolen enough cars by the time he was sixteen to do a little real estate investment on the side. His life had included a few years cruising through the seamy underbellies of the world, and yeah, that was as bad as it sounded. To his credit, he'd done some good in those underbellies, such as it was, considering nothing he'd ever done had changed the course of anything for too damn long. The world, it seemed, was on a constant, inevitable, gravity-enabled slide into anarchy and vice.

And then for no reason, against the odds, there would be a woman like Julia Ann-Marie Bakkert somewhere, and of course, she would be a nun.

Campos didn't know why Garcia had brought the good sisters of St. Joseph with him at this hour, but Sister Julia and Sister Rose weren't who he was worried about this morning. He wasn't even particularly worried about Sister Teresa.

He looked down at the letter Max had handed him a few minutes ago. The script was blockish and straight on the page, the prose wordy, the phrases couched in false praise and subtle threats. Regardless, the damn thing boiled down to a single barbaric command: Give up the woman.

Give up the woman. Jesus. Who in the hell did Diego Garcia think he was?

This morning's meeting had been set up for one reason: an exchange of weapons and money for a courier's pouch with its documents intact. There was no "give up the woman" part.

Of course, there was no money, either.

Goddammit.

To their credit, even in torrential rain, last night's patrol had located the downed Cessna and had set up a perimeter around it. No one was getting near the plane, what was left of it anyway, except the missing hotshot team of Rydell and York-Lytton.

Campos had planned on sending another patrol out this morning to find them, but from the looks of the small army camped on his doorstep, he needed all his men for security.

Because he sure as hell wasn't giving up Lily Robbins.

Rather than housing her in one of his elegant guest suites, he'd had Isidora keep Ms. Robbins with her and her children in the servants' quarters. Isidora's rooms were fairly elegant in and of themselves, and Campos had figured a schoolteacher from Albuquerque would be more comfortable surrounded by another woman and a passel of kids.

According to Isidora's latest report, he'd been right. Ms. Robbins was still asleep.

Just as well.

He handed the letter back to Max, and straightened the knot on his tie.

His leg hurt like hell.

"Jake?"

"Yes?"

"Who has the high ground this morning?"

"We do. Pablo and Tomás are on the rooftops, Pablo on my frequency, and Tomás as your dedicated shooter."

"Good." Both men were expert marksmen. "How many men do you have in place in the warehouse?"

The pallet of weapons wasn't going anywhere, until Campos had the Agency's documents in his hand. Entering into negotiations without the money might have been an insurmountable problem for someone else—for anyone else. Campos had it covered.

"Five guards."

"Where in the hell are Rydell and York-Lytton?"

"We're still trying to raise them on the radio or Rydell's secure phone."

Campos swore under his breath and shrugged into the suit jacket Max was holding for him.

Fucking dawn. The sun had barely broken the horizon, and he was already in Armani.

He had a feeling if anything happened to the two Americans, he was going to get the heat for it. *Dammit.*

"Try again, and keep trying, until we find them. Call Dobbs in Panama. Maybe he knows where in the hell they got off to."

That was the problem with fast-breaking incidents and rushed missions. Things got misplaced—like two million dollars, two full-grown people, and a whole goddamn Land Cruiser.

CHAPTER TWENTY-TWO

Morazán Province, El Salvador

Two things woke Smith from a sound sleep: the erection he'd gotten rubbing up against something so soft and silky and warm, it could only be Honey; and the ringing of his phone. Both of them demanded immediate attention. One was going to get it.

Dammit.

He rolled onto his back and grabbed his phone.

Reception was a wonderful thing.

Right, dammit.

"Smith," he said, reaching over Honey for the radio sticking out of one of the side pockets on his rucksack. "Yes, sir . . . stand by one."

He leaned over her again, digging deeper into the rucksack's side pocket and pulling out his

GPS. He switched it on and reported his location to William Dobbs in Panama.

"Yes, sir. I'll change frequencies and make the call. Yes, sir . . . rain . . . biblical rain . . . yes"—he did a quick visual check of the Land Cruiser and located the briefcase next to the case holding his Heckler & Koch submachine gun—". . . sir. We've got the briefcase . . . yes, sir."

Dobbs went on a bit of a harangue before he gave up the day's radio codes. Smith didn't blame him. Getting lost was pretty damn unacceptable, especially for an operator of his caliber.

"Yes, sir. I'll make the call," he said, and hung up the cell phone.

Swearing softly to himself, he punched the frequency and encryption key into the radio's numeric pad with one hand, while he shucked into his pants with the other, and hoped like hell that someone was manning the radio at Campos's plantation.

Someone would be, of course. Campos had a reputation for running a damn tight ship, but given how things had gone so far, Smith wasn't taking anything for granted.

God, the inside of the Land Cruiser was like a sauna, the windows completely fogged over, the humidity about a hundred and ten percent. The sun was up outside, but barely.

"Come on, baby. Up and at 'em." He leaned down and bit Honey gently on the butt.

She let out a long sigh and rolled onto her back, stretching her arms above her head, one knee bending, so beautifully, gorgeously, so erotically naked—*fuck*. His gaze accidentally slid down the lush curves of her body. The girl was not skinny, not by any stretch of the imagination. What little there was of her had been put in all the right places—some very nice places.

Yeah. Right. Don't go there, Cougar, old boy.

And he wouldn't. He was a professional.

And yet his gaze drifted down to between her legs, soft brown curls, soft pale skin, and a sweet little bikini wax job making her oh-so-just-so.

Right.

Every cell in his body went on instant alert, and only one thing kept his pants on—duty. *Dammit*. Garcia was already at the Campos plantation, according to Dobbs, and the negotiations were about to begin, at dawn, of all the damn strange things. The weapons had been delivered last night, but whatever was in the briefcase was still in the briefcase, and it wasn't anywhere close to where it could be useful.

Smith didn't know Campos, except by reputation. The plantation owner had not been in residence the one other time Smith had been in

Morazán Province. But on this job, they were on the same team, and Rydell was a team player. He hadn't needed Dobbs to tell him he needed to get his ass unlost and get to Campos's coffee farm.

"Whitewater," he said into the radio. "Clothes, Honey. Get dressed."

"Roger that, Whitewater," a man's voice came back at him from over the radio. "Angel Falls fully clothed on this end."

Shit. He hadn't meant to transmit that last part.

"Smith here."

"Jake. My friend said you'd be calling. Give me your coordinates, and I'll tell you where you went wrong."

Smith checked his GPS again, before giving Jake his location.

The last thing he'd expected in return was for his contact to reply with a short laugh.

"Well, you've got a damn good sense of direction."

"How so?"

"The road you're on links up with the one you were supposed to be on, in about five hundred meters. And you're only four kilometers due north of the Cessna."

Sonuvabitch. Smith leaned forward and wiped a section of window clean with his hand, and couldn't see a damn thing. The world was full of fog, inside and outside of the Land Cruiser.

"How far are we from you?"

"Half an hour tops."

"What do you want me to do?" Smith's mission priority was the recovery of the flash drive, but with Garcia already at the plantation, adjustments might need to be made in order to accommodate the whole operation. If Campos needed the briefcase, then the briefcase needed to be delivered.

"Give me five minutes. I'll call back."

"Copy that." Smith stuck the radio in the cargo pocket on his pants. "Come on, Honey. Let's go."

"Go where?" she mumbled, rolling back onto her stomach and settling in again.

He dug his T-shirt out from underneath her and pulled it on over his head. Boots and socks came next. He found hers while he was at it and set them next to her.

"Coffee in two minutes," he said, grabbing an MRE bag out of his rucksack. "Then we're moving out of here, babe. You can do it either dressed or naked. I vote for naked, but it's your call."

"Jerk," she whispered, and he grinned, before kissing her ass one more time.

Opening one of the back doors, he crawled

out of the Land Cruiser and into the day. In the few minutes since he'd woken up, the sun had climbed higher into the sky and was already starting to burn off the fog.

He held up his GPS, then looked to the south. He didn't expect to see the plane. He wanted to see the country. It was steep and hilly, and definitely subalpine, not tropical forest, like closer to the coast.

By the time Honey joined him, looking rumpled and grumpy, he had two cups of a thick rich brew ready—coffee, heavy on the creamer, cocoa, and sugar: breakfast in a cup.

"Nice green shirt," he said, noticing she'd gotten something clean out of her suitcase. She'd also secured her handcuffs to her belt loop, which he thought was damn cute.

"It's not green," she grumbled.

Could have fooled him.

"It's chartreuse."

Of course it was, and now he knew.

"You need to tie those boots, or you're going to end up on your butt, Ms. Chartreuse."

She said something crude, which made him grin, and then she knelt down and tied her boots. She was all wild hair again this morning, the same way she'd been the last time they'd spent the night together, and he had to wonder if it was always like this with her—going to bed with a so-phisticated, elegantly chic woman of the world, and waking up with Sheena of the Jungle.

Depending on how tired he was and how awake he needed to be, sometimes he dropped extra caffeine tabs in his cup. He'd had a few cups of coffee that, sipped slow and steady, had kept him going for a couple of days.

From the looks of her, she could use a little help.

"Do you want a caffeine tablet or two in your coffee, something to kind of get you going?" *And maybe get your eyes open, sweetheart?*

"No," she grumbled. "Regular caffeine is plenty. I usually drink decaf."

Cigars, bourbon, and decaf coffee? So much for her hard-hitting edge.

She took the cup, when he offered it, and walked around toward the front of the Land Cruiser.

"You owe me for saving your ass," she said, and he looked over to where she was standing by the front bumper, looking down the mountain.

"And what would my ass be worth this morning?" he asked.

"How about a hundred bucks?"

He rose from where he'd been kneeling by the

small stove he'd set up, and walked to the front of the Land Cruiser.

Then he reached in his pocket and thumbed off two fifty-dollar bills and stashed them in the front pocket of her pants.

"Close call," he said.

"Damn close," she agreed, and took another sip of coffee.

The right front tire was hanging by a thread on the edge of the road, a whole lot of which had been washed away. A virtual stream of dirt and road base cascaded down the mountainside.

"Maybe we should move the car," she suggested.

"Yeah." Not a bad idea.

"I'm going to wait over there," she said, pointing to the other side of the road, the one still firmly attached to the mountain.

"Good idea." They had spent the night parked in a deep curve, with the mountain track bowing out at each end. In daylight, it was easy to see why so much rain had been funneled on top of them, and why they'd lost their communication reception.

To his credit, he'd been absolutely right about the fifty meters. If they'd driven out of the curve, without going over the side, she could have called her mother in Adams-Morgan, the reception would have been so good.

Of course, odds were that they would have gone straight over the side, and careened just that much closer to the Cessna.

Hell. Considering all the rocking and rolling they'd done in the back of the Land Cruiser, they were lucky to be alive this morning.

Geezus. That was not the sort of obit he wanted at the end of his résumé, or hers.

By the time he got the car repositioned farther down the road, the call came back in. He pulled the map out of the driver's side visor and spread it open on the console. With a pencil in hand, he jotted down the coordinates for the Cessna and got the go-ahead from Campos, via Jake, to retrieve the flash drive, before driving on to the plantation.

"We have a patrol in place at the crash site," Jake said. "They've been there all night, and have a perimeter set up. I'll let them know you're on your way. From where you're at, you need to follow the road east for another kilometer. There'll be a trail crossing, and from there, you're on a footpath, but it's only about three and a half kilometers to the plane, with a little bushwhacking at the end. Our men will be looking for you."

CHAPTER TWENTY-THREE

Campos Plantation, Morazán Province, El Salvador

Well, things were going as well as could be expected—edging toward hell, with a planned side trip to the main warehouse.

"More coffee, Captain Garcia?" Campos asked, signaling Max to bring a fresh pot to the table. "It is my private roast, and I can guarantee you it is excellent."

He and Garcia were sitting alone on the patio, a table full of food set out before them with a television at one end. Two of Garcia's soldiers were positioned against the patio wall, forming his security detail, and Tomás, hidden on the villa's roof, would have both the soldiers squarely in his scope. Max had the hot pot of coffee in one hand and his ever-present Walther PPK concealed inside his waistband. Garcia was simply bristling with armament, and Campos was making do with the Para .45 in the shoulder holster under his suit coat and a Beretta Tomcat he'd dropped into his pants pocket.

The occasion was breakfast, and yes, things would have to deteriorate to an irredeemably grim state before he pulled the combat knife sheathed on his ankle, or, if it became suddenly necessary, stabbed Garcia with the butter knife.

The whole morning smacked of edginess, and after yesterday, he'd hoped for a calmer slide through his meals for the rest of the week. The amazing thing was that he could eat at all.

Sinking his teeth into a raspberry-filled croissant, he poured an extra measure of cream into his own still-steaming cup of coffee. Max didn't let the coffee get cold. Besides his wizardry with the mail, it was the reason Campos kept him on—along with eight years of loyal and dedicated service and the Walther PPK that Max knew very well how to use.

"No, *señor*," Garcia said, sitting stiffly to Campos's left, exactly where Campos wanted him. If things did start to go poorly, Campos had a better shot with Garcia to his left.

"You're not eating, Captain," Campos pointed

out. "Is there something else you would like?" Not that he gave a damn if Garcia ate or not.

He'd taken one hundred percent control of the situation before he'd ever left his bedroom this morning, and he wasn't relinquishing an ounce of it. There was no other way to do business in his line of work, not and come out in one piece or get any kind of a decent meal at all.

So they were eating breakfast, alone, at the place of Campos's choosing, with no women of any kind anywhere in sight and the rest of Garcia's men cooling their heels in the compound, under the watchful eyes of Campos's men and Pablo's .308.

"*Sí*," Garcia said. "I would like to see the weapons and the money I was promised. If not, we have no deal, and the documents will go to the highest bidder."

"Unacceptable, Captain," Campos said around another bite of croissant. "The *gringos* made their wishes very clearly known to me, and they have sent both the weapons and the money as they promised, but there has been a new development, which I would be remiss in ignoring, considering the great trust they have placed in me to work with you on their behalf." And just try to say all that, coherently, no less, on an empty stomach at half past dawn in the goddamn morning.

"What development?" Garcia said, his whole demeanor suddenly wary, with good reason.

Campos made a brief gesture with his hand, and Max stepped forward and turned on the television set. A movie was playing.

"*Salvator mundi,*" Bettine whispered on the screen, her voice a bare thread of sound. "*Salva nos omnes. Kyrie eleison; Christe eleison; Christe eleison...*"

Yes, Campos thought. *Christ have mercy on us all.*

He helped himself to scrambled eggs and re-filled his orange juice—and he drank his coffee and ate.

He ate through Teresa's tear-filled confession, used the remote to skip ahead to her second confession, the one where she mentioned Diego Garcia by name as the father of her child, and continued eating, then fast-forwarded to her beating, and pushed his plate aside.

Garcia was clearly identifiable in the scene.

"Congratulations are in order, I presume?" Campos reached for his coffee and took a sip.

Garcia was livid, but unimpressed. "This has nothing to do with the documents, or my weapons. The United States government does not care about what happens to a disgraced nun."

"No, but the people of Morazán care, and the

people of El Salvador care. The freedom fighters of the Cuerpo Nacional de Libertad might find themselves personae non grata in the very country they are trying to liberate, if this film was to be released to the media in San Salvador."

"You are threatening me with this?" Garcia scoffed. "With hitting a woman?"

And desecrating a sworn bride of Christ, which was by far the more serious infraction, a fact Garcia well knew.

Campos shrugged and directed his attention back to the television. In any court of law, the next scene in the film was definitive, and very, very ugly.

"He was a traitor to the cause, and the price of treason is death," Garcia interceded on his own behalf, before the young soldier's body even hit the floor.

This time, it was Campos who was unimpressed. "Perhaps I should rewind it and turn up the sound, Captain. I believe you stated his crime quite clearly, before you shot him, and it wasn't treason."

Garcia shifted his gaze to his men, and Campos could almost see Tomás's index finger take up the slack on his SR-25's trigger. It would take him half a second each to take out Garcia's men.

"Your desecration of the St. Joseph chapel will

also not go unnoticed by the people of El Salvador," he said.

"There are no Catholics in the White House of Washington, D.C."

"Not this year," Campos agreed. "But there are patriots, make no mistake, Captain, even in the back rooms, and they will all be very unhappy to see how the Cessna pilot died."

"The man crashed his airplane into the side of a mountain," Garcia said, letting down his guard ever so slightly, relaxing into his chair and reaching for his coffee for the first time. "I cannot be held responsible for his death. My men took his body to the priest in Cristobal. This is enough."

Campos picked up the remote and used it to reverse the tape to the scene Lily Robbins had filmed on Tuesday—the death of the American.

"Rumor has it that he was shot down," he said. More than rumor. His men had found the plane last night and found the bullet holes, including a few especially large ones from armor-piercing rounds.

"Perhaps this is true," Garcia agreed. "But it wasn't the CNL who shot his plane."

Campos figured it was, but that was beside the point. The lovely Ms. Robbins had proved his real point for him.

And she was lovely, and in the wrong place at

the wrong time, and in over her head, and he'd hoped to have her out of Morazán before Garcia arrived for their meeting. Everything would be so much simpler if she were already on her way back to Albuquerque.

He signaled Max to top off his cup.

The Campos plantation was famous among a narrow group of cognoscenti for its private reserve coffee: AC-130, Alejandro Campos, one, three, zero. He roasted it on the plantation, and packaged it with an AC-130 Black Label skull-and-crossbones trademarked logo. As a side venture, it didn't bring in much money, but it did add to his legitimacy as a coffee grower.

"It doesn't matter who shot him down, Captain," Campos said, hitting the play button on the remote, "when he died like this."

He settled back into his own chair, deceptively relaxed, and slowly sipped his coffee.

He and Jake had done some editing of the tape last night when they'd made their copies, one of which was already on its way to Dobbs, and another of which he'd sent to the embassy in Guatemala City.

The scene began with a fast pan across the chapel, the camera noticeably handheld, the picture jumping. Campos could imagine how frightened Lily Robbins had been. The picture quality was fairly good, though, and there was no doubt in his mind whose death he was watching—Hal Merchant's.

At least that was the name Campos knew him by.

"What I'm offering, Captain, are the weapons and this tape in exchange for the documents your men found on the Cessna."

The tape was political suicide. Garcia had done himself and his cause irreparable damage with this week's work.

"What about my money?"

"The money buys my silence," Campos said.

Garcia laughed out loud, a short, hearty laugh. "Two million dollars is a lot of silence, my friend."

Not really.

Campos held the man's gaze, steady and sure, until the captain's smile faded.

"Where is Honoria York-Lytton?" Garcia demanded to know. "Sister Julia's sister? She is the one I'm supposed to be speaking with, not you."

"Ms. York-Lytton was delayed by the storm, and I took it upon myself to suggest she stay in San Salvador."

"Then where is my money?" The captain was not laughing now.

The tape reached the end of the scene and the editing he and Jake had done.

"*Fuck you . . . Fuck you . . . Fuck you.*" Hal's last words ran over and over.

Campos couldn't have said it better himself.

He hit the stop button, and a moment's silence descended. He let it sit there between them, weighing on the morning, before he spoke.

"Your weapons arrived very late last night, Captain," he said, rising to his feet. "If you would like to see them, I have them warehoused in one of my buildings."

He gestured toward the courtyard gate, and when Garcia finally stood, he led the way out.

From her and Ari's observation post on a hillside above the Campos compound, Irena watched two women, one a nun, having breakfast on one of the villa's upstairs balconies.

"Do you see the women on the second-floor balcony?" she asked.

"Yes." Lying next to her, flat on his belly, looking through the scope on his Steyer .308 long rifle, Ari confirmed the sighting.

"The nun looks familiar."

Ari lifted his head away from the scope. "You don't know any nuns, Irena."

"She still looks familiar," she said thoughtfully, but was unable to place the blond-haired sister.

"No Rydell yet?"

"No Rydell," she confirmed. "And no Honoria York-Lyt—wait a minute."

She swung her binoculars back along the roofline of the villa, until she had the blond-haired nun in her field of view.

"I'll be damned."

"What?" Ari asked.

"The nun, the blonde, she looks like the woman in the photograph Hans gave us, the one traveling with Rydell."

"He's traveling with a nun?"

"No. That's not Honoria York-Lytton having croissants and coffee, but it is somebody who resembles her."

Ari was quiet for a couple of moments, looking through his scope.

"You're right," he said. "There is a resemblance. Interesting."

"Very." She and Ari had gotten into place shortly before dawn, barely in time to see the CNL drive up in their trucks, not soon enough to be set up for a shot.

"Can you confirm two overwatch shooters?"

Irena made a brief sweep with her binoculars.

"One on the villa's roof and one on the building farthest from the gate."

"Are they targets?"

"If anything starts down there, they're our primary defensive targets." Good strategy, nothing personal. It was never personal. "We'll leave the rest of Campos's men in place, unless they figure out we're here. Then they're gone."

"Have you located the weapons?" Ari asked.

"No, but look who's exiting the villa's courtyard." Out of the corner of her eye, she saw him change the direction he was pointing the rifle from the women on the balcony to the ground-level courtyard.

"The man in the captain's uniform has to be Diego Garcia," he said.

"Yes, and the guy in the Armani suit has to be Alejandro Campos."

"You cannot possibly tell that suit is Armani from this distance."

"Yes, I can," she said. "Stay on him. If this deal is going down, this is where he'll show Garcia the weapons."

"If we were in the market for grenade launchers and sixty-six millimeter LAWs, this would make more sense, Irena, us being here."

He wasn't happy with the situation, and in truth, neither was she. The closer they got to

Rydell, the more complicated everything seemed to become, especially her motives. Panic was not her usual reaction to the unexpected, but her reaction to C. Smith Rydell being alive was starting to feel more and more like panic than the series of cool, rational decisions she'd told herself she was making.

"It's just a job, Ari, nothing more. We'll finish it and go home."

All they had to do was wait for their target.

CHAPTER TWENTY-FOUR

Morazán Province, El Salvador

"I don't like to sweat."

Smith knew that. He knew, because she'd told him a dozen times already. It was like a mantra with her, bubbling up and slipping out about every five minutes by his count—*I don't like to sweat*.

Well, then, she must be one unhappy kitten, because she was sweating, tromping down the trail toward the Cessna, sliding in the mud and scrambling over the rocks—and sweating. Sweat stains darkened her green—excuse him, *chartreuse*— shirt under the arms, around the collar, down the middle of her back, and down the middle of her front. The whole world had turned into a sauna, with pools of water everywhere, everything wet from the storm, and the sun rising higher and higher in the sky and making it all steam. She was damp in the small of her back and on the back of her neck. Moisture beaded her brow. Her hair had discovered a whole new level of wild even from earlier this morning, dandelion wild. He wanted to blow on her, make a wish, kiss her lips.

"I *really* don't like to sweat," she muttered under her breath again, as if he could have possibly missed the headline.

Girls were so different. He didn't mind sweating. Most of his work involved a lot of sweating—humping ninety-pound rucksacks of gear from one indescribably hot and humid spot in the jungle to the next indescribably hot and humid spot.

This morning he was getting off easy, only humping eighty or so pounds, including the black briefcase he'd stuffed into his pack, Zorro's mystery briefcase.

"*Dammit,*" she whispered to herself, when a twig snapped back and caught her on the face.

He'd spent two days in the woods with a Force Recon team once and heard less chatter than he had in the half hour he'd been on the trail with Honey—six guys with a job to do, and they'd managed it without hardly speaking a word.

She came to a sudden stop ahead of him and held her closed fist up in the air, signaling him to stop, too.

Oh, God. He stopped, his hand coming to his chest to hold in he didn't know what—laughter, chagrin, disbelief. *Silent* hand signals. She was bitching and moaning her way down the trail, and finally, when the concept of "silence" actually sank in, it was to give him *silent* hand signals.

Oh, baby, she was no Recon Marine.

Not with that ass.

Darcy Delamere. His grin broadened.

Then he heard it, the sound of someone coming through the brush.

"Lorenzo?" he said softly into his radio.

"*Sí, Smith,*" a man's voice came back at him. "The woman is easy to track."

No kidding. She was like a homing beacon with her little whispered asides.

He and Lorenzo had been in radio contact since he and Honey had veered off the trail to bushwhack the last hundred yards to the plane. Campos's man had assured him the area was clear and secure. They'd been patrolling it all night and morning and had seen no one.

In less than a minute, Lorenzo came into view, and without a word, signaled them to follow him.

The trail grew steadily steeper for the last twenty-five meters to the crash site, before it leveled off. The plane had come to rest in a grove of pine trees, its fuselage remarkably intact. If the pilot could have cleared the hilltop, he would have had a straight shot at the valley below. Instead, it looked like he'd flared just above the trees and fallen through them at about fifty knots. One of the propeller blades was bent backward, indicative of a dead-stick landing where the engine was out. The horizontal tail section and most of the wings had been sheared off, but the craft hadn't burned.

Smith didn't know who the pilot had been, but he was glad the guy hadn't burned.

It had been a nightmare of his, burning. Not himself, but Irena. For months after watching the Piper crash in Afghanistan, he'd woken up in a cold sweat, thinking of her burning inside her plane. Logically, he knew she would have either been dead or unconscious long before the plane crashed, and there wouldn't have been much left of her after the crash, but logic never kept a nightmare at bay—and in his dreams, he'd heard her scream.

He walked toward the front of the craft.

The other two of Campos's men who had been at the site all night were finishing up breakfast on the other side of the plane. A glance back inside the fuselage proved they'd taken refuge in the Cessna to stay out of the storm. They'd also, at some point, tied the craft off to the trees on either side, probably before they'd settled in for the night.

Smith was impressed.

"Good work," he said, pointing to the ropes.

Lorenzo nodded and rattled off a stream of Spanish in explanation, pointing out the hillside and talking about the rain, and especially directing Smith's attention to the mudslide twenty meters farther on.

For Smith's tasking, the security and relative wholeness of the fuselage was imperative. Considering the angle of the slope where it had come to rest, the patrol's foresight in tying the plane off had probably saved the day.

He complimented Lorenzo again, and the man walked over to where the rest of the patrol had set up their stove.

At the front of the Cessna, Smith stood and looked at the nose, then glanced through the broken windshield at the pilot's seat.

The last plane crash site he'd been at had been Irena's. He hadn't really realized it until now.

Her scream is what had always woken him from the nightmare whenever he'd had it, but the cold sweat had come from the vision of her strapped into the Seneca's seat, fighting to get out of the restraints, her hair in flames, a look of horror on her face, and one of her hands spread wide across her belly, clutching something to herself.

"What?" Honey asked, coming to a stop beside him.

He pointed out two half-inch holes in the lower left side of the engine compartment.

"Bullet holes?" she whispered.

He could have told her not to bother to whisper. Campos's men would have instantly known what had happened when they'd seen the holes. There was only one secret left in the Cessna. The one he'd come to get.

"There wasn't any equipment malfunction or pilot error involved in the crash," he said. "The plane was shot down. Look here."

Moving to the right side, he pointed out two more holes, higher and farther aft. They were larger and jagged where the aluminum skin of the plane was punched outward.

"Armor-piercing rounds," he said. "Fifty cal or twelve-point-seven millimeter. Pretty good shots, too."

The heavy bullets had passed diagonally through the engine, probably stopping it immediately.

He looked up the slope. The plane had come to rest about fifty meters from the reverse crest of the hilltop.

Damn, Smith thought. The guy had almost made it. The valley on the other side would have at least given him a chance at a landing.

The pilot's door was open, and Smith peered inside. The impact had driven the instrument panel almost to the back of the empty pilot's seat. There was a lot of dried blood on the seat, and on the windscreen. All the cargo was gone, at least the obvious freight, including the courier's briefcase taken by Garcia's men that had started this whole ball rolling two days ago.

But with luck, there would be one thing left, and it would still be intact—the 2GB flash drive.

He shrugged out of his rucksack and set it on the ground, then levered himself up into the fuselage, with Honey close behind.

She looked around, and her face went oddly flat. He understood. The whole story was starting to sink in—the broken windshield, the crushed instrument panel, the blood on the pilot's seat. Anything that hadn't been torn apart by the crash had been torn apart by Garcia's men, after they'd shot the Cessna out of the sky and then descended on it like a horde of locusts, stripping it almost bare.

And the body—he could see the question written on her face. What had happened to the pilot? Where was he? Or where was the body? Someone had been flying the plane. His blood was everywhere.

But now there was no one.

"Dobbs told me the pilot's body was taken to Cristobal, to the priest there. It will be shipped home."

She nodded and looked at least partly relieved, but her expression remained sad. Death hadn't yet left this fuselage. It was still apparent, still a feeling in the air.

"This...this is a mess," she said. "Do you think the flash drive is even still here?"

"Yes." One look had told him that much.

"I don't have a clue where to begin," she said, looking, but keeping her arms wrapped closely around her waist, not touching, not disturbing anything.

"I do."

He moved forward and knelt between the front seats. The flash drive was concealed inside a shock-resistant compartment in the floor of the airplane, just aft of the center console, in the strongest section of the airframe. With the mid-section of the fuselage reasonably intact, recovery shouldn't be a problem—as long as he was careful.

Using a piece of scrap, he cleared the broken glass and other junk away from between the seats. He was looking for a hatch cover, three inches wide and six inches long, its long axis parallel with the aircraft's centerline. The hatch would be flush with the floor and secured at its edges with what would appear to be six Phillips-head screws equally spaced three inches apart. Only five of the screws were what they seemed. The sixth screw, center right starboard, was a destruct trigger and had to be left tight when the plate was removed. If the screw was loosened along with the others, lifting the plate would ignite a small thermite charge, and the compartment and its contents would both be vaporized. Deformation of the compartment would also ignite the charge, which made it fail-safe.

Needless to say, a little thermite went a long way.

"Honey, move away from the plane," he said when he found the hatch. "I'll be out in a minute."

She didn't question his order, which he appreciated, but once outside, she did call back in.

"Is it booby-trapped?"

"Yes."

There was a long silence, during which he pulled his Leatherman tool out of his pants pocket and started to carefully loosen five of the screws.

"Nobody told me the flash drive was booby-trapped."

No. He didn't suppose anybody had.

"You'd think they would have told me about a booby trap."

No. Not really.

"It's why they sent me," he said, loosening screw number two.

"So you could get blown up, instead of me?"

He stopped whirling the screwdriver on the third screw for a moment.

"I'm not planning on getting blown up." And that was the God's truth.

More silence followed his pronouncement, but not for long.

"I don't see why they couldn't get down here and retrieve their own damn flash drive," she said.

A good point—almost. She'd simply missed one single salient fact.

"Honey, I am 'they.' I'm the one who gets sent to retrieve damn flash drives." He moved to screw number four. "When thermite destruct triggers are put on hatch covers, it's guys like me who open them—very carefully."

"Oh."

He set the Phillips-head to screw number five and gave it a turn. He was not holding his breath.

He never held his breath. Slow and easy, steady and sure, checking each action before it was performed—that was him.

"Thermite?" she said.

Thermite, he silently repeated, lifting the hatch cover off the floor—and slowly letting out the breath he hadn't held.

The compartment was no more than two inches deep, the whole thing about the size of a small automotive glove box, and inside it was a flash drive wrapped in a plastic covering.

"I've got it," he said, and she let out a sigh of relief he heard all the way inside the fuselage.

He secured the flash drive inside one of his cargo pockets. Then he disarmed the destruct device, replaced the hatch cover, and ducked out of the fuselage.

"You've got it?" she asked.

"In my pocket," he said. "Two gigabytes of whatever they sent us down here to get back."

"Thank goodness."

Yeah. Thank goodness.

He closed his knife and looked back inside the plane, his attention drawn by something. Memories, he supposed. He let his gaze go over the destruction wreaked by the crash. There'd been nothing left of Irena's Piper, nothing but a pile of smoldering metal and the damn night-mare.

He knew what she'd been holding to herself in his nightmare, what she'd been clutching so tightly. He'd put it out of his mind so many times, trying to forget, because to remember had made the tragedy so much worse.

She'd been pregnant.

Irena Anastasia Polchenko, the baddest of all the badass girls to ever come his way, had gotten herself *embarazada*. He'd been the lover who had noticed the changes in her body. He'd been the lover she'd confided in—but he hadn't been the father. The honor had gone to Rutger Dolk, an-other contract aviator they'd both known in Afghanistan. Rutger had shipped out at the end of that long-ago April, and by the first of May, Irena had replaced him with Smith.

Yeah, he had plenty of memories. He'd been so damned impressed with himself, right up until the middle of July, when he'd found himself bound and gagged, facedown in the dirt, part of a weapons-for-drugs deal.

Geezus. He'd loved her. Or at least he'd thought it was love. And the baby—he'd actually thought that part was sweet, even if he hadn't been the father. And then a couple of times, he'd wondered if he was the one, if she was carrying his child. The timing had been so damn close, her body growing riper and more lush every time they'd made love.

In his mind there had always been two deaths that day, not one.

And now there were none.

He wiped his hand across his mouth, and looked away, out over the hills and the valleys with their wisps of low-lying fog.

She was alive, and she'd know she'd been spotted, and that made her very, very dangerous.

She would also be a mother by now, and the longer he thought about her having a child, the more he realized how the information could be used against her. She'd know it, too, and suddenly he realized just how much damn trouble he might be in, if she ever found out who had been on that mountainside in Peru—and considering the leaks in the Lima office, he didn't think it would take too damn much effort for her to find out whatever the hell she wanted.

Perfect. Just what he needed to get the day off to a good start—one more goddamn thing to worry about.

CHAPTER TWENTY-FIVE

"Well, this sucks," Honey said a half hour later.

It sure as hell did, Smith thought. They'd made it back to the Land Cruiser from the crash site in two-thirds of the time it had taken to hike the other way, and had been on the road less than ten minutes before they'd come to this crossroad.

Smith had been on the radio with Campos's man, Jake, and he knew the plantation was to the right. But the sign on the post said *"Saint Joseph Escuela y Asilo de Huérfanos—7km,"* and the arrow pointed left. *St. Joseph School and Orphanage.*

"We can't do it." They didn't have a choice. It wasn't just a matter of seven lousy kilometers. "She might not even be there."

"I know."

Dammit.

If Honey York was going to have hot sex with him in back seats, and follow orders, and be reasonable, he was going to fall in love.

"I'll make it up to you."

Crap. Had he just said that? He couldn't believe he'd just said that.

If "I don't like to sweat" was her mantra, "I'll make it up to you" was his. He had a lifetime of saying that to women who had obviously not waited around long enough for him to ever do it.

But he could do it this time.

"Okay, here's the truth: If you want Julia going home with you today, I can make that happen." Sure, he could. He'd been on a couple of two-man "snatch and grab" teams, and even working alone, he didn't think he'd have too much trouble kidnapping one smallish nun, putting her under wraps, and getting her butt on a plane to Washington, D.C., especially since, by the time they got done with today's business, he figured Dobbs and White Rook were going to owe Honey York the moon.

Him, they only owed a paycheck. But she was definitely in the above-the-call-of-duty category.

He looked over at her, and it looked like she

was thinking. Fine by him. She could think on the way to Campos's.

Spinning the steering wheel to the right, he headed the Land Cruiser toward the plantation. Given Garcia's presence, and what Jake called the pace of the negotiations, he'd been told to come in the back way and lie low. Five kilometers due south, he would come to a sign for AC-130 coffee with a skull and crossbones on it, and yeah, from everything he knew about AC-130 gunships, a skull and crossbones fit. He'd grinned when Jake had told him about the sign.

There would be a locked gate, but the guards were authorized to let them pass.

Following the directions would take him along the river and eventually lead him to an old factory on the plantation. His orders were to wait there. If they were needed, they'd be close enough to be handy, and if they weren't needed, they'd be well enough out of it.

Smith was starting to like Alejandro Campos. He liked how carefully he was moving. If the man could manage to get the Agency's documents back without involving Honey any further or putting her in the same room with Diego Garcia, Smith was going to like him even more.

And Zorro's black briefcase? Hell, Smith didn't know where it was fitting in, or how in the hell Campos was getting along without it. But if it really was full of money, and Campos didn't need it to pull off this deal, then he was going to be as impressed as hell.

"I'll talk to her," Honey said. "See if I can convince her this time to come home."

Talk, talk, talk. Personally, he thought there'd been enough talk. A few years of it between Honey and Julia, and little sister was still in the thick of trouble.

"You should just let me grab her," he said. "You two could talk at home."

"Grab her?"

He glanced over, and she was giving him a look—a highly skeptical look.

"Grab. Literally." He wasn't going to sugarcoat it for her. Kidnapping often involved a straight-out grab, and it certainly was the method he was inclined to use with Julia. If that woman had an ounce of reason in her, he sure hadn't seen it.

"You can't just go and grab her."

"Why not?" It was a time-tested method. There were some tactics and techniques involved, sure, but he knew them. He knew them well enough not to—

"She might be pregnant."

—hurt her.

Stop the presses.

"Pregnant?" He slowly and carefully brought the Land Cruiser to a stop. "What do you mean pregnant?"

"With child."

Geezus. And he meant no disrespect.

"Whose child?"

"I shouldn't say."

To hell with that.

"You'd *better* say." For the love of God Almighty. When in the hell had El Salvador become such a hotbed of chaos?

"Diego Garcia."

Well, that made his skin crawl, but finally—finally—he understood why Honoria York-Lytton was sitting next to him in a car on a back road in Morazán Province.

He took a breath and stretched back into his seat.

Fuck.

"You weren't planning on shooting him, were you?" *Please say no,* he thought.

But she didn't say anything.

"You were planning on shooting him, weren't you." It wasn't a question anymore.

"Julia would *never* have consented to sex," she said, tight-jawed. "Never."

He believed her, and that pretty much tied up the whole mission for him, at least her part in it.

"You're going to give me the combination, now, or I'm turning this car around and driving you straight back to San Salvador," he said, and he meant every damn word. He wasn't letting her anywhere near Garcia. "The choice is yours, Honey."

A long stretch of silence ensued.

Fine. He could wait all day, if that's what it took. She wasn't going anywhere, except under his terms.

"Seven, eight, zero, four, four, two," she finally said—and he took his foot off the brake, stepped on the gas, and eased them down the road.

Great. Perfect.

Whatever was going to happen at Campos's, from here on out, would not be happening with Honey York in the middle of it.

He needed Honoria York-Lytton.

Campos had played all his cards, and he still needed Honoria York-Lytton and his briefcase. He had dazzled and amazed Garcia with the pallet of weapons and ordnance. Nobody did weapons and ordnance better than the U.S.A., and to see a stack of the government's finest offerings lying out for the taking was enough to turn any insurgent's head.

It had certainly turned Garcia's. The bastard's eyes had been alight with greed. The captain wanted LAWs and grenade launchers—but not enough to cut the deal on weapons alone.

The threat of the videotape was real. Leaked to the press, the images of Garcia killing the soldier and beating Sister Teresa could permanently damage his career as a captain in the Cuerpo Nacional de Libertad.

But ideology could be difficult to hold on to under the best of circumstances. Guerrilla soldiers bound by a common cause were nearly an anachronism in the reality of today's world. Drugs were the easier way to grasp fortune by the throat. If Garcia could no longer lead an armed resistance to the government, he could undermine it by facilitating the drug trade in his country. He didn't need to be a CNL captain, when the title of Salvadoran drug lord fit him just as well. His infrastructure was in place, and the uniform was practically the same. Very little alteration was needed. An extra epaulet or two, and he'd be on his way.

Campos knew it. Garcia knew it. And so there was a need for cash to sweeten the deal, a half a million to be precise, and Campos had certainly seen men sell out for a whole lot less.

On his side, Garcia had produced ten pages of

the stolen two-hundred-page document, and through Dobbs, Campos had been able to verify its authenticity. Garcia did have the Agency's intelligence, and the deal was getting closer.

Half a million—he grinned. For a day that had gotten off to such a rough start, this one was working out just fine.

All parties had fallen back to their camps, Garcia with his armed men and troop trucks by the front gate, and Campos and Jake on the second floor of the warehouse with the weapons housed on the ground floor with a full cadre of guards.

"Where are they?" Campos asked, glassing the dirt track from the main road to the AC-130 factory.

"They should be coming into sight in a few minutes," Jake said, lifting his radio to his mouth. "Smith, your location?"

Campos heard the man reply and turned to Jake to find out what was said.

"They're two kilometers from the river road now."

Campos nodded.

Raising the binoculars back to his eyes, he ran his gaze over the AC-130 building.

The factory where he roasted and packaged the coffee beans was a concrete, rebar, wooden plank, and corrugated steel fortress located a half a mile from the villa, close to the river and the coffee fields. Small outbuildings sprawled on either side of it. The main building was old, too huge to keep in full production, and a bit of a maze, having been added onto dozens of times over the years.

He glassed the road again, then moved the optics for a brief peek at one of the villa's second-floor balconies, knowing exactly what he'd see. Lily Robbins was having croissants and coffee with Sister Julia, and for the second time since he'd noticed her up there, he wished he was having breakfast with Lily Robbins, too.

But then he let the moment pass.

He was not holding a torch for Jewel, not in any sense of the word, but he had somehow gotten stuck in the aftermath of their breakup. It wasn't that he hadn't moved on, he just hadn't . . . moved. At all.

Sofia was right. He needed to leave El Salvador.

"They're here," Jake said a moment later, and when he looked, Campos saw the black Land Cruiser breaking the trees to the south and making its way toward the old factory.

"I'm going down there," Campos said. "When I have the money, we'll invite Garcia here, to this office, and make the exchange. We'll allow him to bring in one of his trucks and four of his soldiers to pick up the weapons. No more."

"Yes, sir," Jake said.

"Black Land Cruiser heading north on the river road," Ari said.

"Red Toyota pickup leaving the villa compound, moving east." Both vehicles were heading toward a sprawling concrete, wood, and corrugated steel factory down by the river with a big AC-130 skull-and-crossbones sign on one side of it.

"Something's up."

"Campos is driving the red truck. Can you see who's in the Land Cruiser?" Irena asked, focusing her spotting scope on the SUV.

"No. I can't see through the windshield at this angle."

She couldn't see inside either, but she was sure it was Rydell and York-Lytton. They were the only players out of place. Everyone else was here, at Campos's villa, and York-Lytton had a black briefcase she'd brought with her all the way from Panama. Something was in it, and Irena couldn't imagine that anything dangerously handcuffed to the blonde wasn't of vital importance to the current transaction.

"Let's switch," she said, low-crawling to Ari's other side. Two-man sniper-observer teams typically relieved each other at regular intervals, to ease up on eyestrain and keep a fresh shooter on the long gun.

Mostly, though, for this shot, Irena wanted to be on the rifle. The optics on the Steyer had every bit as much resolution as those on her spotting scope. Once in place behind the rifle, she trained it on the Land Cruiser and carefully followed the car up the road, and all the while she was following it through her scope, she was settling in, quieting down, slipping inside the "cocoon" of awareness that would include only her, the rifle, and the target, all three entities bound by a single thread of existence.

"Give me data for the factory," Irena said.

Next to her, Ari measured the distance and the slope angle to the front of the AC-130 building with a laser range finder, and quickly calculated her elevation and spindrift. The ambient conditions were holding steady.

"Set four point nine," he said, and she dialed the elevation in. "Set left zero point one."

She adjusted her windage knob, settled in to her scope, and waited for him to call the wind, the last adjustment made just before the shot.

And they waited, watching the Land Cruiser

and the pickup crawl through the ruts of the road and slowly come to a stop in front of the sprawling old factory.

Her finger slid to the trigger. "Shooter ready," she said softly.

Ari made his call. "Right zero point eight."

She prepared to make the reticle correction as soon as she was on target.

Campos pulled up to the factory, got out of the pickup, and motioned for the Land Cruiser to follow him.

"That's not good," breathed Ari, looking through the spotting scope.

Not at all good, Irena silently agreed, watching Campos open a large sliding door and motion the Land Cruiser into the factory. The vehicle made a left turn, and through the open passenger window, over the head of a blond-haired woman, she caught a fleeting glimpse of the driver—C. Smith Rydell, ID positive.

It wasn't enough. A half-second exposure with a clean line of sight didn't give her enough time to compensate for the target's lateral motion.

Fuming, she followed the Land Cruiser's progress with her sights and watched the angle of the vehicle block her shot. Then the SUV disappeared completely inside the factory.

She took her finger off the trigger and swore

under her breath. Not firing had been the correct decision. Head shots at six hundred meters
were tricky things, even on a stationary target.
But damn, she'd been close, so close to accom-
plishing her mission.

"Stay on the door," Ari said. "I'll give you another wind call if he comes out."

"*Da*," she said, not moving. *Yes*.

But the odds were against them getting another shot. Ari knew it as well as she did. Rydell
and his passenger had been taken into the building to get them under cover, and that's probably
exactly where they would stay—under cover.

After ten minutes, Ari leaned back on his el-
bow and gave her a long look.

"How do you wish to proceed?" he asked.

"We need to get down there," she said. "The
odds will be better close in."

They hadn't gotten the long shot, and she
wasn't prepared to spend hours or days waiting
for another. Their position was vulnerable. Their
rental car was parked in a market where it
wouldn't be noticed for one day, but would surely
draw attention for two.

"Then we need to find a way in—and back
out," he said.

"*Da*," she said, putting her eye back to the scope
and scanning the terrain down by the factory. "Do

you see the opening in the low bluff above the river? Seventy meters from the factory's back door?"

"Yes."

"What do you think it is?"

"Some sort of opening, about a meter across, maybe a drain into the river."

"It's bricked, looks like a tunnel. We'll enter there."

CHAPTER TWENTY-SIX

Honey stepped out of the Land Cruiser into the cool, dark interior of the AC-130 building and was immediately awash in the soothing scent of coffee. Good thing, because the old place was a little creepy from the outside, too big, and really old and broken-down in a lot of places. Smith was right behind her, carrying his rucksack and a wicked-looking weapon he'd told her was a sub-machine gun.

They entered a large, open room, which immediately put her more at ease. Wooden-floored, with concrete walls painted a warm, rustic yellow, the place had a certain rough-hewn elegance. A set of double doors opened toward the back, leading into the rest of the factory. Thick, multipaned windows looked out toward the river.

There were a number of large wooden trestle tables in the room, and Smith immediately commandeered one, laying his rucksack on it and opening the pack to pull out the briefcase.

That's what they were here to do, to finally make the delivery she'd been recruited for, or blackmailed into, depending on her mood, by Mr. Cassle less than forty-eight hours ago.

She was running out of time.

Jake, the man on the radio, had let them know Alejandro Campos was on his way. With the money delivered, and the flash drive retrieved, she wondered if she'd be released from any further duty. Campos had the weapons, and he was already dealing with Garcia, who had the documents. She wasn't sure there was any place for her in that part of the deal, or if there should be any place, considering her feelings.

She needed to get to St. Joseph.

And she wanted to nail Garcia's ass to a wall and ask him what he'd done to her sister.

Smith was right. Shooting the rebel captain had crossed her mind more than once, more than twice. There had been a couple of nights since her talk with Father Bartolo when she'd thought of little else. The old priest had been so self-righteous in his accusations, adamant and horrified, and full of threats and bluster, all of it directed at the sisters of St. Joseph, the whores of Cristobal. Julia, having once been married, had come under especially virulent attack—and then, after he'd worked himself into a lather, he'd screamed "The whore is pregnant!" and hung up.

Alarming, to say the least.

He'd only accepted her subsequent phone call through the intervention of his prelate and with a promise of a hefty donation to St. Mary's Parish. All she'd gotten for her trouble and her cash, though, was a guise of normalcy, prayers for her soul, and an assurance that God's will would prevail—another extremely alarming pronouncement.

And Julia in the middle of all of it, alone and isolated in the mountains of El Salvador with whores and rebels. Honey had seen no choice but to come. In truth, she couldn't have gotten here fast enough—and look at her, tumbled and muddy, with secret briefcases, and armies at the gates, and hiding out in old buildings with a man named Cougar.

He looked every inch a soldier this morning, armed with a pistol he'd holstered on his thigh and with a knife sheathed on his belt.

Honey had a greeting prepared for their host, something cool and professional, but when

Alejandro Campos strode through the door into the main room, all she could do was stare.

Oh, my, she thought. *Oh, my dear God, my.*

"Campos." Smith stepped forward and held out his hand, and the most beautiful, and most beautifully flawed, man in the world took it in his grip.

"Rydell," Campos said, then shifted his attention to her.

She did a quick check and confirmed that yes, indeed, her mouth had fallen open, and she closed it. There was nothing to be done about her sweaty shirt and her wild hair.

"Ms. York-Lytton." He made a slight bow. *"Encantado."*

She didn't speak Spanish, but she knew exactly what he'd said: *I'm charmed.*

So was she, ridiculously charmed. The last thing she'd expected was a gorgeous man in Armani.

Good Lord, he was tailored to perfection: black suit, crisp white shirt, even in this humidity, and a red silk tie that looked as if an artist had poured watercolors down it.

He had green eyes shot through with brown and gray, chiseled features, and dark, midnight-colored hair pulled back at the nape of his neck and held in place with a discreet band. He also had a scar running the length of his face.

"If you will?" he said, gesturing at the brief-case and getting straight to the point. *"Por favor."* Please.

She most certainly did please, feeling an unexpected sense of excitement. She'd dragged the damn thing with her all the way from Washington, D.C., without a clue as to what exactly was in it—and now she was about to find out.

She stepped forward and entered the six digits she had of the combination, three numbers for each of the cipher locks on the briefcase. Money was the likely contents, but she didn't know for sure. When she was finished, Campos stepped around the table and looked at what she'd done, and then he picked up the case and left, disappearing up a set of stairs at the far end of the room.

Her mouth fell open again.

That was it?

"But—" she said, turning to look at Smith. "But . . . but—"

He was grinning. "Did you think he was going to let you see what was inside?"

"Yes." Yes, she had. Most definitely. "I'm the one who brought it all the way here."

"For which I'm sure he is very grateful."

She couldn't believe it.

"So what's in it?" she asked.

"Money, I'd guess."

"But how much?"

"You're too curious."

"And you aren't?" She couldn't believe it.

He shook his head. "Not about the contents of cipher-locked briefcases. In this business, Honey, it's important to concentrate on your own job. It was your job to get it here, my job to protect you, and his job to deal with whatever is inside and use it. Next week, for me, it could easily be another briefcase, and another guy, and another deal going down."

Intellectually, she understood exactly what he was saying. It made perfect sense—and she still wanted to know what was in the black case marked with the letter Z. *Dammit.*

"What about another woman?" The words came out of nowhere, surprising her—and disappointing the hell out of her. Good God, how could she have said something so . . . so juvenile?

He let out a laugh. "I think it's going to take me more than a week to recover from you, sweetheart."

She gave him a look of pure annoyance, doing her best to salvage an embarrassing moment, and was about to ask him what in the world he meant—he had so much nerve—when his radio came to life.

At the same time, Campos came back down the stairs with the briefcase, almost at a run.

"We have troop movement," he said.

Smith nodded, said, "Yes," into the radio, and listened intently, while moving back to where he'd left his rucksack and the submachine gun on the table.

Campos strode to the front window, looked out, and swore under his breath. Then he turned to her.

"It has been a pleasure, Ms. York-Lytton," he said. "But if you would be so kind as to leave. Now." He gestured toward the doors leading into the building, before turning to Smith. "There is a passageway in the basement boiler room that leads to the river. I highly recommend you use it. And Ms. York-Lytton"—he glanced in her direction again—"your sister is at the villa. She arrived this morning with Garcia and the other nuns from St. Joseph."

The man had the most interesting way of reducing her to poleaxed surprise. Julia was here?

The news made her heart race, but it was also just more disaster piled on a disaster. This was the last place she wanted Julia to be, in the middle of all this.

She looked back out the window, and was amazed how quickly things had gone to hell. Hadn't she just thought her part in all this was over? And now she had to wonder if maybe the whole shebang was over.

Three trucks full of soldiers had roared up outside, one coming all the way to the factory, the other two trucks stopping about a hundred yards away. Dozens of men were piling out of the distant vehicles. Only five exited the truck stopped at the door—one of them Diego Garcia.

Whatever he was planning, she doubted if it was going to be to the advantage of anyone in the coffee plant—a point brought suddenly and graphically home by the appearance of the strange-looking shotgun-like weapons wielded by the soldiers with Garcia.

"M-79s," Smith said. "Forty-millimeter grenade launchers."

Grenades?

Dear God.

"Go," Campos ordered, unnecessarily. Smith had already shrugged into his rucksack, grabbed the submachine gun, and had ahold of her arm. He hustled her through the double doors, and Campos slammed them shut.

She heard a bar drop on the other side, which was not a comfort, not when she turned around.

No.

The one word was very clear in her mind, very succinct, and very, very true.

No, she was not going into any basement, not in this place.

Sunshine streaked through holes far up in the top of the building, but the contrast of the bright shafts of light only served to deepen the shadows surrounding the stories of rafters, catwalks, and freight elevators looming up on either side of the cavernous room. Down on the main floor, smoke rose from the depths of an old iron machine as it squealed and rumbled, and groaned with moving parts, the whole thing sounding like it was on the verge of exploding or breaking down.

There were cobwebs.

Big ones—and she knew exactly what that meant.

Spiders. Big ones.

There were bats.

She couldn't see them, but she knew they were there. The place was a damn cave, damp and dark and eerily still. Oh, there was noise from the machine, but nothing else moved in the whole place.

It looked like it was waiting.

Probably for her.

Oh, yeah.

She took a step back, an inadvertent retreat.

"I think—"

"Don't," Smith said, taking hold of her and moving her along at a quick pace. Their footsteps echoed on the wooden landing above the factory floor. Flights of stairs snaked down the walls everywhere she looked.

Snakes.

She couldn't believe it had taken her thirty seconds to think of snakes—and they'd be in the basement, probably hanging around any secret passageway to the river.

This was insane.

"I have a better plan," she insisted, having to half run to keep up with him.

"No, you don't."

"I'm not going down into any basement in here. This place is . . . is—"

"That's how we get to the river."

Us and the snakes, she thought.

"Let's just go out one of these windows, or find a door, and—"

He pulled her to a quick stop and stared down at her for the space of a breath, then two, and she realized he didn't look like the man she'd made love with in the back of the Land Cruiser. He looked like the man she'd met four months ago in the Hotel Palacio. Hard.

"There are soldiers out there, Honey, and the

best way for us to evade them is by getting as far away from here as possible without being seen, which means the basement passage to the river."

She didn't care. She had a bad feeling about the basement.

"I have a bad feeling about the basement."

He didn't look happy to hear it.

"Bad feeling?"

"Yes."

He gave a short quiet nod. "Okay, well, I've got a bad feeling, too, and my bad feeling is all about getting blown to friggin' smithereens by a goddamn grenade."

"That sounds pretty bad."

"It is." Guaranteed. He'd seen it. "Now let's move out."

CHAPTER TWENTY-SEVEN

That was the problem with small delays, Campos thought. They turned into huge problems. If Rydell and York-Lytton had not gotten lost, he would have had the cash at the villa and been able to expedite this damn deal, and be done with it by now.

But no. The short drive he'd had to make to the factory had turned the whole thing into a disaster. Give some people time to think, people like Diego Garcia, and you could bet they'd think up something stupid.

What was the captain planning out there? A Salvadoran standoff?

"Jake," he said into the radio, "what have we got here?"

"The other half of Garcia's army."

So this wasn't the group from the front gate. Garcia had dreamed up this piece of strategy long before he'd shown up at dawn. There was just no trusting some people.

Most people.

What a pain in the butt.

"If I end up having to give him all two million to save my ass, we're going to have to go in there tonight and get it back."

"I know, boss."

Goddammit. The last place he wanted to spend his evening was farther north on the Torola River, sneaking and crawling around in the woods, trying to steal two million dollars he should have been able to hold on to without so damn much trouble.

Diego Garcia had been a good CIA asset for the last ten years, but this whole deal with the plane, and the money, and the courier's pouch, not to mention the weapons, had the ring of a final hurrah, and this move, with the soldiers and the grenades, that was a pure, no-holds-barred and burn-your-bridges exit strategy. The man must have let a few good drug deals go to his head.

Rebel insurgency could be a good business, sure, but it paled in comparison to the money to be made in drugs. Nobody would deny it, but

Campos wasn't at all sure Garcia comprehended the intensely competitive nature of cocaine.

As a Salvadoran guerrilla leader, his enemies numbered two: the Salvadoran government and, give or take on any day of the week, the U.S. government. As a *narcotraficante* that number extrapolated and exploded.

Hell. The *pendejo* had made a bad decision, and if Campos couldn't get his end of it worked out real damn quick, he was going to get burned.

Or he could call it quits right now, have Jake lock everything down on his end, get out the LAWs, and start this party.

But first he needed to get those damn documents. That was the job.

"Señor Campos!" Garcia called from outside, demanding and getting his full attention.

Goddammit, this was going to cost him.

"Hold steady on your end, Jake. If I'm not back at the villa in an hour, or if anything blows up over here, I expect to be avenged in great style. My memoirs are in the wall safe in my office."

"Yeah," Jake said. "That's where I've been keeping mine, too."

Campos almost grinned, but the situation was just too damn grim.

"He's got three trucks here, big ones," he said. "They'd make great targets."

"Roger that."

Half a friggin' mile, and he'd gotten ambushed in his own backyard.

He slipped the radio into his pants pocket and pulled out his phone.

Oh, yeah, this was going to cost him, all right.

He punched in a coded number and waited for a long series of connections to be made.

When the call was finally answered in Cali, Colombia, he sold himself down the river to save Uncle Sam one more time.

"Tell Miguel Carranza it's Alejandro Campos."

If anyone could call off the dogs at his door, it was the head of the Cali cartel.

"Did you see that?" Honey asked.

"Yes." Smith had, a sudden movement below them on the factory floor.

"I-I don't think it's just the wind or something. I don't think there is any wind in here."

No, there wasn't. Not a breath of it.

Peering down into the gloom, he was betting on rats, quite a few, like about a hundred or more, a slow-moving wave of a hundred or more rats who probably owned the mortgage on this place.

Rats. Okay. He didn't mind rats.

"Just stay behind me," he said.

Campos had said the passageway was in a boiler room, which shouldn't be too hard to find once they got to the basement. Smith bet the flight of stairs disappearing under the floor on the other side of the factory was just the ticket.

"Did you see that?" she asked, almost tripping over him in her haste to get closer.

Yeah, he'd seen it—more rats, a couple dozen scurrying through the shadows cast by a tower of crates at the bottom of the stairs. Fifty- and hundred-pound sacks of coffee beans were piled every which way on the main floor, stacked against pylons, making small mountains against the walls, and providing excellent cover for the furry little bastards.

"Stay close." He loved giving orders she didn't have any trouble obeying.

She was good for another thirty seconds.

"What was that?"

"What was what?" If they were going to talk about every rat she saw, this was going to be the chattiest escape in the history of the world. He had a plan. Once they made it to the river, they'd circle back around to the villa. He'd seen a Beech Baron parked in a hangar close to the main house, and where there was a plane, there was bound to be a pilot. Flying out of Morazán would beat the hell out of driving.

Of course, his plan only worked if the whole place wasn't going up in flames and smoke by the time they got there.

"That." She grabbed onto his waistband, the word ending on a whispered squeal.

"There might be a couple of rats in here." Okay, more than a couple, more than a hundred, more than a couple of hundred.

Her hand tightened on his pants. "Rats?"

"Honey, rats are the least of our problems."

The rattling of the doors above them proved his point. An explosion outside slammed his point home with a vengeance. He doubled their pace, loosening her hand from his pants and taking hold of her arm.

Weapon at the ready, he hustled her across the main factory floor, breaking into a run when the way was clear, keeping as much machinery as possible between them and the stairs they'd just come down.

When voices sounded above them, he pulled her in front of him and gave her a small push.

"Go go go," he commanded.

"Alto!" The command came from above them. *Stop!*

And then somebody goddamn shot at them, the bullet pinging off the wall above his head.

Shit.

"Go! Now!"

She started down the stairs, him hot on her heels, until she made an abrupt about-turn and started back up at double speed, trying to push by him, her breath coming fast, her face white.

"Oh...oh, God, oh, so help...help." Her words were barely coherent. One look down explained it. She'd started a riot.

A rat riot.

They were streaming by her, running over her boots, running over each other, half crawling up her legs, squeaking and pitter-pattering, sharp nails scraping on the stairs, bodies piling over each other, scrambling, hundreds of the beasts.

Okay. Whatever. He didn't change directions, not for a second, and he didn't miss a step. He kept going down, sweeping the damn things off the steps with his boots, and crushing the ones that didn't move quick enough, and by God, he took Honey with him, hauling her close to his side, lifting her off the stairs.

When he put her down, he kept her moving despite her gasped protests and her ineffective attempt to stay on her tiptoes. Above them, booted feet pounded across the factory.

At the top of the stairs, some *pendejo* took the initiative and squeezed a few bursts of automatic weapon fire off into the basement.

Goddammit. Guerrillas behind them, rats in the middle, and no boiler room or secret passageway in sight, he couldn't believe he'd allowed himself and Honey to get caught like goddamn rats in a—

Rats.

When he heard feet hit the stairs, he pushed her behind a piece of rusting machinery and returned fire.

A rebel soldier let out a cry and fell the rest of the way down the stairs, creating momentary gridlock.

Rats.

If he'd been a damn rat with the run of the AC-130 coffee factory, he'd be opting for a riverside condo.

Follow the rats, yeah, that was classic combat strategy.

Sure it was.

Wherever they were coming in was where he and Honey were going out. He grabbed her again and took off running, pushing her ahead of him against the flow of all those running rats.

CHAPTER TWENTY-EIGHT

Campos's phone rang and rang in Diego Garcia's pocket, confiscated by the captain along with his .45 and his sheath knife. He'd palmed his Beretta Tomcat and his radio, so figured he was actually up by two, and before he'd lost his phone, he had made personal contact with Miguel Carranza.

Carranza had said he would consider his request.

Muy bien. Very well. But "consider" wasn't quite going to cut it, not when Garcia had ordered his soldiers to blow up one of the coffee sheds, an ill-thought-out act of intimidation Jake was going to take as a "green light" for mayhem.

And not when the captain's men were firing off rounds in his factory.

"Ms. York-Lytton will be worth far more to you alive," Campos suggested, dialing the combination into the cipher locks on the briefcase.

"Just open *la cartera, señor*."

Of course, if Carranza decided not to interfere, Campos would be saved from the bother of a return favor, which was no small thing. He wasn't sure he had the strength anymore for a Cali cartel payback. The risk in such a proposition could get unbearably high.

Also on the bright side, such as it was, Garcia had brought the CIA documents with him. They were in a brown briefcase on the table. The captain had planned to immediately make the exchange with Honoria York-Lytton for the two million dollars.

Campos could have warned him that nobody's plans were working out this morning, but kept silent. The truth would out soon enough—in about three seconds, to be exact. With the combinations dialed in, he popped open the briefcase and hoped for the best.

There was a long moment of silence as Garcia looked inside at the neat piles of cash tidily bricked into stacks and secured with paper bands.

"It is not enough," the captain said.

That was strictly a point-of-view problem, and

from Campos's point of view, half a million dollars was more than enough for the documents Garcia had stolen out of the Cessna.

But Campos wasn't getting paid for his personal opinions, not this morning.

"The woman," he said coldly. "She's stolen your money, Captain."

Garcia leveled a suspicious glare in his direction. "And not you?"

He took a step back from the briefcase, his hands raised. "For myself, I might have taken something, but I have a situation, and I cannot afford to lose my North American friends under my current circumstances. No, *Capitán,* I was told there would be two million dollars in a black briefcase to be delivered to me by Honoria York-Lytton." He gestured at the stacks of cash. "Perhaps this explains why she was so quick to leave once you arrived."

Garcia's gaze slid to the doors opening into the factory. He didn't look convinced.

"Perhaps," he said. "But the doors were barred from this side, *señor.*"

He was going to ignore that little piece of investigative reporting.

"Wherever she put the money is between here and San Salvador. I was assured, *Capitán,* that it was securely put on the plane with her in Panama City."

"The money came directly from Washington."

"*Exactamente.*"

Garcia thought for another few seconds, during which another burst of weapon fire sounded in the factory, and during which Campos worried that if he didn't hurry the hell up, any decision was going to be moot. Garcia had sent four of his five-man squad after the woman, which meant the odds were five to one, and that was counting Rydell, not Ms. York-Lytton. For himself, the odds were two to one, more than workable, especially when the two didn't know he was armed.

"*Césense disparando!*" Garcia finally ordered, talking into his radio. *Cease fire.*

Campos breathed a sigh of relief.

"We will take the woman alive," Garcia said.

Yes, Campos thought. Alive was good.

Dead was good, Smith thought, looking down at the last asshole to take a shot at him and Honey. The basement was a damn maze, full of old machine parts and discarded furniture, and stacks and piles of crates and junk. In order to get a clear shot, he'd had to circle back, and in order to circle back, he'd had to stash Honey someplace safe. He'd chosen the tunnel.

They'd finally found it at the back of the boiler room by doing exactly what he'd hoped would work—following the rats. He'd hated leaving her there, but the guy was dead, and that was three down, and one more to go, the scared one, the one trying to get back to the stairs and get the hell out of the basement.

He wasn't going to make it.

The bastard was too scared not to make a mistake, and when he did, Smith raised his submachine gun and squeezed the trigger.

Ohmigod.

Ohmigod.

Ohmigod.

Honey was holding herself so still in the tunnel she could hardly breathe. The faintest ray of light shone in from a long way away, but truly, it almost made things worse.

Because she could see them.

The rats.

Everywhere.

This was their home.

They weren't frightened here, like they'd been in the factory. They weren't running. They were milling about—milling about her feet, and milling about her legs, resting their front paws on her calves and sniffing her knees. They were touching her, crawling over her boots, and she was ankle-deep in water. They were big, and she was scared spitless, trembling from the top of her head to her toes, and trying to be so still.

The tunnel was made out of bricks, much of it crumbling, which gave the rats a foothold on the walls. She didn't dare look, but she thought there was one directly behind her, looking over her shoulder. She could almost feel its breath in her ear...almost see it reaching out with a long, slender leg, claws extending, its snakelike tail whipping back and forth as it readied itself... readied itself—

To pounce.

Fear, pure and stark, flashed through Honey's entire body in one paralyzing instant—and then she was running.

Running for her life, hell-bent, going the only way there was—out, toward the light, toward the end of the tunnel, her feet pounding, until they completely slipped out from under her.

CHAPTER TWENTY-NINE

Now, where in the world had she gotten off to? Smith wondered, stepping into the tunnel. She should be right here, right by the entrance. By God, when he put somebody someplace he expected them to stay the hell put, even if he'd stuck them right smack-dab in the middle of their worst phobic nightmare.

In his own defense, he hadn't had a choice, but that didn't solve the damn problem, did it?

Behind him, he heard the sound of voices approaching. He looked both ways, out into the boiler room, and down the long brick passage. There was only one way she could have gone, and he took it, heading for the light.

Honey knew what the term "maytagged" meant. It was an old river runner's way of saying "getting the stuffing whomped out of you." Her brother, the great adventurer, Haydon, had gotten maytagged in Westwater on the Colorado River, a classic clock-cleaning. Honey had never been maytagged—until today.

There wasn't any room for thought in the experience. It was purely visceral, every chaotic, agonizing, panic-inducing split second of it. Being churned up and down in a river current that wouldn't let go of her limp, disoriented body was not how she'd envisioned her end.

But there she was, too tired to thrash, not knowing which way was up, and going around one more time.

Then it spit her out.

She gasped in a lungful of air and realized a hand had ahold of the back of her T-shirt and was hauling her through the water. She looked and was surprised to see a large, dark-haired man, a stranger.

On shore, a woman was saying something, but Honey couldn't hear the words, only the voice. She tried to listen, but it took every ounce of concentration she could muster to keep her head above the water, to keep the river from washing into her mouth with every breath. Finally, she felt the river bottom, but she couldn't get her legs under her.

"Is she alive?"

"Yes, *patrona*."

The dark-haired man dragged her up on the bank and dropped to his knees. Honey couldn't even get to her knees. She lay there, exhausted, trying to keep her face out of the mud.

"That was a fight, Ari," the woman said. "The river almost won."

The man said something under his breath, and the woman gave a short laugh.

"You're an ox. I didn't doubt you for a moment."

Honey heard the woman draw closer, and when she knelt down, Honey could see her face.

"Honoria?" she said, bringing her hand to Honey's face and smoothing a tangled skein of hair off her cheek. She had a gentle touch.

Long dark braid, pale gray eyes, exquisitely elegant face, the woman was all slender legs, squared shoulders, and supreme confidence. It radiated out of every cell in her body. Honey had never felt anything like it.

"Honey," she said, and barely recognized her own voice, it was so harsh and raspy.

God, she hurt. She felt sick and beaten, and she could hardly breathe. She was going to have bruises on top of bruises. There were boulders in the river, and she'd been smashed up against them at least three times.

One of the woman's eyebrows arched in a graceful curve. "Honey? How sweet." And then she laughed again. "Where is Rydell, Honey?"

"Behind me. In the . . . the factory. There are men, soldiers, shooting, chasing us."

The woman's smile faded, and she looked up toward the man. "We need to move to cover."

"Yes, *patrona*."

The woman caught Honey's gaze again and smoothed her hand across Honey's brow.

"Your ankle is broken," the woman said calmly, her voice so soothing. "So don't try to get up and run off anywhere."

And with that, she rose to her feet and walked away, leaving Honey in the mud.

The first thing Smith saw when he got to the end of the tunnel was Honey lying on the bank, not moving. Then he saw the red laser dot painting the back of her head—and it made his blood run cold.

She was in somebody's sights.

"Hello, Rydell. It's been a long time," a woman

said, her voice coming from out of the trees farther up the shore.

Not long enough. *Sonuvabitch*.

The red dot leveled at Honey's skull did not waver. The hand holding the laser-sighted gun was inhumanly steady. Red Dog was that steady. Kid Chaos was that steady. And so was Irena Polchenko.

Even after six years, he didn't doubt the voice.

"You're not here for this woman, Irena," he said. This was not going to happen, not Honey's death, not today.

"No. You're right, Rydell. I came all this way for you. After Peru, I didn't think I could afford not to come after you."

Fuck. He'd been right.

He lifted his hands to either side of his head, palms out in surrender. "To finish the job?"

"To correct a mistake. How did Abdurrashid miss?"

"He didn't miss. He never took the shot."

"I heard the shot, Rydell."

He was looking into the grove of trees, trying to locate her. "You heard Tirandaz shoot Abdurrashid. He's the one who took the Stingers that day. It was a classic double-cross. Who went down in your Piper in the Hindu Kush?"

"Some fool who thought he'd gotten a good

price for a plane by besting a woman in negotiating a deal."

A fool was right. If there was one thing Smith had learned over the years, it was never to underestimate a woman based on gender alone—with a few exceptions.

His gaze fell on Honey, and a couple more emotions than he was used to having flooded into his system. There were limits on how much physical abuse a Park Avenue princess could take without breaking.

He'd broken her today, her ankle for sure, from the odd angle of her foot, maybe a few other things.

He took a breath and forced his gaze back into the trees.

"If you came for me, it's me you should take." And he knew it meant "take out."

"I could take you both."

"I know perfectly well what this is about, Irena, and I've taken precautions." He was a pretty good liar, even on an off day. When the stakes were high, he tended to be a great liar.

"Precautions?" There was the barest hint of doubt in her voice.

He liked it.

"Joint Ops Central in Lima is an intelligence nightmare. I'm impressed with how fast you've been able to work, but I'm not surprised you found out it was me on the surveillance op. I took out some insurance, just in case."

"What kind of insurance?"

He could hear someone splashing down the tunnel, maybe more than one person. They weren't talking, whoever they were, but he didn't dare turn around and look.

"The kind where as long as I'm alive, your secret goes nowhere, and the minute I die, five guys at the DEA in Washington, D.C., get a time-delayed e-mail explaining what they need to look for in order to bring you down. As long as I keep coding in the delay, the e-mail stays put in a draft file. The minute the timer goes off on the draft file, the e-mail is automatically sent. And, Irena?"

"Yes."

"The computer housing the e-mail is not my personal computer. It's not at my house, or in my office."

"I suppose you are now including the woman in your insurance policy."

"Absofuckinglutely."

From behind him, he heard Campos's voice. "Do you have a clear shot?"

"No," he said very quietly. "She's in the trees, and I doubt if she's alone."

"I saw your handiwork in the basement. Good job," Campos said. "I added one more to the pile, and I have Garcia right here with me, along with the CIA's documents in a brown briefcase, and a certain amount of money in the black one."

Certain amount? Smith could guess what that meant.

"How much?"

"Five hundred thousand."

"I have cash, Irena," he called out louder. "And a promise to keep my word. You'll know if I break it, but I won't. Your secret is no part of what we do, and neither is the woman. Let her go. Take the money."

Smith knew he was a perfect target, and he knew every breath he took could be his last. If she called his bluff, he'd never know it.

"If I die here, and she kills Honey, would you please track her to the ends of the earth and put a bullet in her brain?" he said softly to Campos.

The momentary silence told him the guy was considering his answer carefully. Smith liked that, no matter which way he replied.

"For the killing of an *inocente*? Yes. It's enough that we die, when our time comes."

"Sentimental fools," Garcia said harshly. "You will both die for this day's work."

"Hand me the briefcase," Smith said, reaching his hand back.

"No!" Garcia shouted. "The money is mine. The deal is mine. My men will come and—"

A huge explosion rocked the earth, and then another. The tunnel shuddered, but held, as a fireball rolled up into the sky from the direction of the river road and was quickly followed by another.

Truck versus LAW, Rydell thought. *LAW wins every time.*

"The money, Rydell," Irena yelled—and he took the case from Campos and slung it out along the edge of the river. It sailed thirty feet before landing near the trees—and in that time, Diego Garcia died. It happened in an instant. The captain lunged after the briefcase, and the red dot moved from Honey's head to Garcia's chest, *pop pop,* and it was over, and the red dot was back and holding steady on Honey.

Geezus, Smith thought. He needed to be spending more time on the firing range.

Behind him, Campos let out a short breath. "Did you see that?"

"Hell, yeah."

A large, dark-haired man came out of the trees to retrieve the briefcase, and then Irena spoke again. "Tell Alejandro Campos the hit is a gift from Miguel Carranza. The money I'm taking from you, Rydell. What is the combination on the locks?"

From behind him in the tunnel, Campos recited the numbers.

"Seven, eight, zero, four, four, two across the top," Smith said loud enough for his voice to carry. "And the same backward across the bottom."

He was answered with silence, until finally, she confirmed.

"All is as it should be."

The red dot never wavered from Honey.

Then, to his surprise, Irena stepped out from behind the trees and gave him a short nod.

"*Dos vidanya.* Until next time," she said, and melted back into the copse. Two seconds later, the red dot disappeared from the back of Honey's head.

It took him less than that to swing himself around the crumbling edge of the tunnel, and less than thirty seconds to get down the bank to the shore. He'd understood what had happened to her the minute he'd seen her so wet and muddy on the shore. The bank under the passageway had been eroded away, especially after last night's rain, and the floor at the end of the tunnel had collapsed. Anyone caught unexpectedly by the fact would have fallen into the churning eddy of the river below.

Goddamn. The thought frightened him almost as much as the way she looked.

"Honey," he said, gently touching her face and looking her over from head to toe. There wasn't any blood, and no head wounds, and when she moved her hand to take hold of his, he felt a sense of relief.

"My ankle," she said, her voice a little raw.

"Yeah, baby. I think it's broken. Do you hurt anywhere else?"

"No . . . no, I—" She reached up for him, and he pulled her into his arms.

In the distance, he could hear Campos on the radio, calling for transportation.

CHAPTER THIRTY

Campos's home was in an uproar: Jake outside directing traffic, rebels, and the fallout of their early morning fracas; Rydell in Campos's largest guest suite, hovering over Honey; Sister Julia in the guest suite, hovering over Honey; Sofia in the guest suite, hovering over and working on Honey; three of Isidora's littlest ones in the guest suite, making nuisances of themselves; and Campos only there as a concerned host.

The woman's ankle was broken. Campos had once been shot and received less attention. Hell, he'd been shot yesterday and received less attention.

"Conchetta, Paco, Rosella, *váyanse*." He shooed the children out and wondered if there would be lunch today. He supposed he could go to the kitchen and find out. As he recalled, Lily Robbins was in the kitchen with Isidora. Possibly, they were making lunch.

He hoped quite a lot of it.

A few officers from the Salvadoran army had flown in by helicopter to verify Garcia's death, with Campos's men holding the rebel soldiers until Salvadoran troops arrived to take them into custody.

He wasn't planning on feeding the rebel soldiers, but the officers should have a table.

He wasn't planning on delivering Rydell's fax, either, the one telling the man his partner in Lima had been killed. Plenty of other people had that piece of bad news. Rydell would hear it soon enough.

The sound of crying coming from the next suite down the hall had him stopping to take a look. Ah, yes. Sister Teresa.

He'd have to take her in, create a place for her on his staff. Isidora would figure it all out for him. The church certainly wasn't going to allow her to stay at St. Joseph, not even with Sister Rose as her advocate. No, the woman was an outcast, with two dead lovers and a heap of broken vows.

When he reached the kitchen, he stopped just outside the door and looked in. Ms. Robbins was, indeed, helping Isidora, the two of them making a good team, even with Lily's less-than-fluent Spanish. Food preparation, he decided, was probably one of the universal languages, like math. Everyone who'd ever been in a kitchen knew how one worked.

Jewel had never cooked a meal in her life.

He hadn't minded.

Miguel Carranza had rather miraculously contracted a nearly instantaneous hit on Diego Garcia in response to his phone call this morning, going above and beyond the request, and he minded that very much. Payback was going to be hell. His only hope lay in the assassin. Possibly, there was something in the conversation between Irena Polchenko and Rydell that he could use to his advantage with Miguel Carranza.

He'd have to think that one through very carefully.

Lunch smelled divine, with soup pots steaming, and meat roasting, and Lily wrapped in a white chef's apron. He liked lanky women, and Lily Robbins was lanky with cleavage, a fantasy come true. Another time, another place, maybe he could have indulged. But with the state of his life, it would take twenty years and another country before he could involve himself with someone like Lily Robbins, a schoolteacher, for crying out loud.

Schoolteachers frowned on drug dealers, and for all intents and purposes, he was a drug dealer, and he meant *all* intents and purposes. There was no hedging those bets, not as long as he was in El Salvador. His cover was deep and hard-won, and his life depended on it. So no, there would be no Lily Robbins in his future.

But he could take her home. By anyone's standards, he had pulled off the coup of the week, if not the whole damn month. The mission was an unqualified success. They had the documents, the flash drive, and three fourths of the money, the mil and a half he'd put in his safe in the AC-130 building.

For that, between the CIA and State, there shouldn't be any problem fulfilling his request for a private jet to meet them in San Salvador this afternoon. After lunch, with Sofia's approval for Honey to travel, he was planning on flying Rydell, Honey, Sister Julia, and Lily in his Beech to Ilopango. From there, they'd board the jet to Albuquerque, and from Albuquerque, he'd take the York-Lytton sisters to Washington, D.C., and probably Rydell as well. The man didn't look inclined to leave Honey's side. A couple of days out of Morazán wasn't such a bad idea for him, either. Too bad he couldn't spend them in Albuquerque.

Going home would be a nice surprise to Ms. Robbins, and he was grateful he could offer her at least that.

Thirty thousand feet over the Gulf of Mexico had never looked so good to Honey, in no small part because of the man sleeping at her side, and Julia.

Julia was coming home.

"I still can't believe Father Bartolo implied I was the one who was pregnant," Julia said, shaking her head.

"Well, remember, I said he only implied it. He didn't state it as a fact."

"But it's why you came, Honey, and look what happened. Good Lord, you've been in danger the whole time, and you got hurt." Julia reached over from her seat and took Honey's hand. "I'm so sorry, Honey."

"You're not the reason I got hurt," she said for the hundredth time. "That had to do with crumbling tunnels and raging rivers."

"Which you wouldn't have been anywhere near, if not for—"

"Shhh," Honey interrupted her sister. "The

only thing I can possibly blame you for is not writing enough for at least a few letters to get through."

The state of the mail system in Morazán was exemplary. But there was a bit of a hitch between St. Joseph School and Orphanage and the post in Cristobal, where the mail was processed. The hitch, they'd decided, being the cook's helper whose job it was to gather the mail from the school's drop box and make sure it all safely arrived in Cristobal. Julia had promised to check the pack bags the boy used on his burro when she returned. They were both guessing there would be old letters stuffed here and there in the bags, or crumpled up in the corners.

And there it was, despite everything, the hard truth. Julia was going to Washington, D.C., with Honey, yes, and was happy to be visiting her family, but then she was going home, and home was St. Joseph.

It wasn't just the lack of letters that made keeping in touch so difficult. It was the work, Julia had said. Between the children, and teaching, and her devotions, there was little time left to dwell on the outside world, and therein lay her peace and her hope.

The work was a comfort to her.

Honey would never deny Julia her comfort.

They'd been through too much together, and if ever Julia was in need, Honey would always be there, the young woman was so very precious to her. But perhaps it was time to try to at least begin to let go. Or maybe not. Even the thought hurt.

El Salvador wasn't the only country in the world with orphans, but it was the country with Julia's orphans, and Honey had a feeling Alejandro Campos would be a more reliable connection than Garcia. Though Julia had assured her that whatever the man's faults, and they had been legion, Diego Garcia had been a great help to St. Joseph.

And if Campos fell through for her, she had Brett Jenkins III in Panama City who would always take her calls, and the elusive Mr. Cassle who knew everything and everybody. But mostly she had Smith, at least for now, and at thirty thousand feet and heading home, for now was enough.

Lily had never flown in a private jet before. Neither had she ever seen a grenade explode, or a truck explode, or seen a cold-blooded murder, or watched a man die. The experiences had marked her for life. She would never forget the pilot's death, or the young soldier's final plea.

"Would you like another soda, Ms. Robbins? Or wine?" the man across from her asked.

She wouldn't forget him, either, Alejandro Campos. She hadn't expected to witness violence in El Salvador, but its existence there did not surprise her.

He surprised her, in every way.

From the moment she'd walked into his kitchen, soaking wet and frightened, he had treated her with kindness. The biggest drug dealer in Morazán Province was the most gracious man she'd ever met, and she didn't know if that said something about American men, or the men in Albuquerque, or if it simply said something about Alejandro Campos.

"Wine would be nice. Chardonnay."

He lifted his hand, and his servant, Max, brought the Chardonnay out of the galley and poured her a glass.

"Now, where were we?" Mr. Campos said. "With Diane, right? One of the girls in your tenth grade Advanced Placement human geography class? You were saying her essay on Native Americans had proven to be exceptionally insightful."

Yes, that's exactly what she'd been saying, and Mr. Campos had been listening, and so it had been going for the last four hours. She couldn't remember the last time she'd held a man's attention quite so thoroughly, at least with her clothes on. Her ex-husband, Tom, had always noticed her naked, but even sex had started to wear thin for them by the end.

"Yes," she said. "Diane managed to fairly successfully integrate a theory on tribal identity with a position on genetic memory put forth by James Waddel in his book on the Celts." And so it had gone, and so it went, topic after topic, with Mr. Campos sometimes resting his chin in his hand and watching her with rapt attention as she rambled on about high school whatnot and geographical flotsam.

By the next change in subject, he had pulled a pen out of his coat pocket and requested a piece of paper from Max.

"I'm going to give you a phone number," he said, jotting it down on the paper. "For obvious reasons, I don't carry business cards, and this number I'm giving you will not connect you directly with me." He looked up and smiled, and the warmth of the expression went straight through her. "I don't suppose that sounds very commendable, does it?"

"I'm fine with that," she said, for some reason knowing she did not want to lose touch with him, if it was at all possible.

"Good," he said, and continued writing. "If, for whatever reason, you ever need to contact me, this number will suffice. I pick up my messages every day, and am usually able to return calls within a day or two."

He folded the paper in half and handed it over.

"If you need me, Ms. Robbins, or if I can be of service, don't hesitate to call. And now, if you'll excuse me, I believe we're ready to begin our descent into Albuquerque. It has been a pleasure." He rose from his seat and gave her a short bow, before heading into the cockpit.

She looked over at the other passengers. Sister Julia liked Campos, and so did the man named Rydell. Lily hadn't really had a chance to talk with Sister Julia's sister, but none of these people seemed to either notice or care what the enigmatic Mr. Campos did for a living.

Glancing down, she opened the paper and looked at the number. She would never use it, of course. What possible need could a schoolteacher from New Mexico ever have for a drug dealer from El Salvador?

None, she hoped.

She hoped it with all her heart—and yet she was glad to have the number.

CHAPTER **THIRTY-ONE**

Denver, Colorado

Of all the strange twists of the day, this was by far the most interesting, Campos thought. Absolutely fascinating, and probably, considering his real line of work, after this many years, inevitable.

In Albuquerque, Rydell had made a request for a change in destination from Washington, D.C., to Denver. From there, he'd promised Campos, he would see the women home.

Granting the request had been a matter of course. Campos liked Denver for a lot of reasons, some of them very personal. He knew the city, but he hadn't been there in years, for a lot of reasons, some of them very personal, like the one driving across the tarmac, heading for the jet.

The sun was just beginning to set on a long

summer day in the Mile High City, but he would have recognized Corinna anywhere. The 1967 Pontiac GTO was pure classic, a navy blue beast with a Ram Air 400 under the hood and a four-speed on deck.

The young man getting out from behind the steering wheel, Kid Chaos, was also easily recognizable, but only because he was the spitting image of his brother, J. T. Chronopolous.

Yeah, he'd heard the news about J.T. a few years ago and cried himself to sleep with a bottle of Scotch for a week, and then done it again a month later, and a month later after that. J.T. had been the best of them, always.

His loss still hurt.

Campos watched Kid walk across the tarmac to greet Rydell and the two women, and he saw the curious glance the younger man tossed in his direction—but that was as far as it would go. Kid would not recognize him, especially from a distance, not in sunglasses, with long hair, and a Hugo Boss suit.

He'd stayed by the jet specifically to keep that distance. He always kept his distance.

But a few yards of distance and a pair of sunglasses weren't enough to hide him from the man getting out of the passenger side of the Goat.

Christ. Dylan Hart.

Campos almost grinned. Yeah, there had been a few years when he'd thought they were one and the same.

Dylan was talking into a cell phone, until the boss of SDF Steele Street locked his gaze on a man he must have thought he'd never see again.

Campos couldn't have called; that wasn't the way the deal worked. And yet he knew Dylan must have wondered about him. They all must have wondered, Hawkins, and Creed, and Quinn, and J.T.

Water under the bridge, he thought. He'd made his choice, and the only regrets he'd had were recent.

He saw Dylan say something brief into the phone, then close the cell and drop it in his pocket—and all the while, his gaze was steady across the tarmac, his expression unreadable.

When the pilot poked his head out of the hatch to say they were good to go, Campos acknowledged him with a glance, then looked back to Dylan. Rydell, and the women, and Kid were busy getting into Corinna, and Campos doubted if any of them saw Dylan give him a short salute.

But he saw it, and that's what counted.

He nodded, once, the barest movement, then turned and walked back up the ramp.

CHAPTER **THIRTY-TWO**

738 Steele Street, Denver, Colorado

"You're staring at my ass."

"Yes, I am." It's what he did in the mornings, when she woke up and spent the first hour lying around in bed.

"You've been staring at my ass for three weeks."

"And it's looking good, babe."

"We've got to stop meeting like this."

"No, we don't." He liked meeting like this, over her bare ass, a hot-off-the-presses copy of the *Rocky Mountain News*, and a steaming cup of coffee. It was so perfect, he planned on doing it every day for the rest of his life. He just hadn't told her yet.

"You've got to stop reading that local rag and get some real news," she said from her end of the bed, where she'd spread out the Sunday edition of *The Washington Post.*

"And what does Darcy Delamere have to say today?"

"Not much," she admitted. "The girl hasn't been getting around to many parties lately."

"Well, I heard she broke her ankle." He took a sip of coffee.

Green eyes slanted him a teasing look from over a shoulder so soft and creamy, he dreamed about it.

"I heard she got a new lover and hasn't been out of bed since May." She wiggled her eyebrows at him.

Normally, he would have laughed, but she'd just given him a really great idea.

"You want to do it in the kitchen again?"

"No," she said, surprising him. They'd had a great time in the kitchen. "I think I still have meringue on my butt from last night."

"No, you don't." He'd gotten it all. With his tongue. How could she have forgotten?

"Nope. I think there's still a little bit back there."

He was looking right at her ass, and he could guarantee there wasn't a—oh.

"Oh, yeah. I think you're right." Of course she was right. She thrived on being right, especially about things like meringue on her butt, and how many Salvadoran orphans she could support through the Kardon Foundation, and what scuzzball politician she could take down next week in Washington, D.C.

The girl was multifaceted.

Kind of like the diamond burning a hole in his pants pocket. He glanced over and saw his slacks in a pile on the floor. They were lying right next to a little black dress, the classic little black dress he'd taken off her last night.

Blondes looked good in black.

Of course, they looked better naked, but right next to naked was black, as in lace, and after lace, he'd take spandex, and after spandex, he'd take above-the-knee, jersey knit, little black dresses.

"I have a proposition for you," he said, and that got her interest.

"Is this anything like the proposition you gave me last week in Osaka?"

"No." That proposition had been very Oriental, with a bit of accompanying paraphernalia, and a little bit of this and that, and she'd loved it, and he'd loved her loving it.

"Is it like the proposition you gave me two weeks ago in Key West?"

"Ah, no." He grinned. Key West had been fun.

She was fun, and a good traveler. He could see why her brothers invited her on all their adventures.

"Hmmmm," she mused. "Not Osaka, not Key West. Is this like that Houston Hustle you showed me?"

He shook his head, and her brows drew together.

"So what, exactly, have you dreamed up... Cougar?"

He did laugh at that, and reached down to pull her up next to him. "How's the ankle feeling today?"

"Good." She snuggled in close, but wasn't dissuaded. That was the reporter in her. "So tell me what you've got in mind."

"Collusion," he said, going for broke. "And delusion."

She was a quick girl, with a damn good memory. She looked up at him, her expression serious. "That's what you called the chapter you were going to write on marriage in San Luis."

"And you called yours 'Sanctioned Oppression in Patriarchal Societies.'"

She was quiet for a long time, real quiet, and just looking at him, and he began to wonder if he'd really jumped the gun.

"We're having an awful lot of fun together," she said.

"It's more than fun, Honey, and you know it." And it was. He didn't know how to describe what he felt for her, except it was different from all the wild hormone lust he was used to calling love. For all the hot sex, it was the connection he craved with her. Watching her think had become his favorite pastime. Ninety percent of the women he'd ever dated had been smart, and funny, and beautiful, and the other ten percent simply hadn't been funny—and okay, yeah, there were a few in there who maybe simply hadn't been smart.

But that wasn't it with Honey. She was everything any guy would want, and none of that was why he wanted her.

"I have something kind of crazy to tell you," he said.

"Crazier than us getting married?"

"Yes," he said slowly. "It's about the day we met."

"That wasn't crazy," she said. "That was kismet."

"Yeah, that's what I mean. I remembered something a couple of weeks ago, about my mother, and it got me thinking about the day we met."

"Thinking what?" she asked, when he paused.

"Well, normally, I am not the sort of operator

who leaves his observation position to save a woman who isn't a part of my mission. But when I saw you there, I barely even thought. I just moved. I mean, I love how it worked out, but I've always wondered why I got out of my chair and left my beer."

She looked a little skeptical at that. "And?"

"And it was because of the dress, the polka-dot dress. My mother was wearing a polka-dot dress in the photograph I told you about, the one I looked at hundreds of times as a kid, the one that shows where she was hurt, and there you are, another woman in a polka-dot dress, and man, I can see the hurt coming for you from a mile away. So I just get up and move."

"Wow," she said softly.

"But that's not the amazing thing."

"It isn't?"

"No," he said. "The amazing thing is that you turned out to be the perfect person for me."

Her arms came around him really tightly. "And that's why you think we should get married?"

"No," he said, holding her closer and smoothing his hand up the satiny curve of her back. "I think we should get married because I love you, Honey, and I want to be there for you through all the thick and thin of it."

"I want to be there for you, too."

"Is that a yes?"

She stretched up and kissed him, once, sweetly on the cheek. "It's a yes for now, but after we're married, I think we should go steady for a while, until we get through the break-in period."

"Break-in period?" He liked the sound of that. "Isn't that what we've been doing for the last three weeks? Breaking in?"

"Yes," she said. "But we've got a ways to go, yet."

"Here," he said, leaning over the side of the bed and fishing around in his pocket until he found the ring. "Maybe this will help."

"Ohmigosh, Smith," she gasped. "It's beautiful."

Yeah, he liked the way it looked. It was platinum, with a couple of stones in one spot, and kind of a bigger stone in the middle.

"I thought this part was neat," he said, pointing out a sweep of really tiny diamonds encrusted on the band. He'd loved all the concentrated sparkle of it, and he'd figured she would, too. It reminded him of her, the cool platinum and brilliance of the ring, and then the unexpected part, the hot center and the sparkle of all the tiniest diamonds.

"The pavé," she said, slipping it on her finger and holding it up into the light.

Yeah, the pavé, he thought. He was all about the pavé—but he wasn't going to tell her just yet. He'd spilled enough of his heart on the table for now. He'd save the pavé part for later, after the break-in period.

ABOUT THE AUTHOR

TARA JANZEN lives in Colorado with her husband, children, and two dogs, and is now at work on her next novel. Of the mind that love truly is what makes the world go 'round, she can be contacted at *www.tarajanzen.com*. Happy reading!

READ ON
FOR A SNEAK PEEK AT

CUTTING LOOSE

BY TARA JANZEN

COMING FROM DELL
IN WINTER 2008

TARA JANZEN

Author of *On the Loose*

A mission
so hot, it's off
the charts...

Cutting
LOOSE

CUTTING LOOSE
ON SALE WINTER 2008

CHAPTER **ONE**

Langley, Virginia

Alejandro Campos slowed his rented black Mercedes to a crawl, carefully negotiating a serpentine series of heavy gray concrete pylons approaching the security checkpoint at the main entrance to CIA headquarters. The positioning of the barricades looked haphazard.

It wasn't.

NASA's astrodynamics lab in Huntington had designed the maze. At four miles an hour or less, traffic flowed smoothly through the pattern. Anything over four mph guaranteed smashing a quarter panel against a pylon at an angle guaranteed to put a vehicle broadside to a guaranteed line of fire from the armored guard station at the end of the serpentine.

The CIA liked their guarantees.

They liked their double guarantees, like the mirrored third-story windows in the main building overlooking the approach. Behind the windows was another NASA-designed product, an array of computer-directed weaponry with a broad range of capabilities, from putting a bullet neatly through a single driver's eyeball to turning an armored vehicle into a smoking tangle of twisted metal—or to do anything in between, depending on the perceived threat level. In terms of firepower, the imposing guard station at street level was mostly for show.

Even so, the security officer at the checkpoint was carrying a custom single-action .45 caliber sidearm in a tactical SWS polymer holster with four spare magazines on his duty belt. The pistol's rosewood grips showed wear marks, an indication of the amount of use it got—plenty, probably at one of the agency's off-site high-tech qualification ranges.

Campos pulled the Mercedes to a stop, and the officer approached the driver's window, simultaneously pressing a switch on his multifunction communications device. Everything that happened during the officer's contact with the vehicle, both audio and video, would be transmitted in real time to the control center's computer inside the main building.

Campos rolled his window down and deliberately placed both hands, palms open, on top of the steering wheel.

"Good morning, sir," the officer said pleasantly. "Could I see your entry authorization?"

The guy was hard and lean, about thirty-five, with a layer of Kevlar soft body armor just visible inside the open collar of his uniform shirt.

"Certainly," Campos said, reaching onto the dash, securing a business card, and handing it over. There wasn't a doubt in his mind that besides being courteous and efficient, the guard was capable of handling most situations without third-story assistance.

The man entered the numeric sequence written on the back of the card into a PDA and viewed the response on the screen.

"Look directly at me," he instructed, then aimed the lens of the PDA's digital camera toward Campos. He compared the image with whatever else was on the screen. "Is there anything more you would like to tell me, sir?"

"Zachary," Campos said, just loudly enough for the officer to hear him clearly.

Zachary Prade—the name he'd used the first time he'd come to Langley, and according to his orders, the name they were giving back to him, at least for a while. Alejandro Campos had served its purpose.

It was the way of things.

The guard nodded and handed him a visitor's pass.

"I'm clearing you for building entry, but not through security screening. Park your vehicle in the Alpha Two section on your right, proceed inside the main entrance, and wait outside of screening for your escort. Should pick you up within ten minutes. Any questions?"

"No," he said, and put the Mercedes in gear.

A few minutes later, he was heading for the building, and it occurred to him that in all his years with the CIA, this was the first time he had ever, literally or figuratively, walked in through the front door.

Four sublevels down, his escort swiped a keycard through the cipher-lock reader on a door marked "Forensics." The temperature inside the room was a good ten degrees cooler than the hallway, which made his suit jacket almost comfortable.

Campos noted three rows of what appeared to be oversized stainless-steel filing drawers set into the wall on the left, an assortment of analytical instruments along the remaining walls, and a steel examining table in the center of the room.

Perfect. A morgue.

He wasn't surprised.

Given his involvement in a recent debacle in El Salvador and his report, he could even guess who the guest of honor would be. *Hell*.

There were three individuals already in the room, two men and a woman. They were standing close to the table and the thick black body bag laying on top of it, unzipped. He recognized the woman and one of the men immediately, then recognized the other man, but only just barely. Despite an active, some might say *hyper*-active, history of correspondence between the two of them, conducted through various cut-outs, intermediaries, and back channels, he hadn't actually seen the man who had recruited him in over twelve years.

"Hello, Zach," the man said, turning to face him but leaving both hands inside the deep pockets of his lab coat.

"Alex," he said, acknowledging the case officer. "Are you planning on telling me what's important enough to terminate my cover?"

On the flight up from San Salvador, all by himself, he'd compiled a pretty good short list of reasons for Alejandro Campos to disappear, and his partner, Joya Molara Gualterio, could probably add, oh, a million or so even better reasons why his butt had needed to be pulled out of Central America. Even his doctor had thought it was time for him to go. He had no problem with that part. He'd get reassigned.

Okay, "no problem" was stretching things a bit. He had a couple of problems with it, all of them personal. But this little trip to Langley had required a catalyst beyond any reason to pull him out of deep cover—and that's what had been eating him since he'd gotten the call. A lot of shit had hit the fan in El Salvador three weeks ago, and suddenly, after twelve years, he was face-to-face with his boss. It wasn't a coincidence, not in his business.

"Yes, of course," Alex answered, a look of weariness passing over his features. "But, as always, first things first."

"Right. And what exactly might those be?" he asked evenly, already knowing at least part of the answer. Hell, it was stretched out on the table.

"First of all, Zach," Alex said, "allow me to introduce Charles Kesselring and Amanda van Zandt. Charles is Deputy Director, Operations, and Amanda is Deputy Director, Intelligence." The two senior officers each gave Zach a polite nod, which he returned.

The introductions were required by agency protocol, but were completely unnecessary. He knew perfectly well who the current DDO and DDI were, and he knew that having the two of them in the same place, especially this place, at the same time, probably meant a situation serious enough to have foreign policy implications—the catalyst, and the reason he'd been popping antacids since he'd gotten on the plane early this morning.

"And," Alex continued, "may I regretfully direct your attention to the body of Mark Devlin, recently killed while on assignment in Central America." The body bag. The guest of honor, literally.

Zach recognized the dead man as one of the agency's contract aviators, a hardcore former Marine who had been a frequent visitor at Alejandro Campos's plantation in northern El Salvador. He had known the man by another name, a name that would never again be spoken by anyone inside the agency.

"Your most recent field report included a videotape of Devlin's death at the hands of CNL guerrillas after his Cessna was shot down in Morazán," Alex said. "This tape was filmed by one Lily Robbins, an American schoolteacher from Albuquerque, New Mexico, whose return to the States you expedited at the conclusion of the Morazán incident. We are here to discuss Robbins's possible connection with the flash drive from Devlin's downed aircraft."

Zach recalled the incident in painful detail. Smith Rydell, a DOD operator, had recovered a classified flash drive from the CIA's Cessna, days after the critically injured Devlin had been captured by the CNL. No one on the U.S. side had been aware of the pilot's fate until the guerrillas, in an uncharacteristic gesture of decency, had delivered his body to the Catholic mission in San Cristobal for transport back to the States. After that, the entire incident had exploded into a violent tangle of conflicting agendas involving more actors and intrigue than an Italian opera, including cocaine smugglers, arms dealers, international assassins, and Salvadoran insurgents, not to mention deep-cover CIA intelligence assets. The agency had at first suspected Lily Robbins of being an agent for at least one of the players in the drama, but eventually agreed with Zach's assessment that she had simply been in the wrong place at the wrong time.

At least they *had* been in agreement, but now—well, now he wished he had a couple more antacids to pop.

"What kind of connection are you thinking?" he asked evenly.

Van Zandt picked up the conversation, speaking with a clear, refined eastern accent.

Zach guessed Vassar, or maybe Yale, definitely not Albuquerque.

"We have downloaded and analyzed the contents of the flash drive," she said. "The files are extensive, mostly routine field reports and other regional data. The largest file, however, initially downloads as an overwritten area of the device's memory, appearing to contain only random bytes with no recoverable data." She paused, her gaze holding his.

"I'm guessing 'appearing to contain' is the operative part of that sentence," he prompted.

"Correct," she said. "Using the appropriate algorithm, the file can be reordered into random character strings. That, by itself, doesn't accomplish anything of value. When paired with the proper literal key, however, the file becomes readable. In this case, the encoded file was created using a true random one-time literal key."

Zach knew about literal keys. The cryptographic method was centuries old, and had fallen out of favor in the computer age. The technique involved mapping plain-text characters through random characters to create encoded text. If done properly, the only thing a cryptographer could tell from the encoded text alone was that each character was somewhere in the alphabet from A to Z, with each letter being equally probable, assuming that the plain-text had started out as English. In other words, a computer could make the encoded text mean anything at all, with equal odds of success for each decryption version. Systematic computer codes, including computer-generated pseudo-random keys, could eventually be broken by other computers. Codes using true random keys, however, could be broken only if the same key were used repeatedly. If the key was only used once, computer analysis could not recover the plain text.

Kesselring spoke next. "Normally, of course, both the originator and the recipient would possess the same literal key. In this case, for reasons that are not pertinent to this discussion, the only copy of the key accompanied the encoded file. One of Devlin's transport options for such data was a macramé bracelet with a polymer strand containing a series of microdots woven into it. Very low-tech in this modern age, but still quite effective, especially since so few examiners even look for it." He activated a laptop computer screen on a table next to Devlin's body. "Our medical examiner scanned Devlin's wrists and found a pattern of hemp fibers embedded into the skin on the left one. Here's a color-enhanced image of the pattern." Kesselring paused to let Zach take a close look at the purplish chain-link outline. "Your report states that Ms. Robbins was in physical contact with Devlin just before he died. Her tape shows clearly that Devlin had nothing on his wrist at the time of his death. The report also states that she was wearing various items of personal adornment when she arrived at your residence. Could a fiber bracelet such as this have been one of those items?"

Zach drew a long breath. "Yes," he said finally. Lily Robbins had been wearing all sorts of jewelry the night she'd shown up at his plantation, soaking wet from a rain storm, packing a guerrilla *capitán*'s engraved pistol, and obviously in more trouble than he'd thought—and he'd thought she'd been in plenty.

And dammit, he'd found the catalyst, the connection, and the reason he'd been called all the way back home—a damn piece of macramé.

"It's entirely likely Ms. Robbins has your key," he finished, even as he wondered why in the hell a schoolteacher would have taken a cheap bracelet off a dying man.

"Likely enough to send you to find her and look for it," Kesselring agreed. "There are a few more things you need to be aware of, though. First, the only individuals on this end who know of the key's existence are the four of us in this room. Second, we consider it entirely possible that Devlin was photographed after he was captured. Third, there are some pretty clever folks who serve—ah—other interests, and those folks just might figure out that he left without something he arrived with. If we can guess what it is and where it is, then so can they. Best case, you locate Ms. Robbins, recover the bracelet, it turns out to be what we think it is, you return without incident, and that's the end of it. Worst case . . ."

"I get it," Zach said. And he did, dammit.

"You'll maintain your current identity and use your existing resources for this, at least to begin with," Van Zandt said. "Alex will brief you on the risk assessment, operational details, and options. Do you have further questions for Charles or myself?"

"No, ma'am," he said, not even considering asking what was in the file.

With another short nod, Van Zandt left the room. Kesselring was close behind her, leaving Zach with Alex and what would undoubtedly become an hours-long briefing.

Alex gestured toward a door at the other end of the room, and Zach followed him out into another hallway.

"Report only to me on this," Alex said.

"Yes, sir." It was an order, not a request.

"And this was sent down from State for you." The older man handed him a sealed envelope.

Zach opened it while they walked, and pulled out the single sheet of paper. There were six words on it.

A fleeting grin curved his mouth. *Geezus*. He read the note again, then refolded it into the envelope and stuck the whole thing in his pocket.

Geezus.

"I don't know what's in the letter," Alex said, "but considering where it came from, I can guess. The State Department is in this thing up to their neck, right along with us. They're the ones who pulled the DOD in on the Salvadoran deal. It was all back room politics, down to the inclusion of one of the DOD's covert operators, Smith Rydell. The important thing for you to remember is that when Amanda spoke about 'existing resources,' she meant everything. You've got ties to Rydell's team in Denver, Special Defense Force. Use them. Shake these guys down, if you need to, and make sure we come out on top. After our briefing, you'll be leaving from Dulles and heading to Denver ASAP."

"Yes, sir." He didn't have a problem with going to Denver before he picked up the woman in Albuquerque. He sure as hell didn't think he'd be shaking down the SDF team, though, at least not as his first order of business. Later, if Lily Robbins didn't pan out, he'd do whatever it took to get the job done.

But going to Denver was a good idea.

His grin returned for another fleeting second. He thought it was a damn good idea, but not for any reason Alex would understand, because for all his Ivy League education and brilliance, Alex was no mechanic.